OXFORD ENGLISH NOVELS

General Editor: JAMES KINSLEY

ALICE'S ADVENTURES IN WONDERLAND

and

THROUGH THE LOOKING-GLASS

LEWIS CARROLL

ALICE'S ADVENTURES IN WONDERLAND

and

THROUGH THE LOOKING-GLASS

AND WHAT ALICE FOUND THERE

With illustrations by John Tenniel

Edited with an Introduction by
ROGER LANCELYN GREEN

LONDON
OXFORD UNIVERSITY PRESS
NEW YORK   TORONTO
1971

Oxford University Press, Ely House, London W. 1

GLASGOW NEW YORK TORONTO MELBOURNE WELLINGTON
CAPE TOWN SALISBURY IBADAN NAIROBI DAR ES SALAAM LUSAKA ADDIS ABABA
BOMBAY CALCUTTA MADRAS KARACHI LAHORE DACCA
KUALA LUMPUR SINGAPORE HONG KONG TOKYO

ISBN 0 19 255341 0

PRINTED IN GREAT BRITAIN

CONTENTS

INTRODUCTION

'CARROLL ought now to be taking his place among the novelists', wrote Kathleen Tillotson in 1950. 'Henry Kingsley, a novelist himself, was not speaking at random when he called *Through the Looking-Glass* "the finest book since *Martin Chuzzlewit*". . . . The *Looking-Glass* characters are defined and memorable in the same way as those of Dickens, and of no other novelist.'[1]

Such an assertion goes some way towards explaining the presence of *Alice* in this series of English Novels, though in any strict terminology it is no more a novel than *The Princess and Curdie*, *The Wind in the Willows*, or *Winnie-the-Pooh*— and considerably less so than *The Carved Lions*, *Little Lord Fauntleroy*, or *Swallows and Amazons*. In fact, it stands supreme in a definite branch of literature which, for convenience, we call the Children's Book, and is no more a novel than it is a play or an epic poem.

But, undoubtedly, there are a number of such books which transcend their original audience and are appreciated as much—and in time, more—by adults as by the children for whom they were written. 'A children's story which is enjoyed only by children is a bad children's story. The good ones last', said C. S. Lewis in 1952,[2] and he pointed out that the reason for writing one should be 'because a children's story is the best art-form for something you have to say'.

It is because *Alice*—or *The Rose and the Ring* or *Prince Prigio* or *The Hobbit*, or any of those mentioned above—is so good an example of its own art-form that it 'lasts', that it is so widely enjoyed by adult readers, not because it is more like

[1] Kathleen Tillotson, 'Lewis Carroll and the Kitten on the Hearth', *English*, viii. 45 (1950), 138.

[2] C. S. Lewis, 'On Three Ways of Writing for Children', a lecture read to the Library Association and published in its *Proceedings* (1952); collected in his *Of Other Worlds* (1966).

a novel than a fairy fantasy. If it were, it would mean that it was a bad children's story—which can hardly be true of the most popular example of the *genre* in the language. This should also answer various attempts that have been made to prove that *Alice* is really a carefully constructed allegory satirizing the political and religious controversies of the day[1] —or even, as recently suggested, a completely pointless mish-mash of Jewish religious symbolism.[2]

Behind all attempts to change its category lies the conscious or subconscious desire to prove that *Alice* is really not a children's book at all, and is enjoyed only by adults. Perhaps relatively fewer children read it now than fifty years ago. If so, this may in part be due to the fact that fantasy and 'nonsense' of the Lewis Carroll variety grow steadily more alien to the more 'realistic' children of today. As the vast majority of books now set before children do not stretch their vocabulary (or, often, their imagination) at as early an age as in Victorian times, *Alice* also frequently seems too babyish now by the time it can be read with ease. Dodgson's stories were read out loud to their earliest audiences, or read by children whose taste for fantasy and fairy-tale lasted longer than among the majority of readers today.

More adults enjoy Lewis Carroll than any other children's author, though a select few—it may be MacDonald or Milne, Kipling or Tolkien, Lang or C. S. Lewis—are probably not as far behind as is commonly supposed, just as Rider Haggard and Conan Doyle retain their place securely among much greater novelists and story-tellers. *Alice*, it is maintained, contains much that can be appreciated only by the adult reader; the same is true of many other writers whom we enjoyed first in childhood or youth, but *Alice*, none the less, deserves its

[1] Shane Leslie, 'Lewis Carroll and the Oxford Movement', in the *London Mercury*, xxviii (July 1933); Alexander L. Taylor, *The White Knight: A Study of C. L. Dodgson* (1952). There was also an attempt to prove that *Alice* was based on intimate knowledge of the 'Bed Chamber Crisis' of 1839 (including many details not available until after Dodgson's death)—still, presumably, unpublished; and doubtless others.

[2] Abraham Ettleson, M.D., *Lewis Carroll's 'Through the Looking-Glass' Decoded* (New York, 1966).

pre-eminent position in its own branch of literature. There is satire, allusion, even intentional symbolism in *Alice* that in most cases can be understood and enjoyed consciously only by older readers; but there is as much (not quite so success-fully woven into the fabric) in *The Rose and the Ring*—rather less in *Prince Prigio* or *Just So Stories* or *Pooh*. These deeper meanings seem to give an added dimension, and with it some measure of immortality to humorous fantasy, in the same way that the more serious background allegory or symbolism does to the imaginative adventure stories of writers like George MacDonald and C. S. Lewis, or Rider Haggard and J. R. R. Tolkien.

In spite of its apparently calculated adult background, most of *Alice's Adventures in Wonderland* was told spontaneously to three little girls and written down from memory for their private amusement, before being expanded for the larger audience of whom its author had no thought when telling or writing the original version.

The facts are surely over-familiar. Charles Lutwidge Dodgson, thirty-year-old mathematical lecturer at Christ Church, took the three small daughters of Dean Liddell up the Thames from Oxford to Godstow, with the assistance of his friend Robinson Duckworth, Fellow of Trinity, on 4 July 1862. They 'had tea on the bank there, and did not reach Christ Church again till quarter past eight', Dodgson wrote in his *Diary*, and added, 'On which occasion I told the fairy-tale of *Alice's Adventures Underground*, which I undertook to write out for Alice.'

Duckworth recorded that:

The story was actually composed and spoken *over my shoulder* for the benefit of Alice Liddell. [He rowed stroke and Dodgson rowed bow]. I remember turning round and saying: 'Dodgson, is this an extemporary romance of yours?' And he replied: 'Yes, I'm inventing as we go along.' I also remember how, when we had conducted the three children back to the Deanery, Alice said, as she bade us good-night, 'Oh, Mr. Dodgson, I wish you would write out Alice's Adventures for me!' He said he would try, and he

afterwards told me that he sat up nearly the whole night, com-
mitting to a M.S. book his recollections of the drolleries with which
he had enlivened the afternoon.[1]

Alice herself remembered that 'the stories he told us that
afternoon must have been better than usual, because I have
such a distinct recollection of the expedition, and also, on the
next day, I started to pester him to write down the story for
me'.[2] This squares more closely with Dodgson's note in his
Diary (written some time later, however), 'Headings written
out on my way to London' (5 July 1862), when the Liddell
children travelled on the same train. And twenty-four years
later he wrote: 'I distinctly remember how, in a desperate
attempt to strike out some new line in fairy-lore, I had sent
my heroine straight down a rabbit-hole, to begin with, without the least idea what was to happen afterwards.'[3]

Having got Alice down into the hall underground, Dodgson
turned back for inspiration to a disastrous picnic that had
taken place two weeks previously, which he thus described in
his *Diary*:

17 June 1862. Expedition to Nuneham. Duckworth (of Trinity)
and Ina, Alice and Edith came with us [Dodgson himself, his sisters
Frances and Elizabeth, and his aunt Lucy Lutwidge, who were on
a visit to him]. We set out about 12.30 and got to Nuneham about 2:
dined there, and then walked in the park and set off for home
about 4.30. About a mile above Nuneham heavy rain came on, and
after bearing it a short time I settled that we had better leave the
boat and walk: three miles of this drenched us all pretty well. I went
on first with the children as they could walk much faster than
Elizabeth, and took them to the only house I knew in Sandford,
Mrs. Broughton's, where Ranken lodges. I left them with her to
get their clothes dried, and went off to find a vehicle, but none was

---

[1] Robinson Duckworth in *The Lewis Carroll Picture Book*, ed. Stuart Dodgson
Collingwood (1899), pp. 359–60.
[2] 'Alice's Recollections of Carrollian Days, told to her son, Caryl Hargreaves',
Cornhill Magazine (July 1932).
[3] Lewis Carroll, 'Alice on the Stage', in *The Theatre* (April 1887). Reprinted in
The Lewis Carroll Picture Book (1899), pp. 163–74; and *The Works of Lewis Carroll*,
ed. Roger Lancelyn Green (1965), pp. 234–8.

to be had there, so on the others arriving, Duckworth and I walked on to Iffley, whence we sent them a fly. We all had tea in my rooms about 8.30, after which I took the children home.

The story as told to the children and written down for Alice as *Alice's Adventures Underground* was altered at this point when Dodgson was preparing the book for publication as *Alice's Adventures in Wonderland*. The original version ran as follows (after p. 23):

. . . They were indeed a curious party that assembled on the bank—the birds with draggled feathers, the animals with their fur clinging close to them—all dripping wet, cross, and uncomfortable. The first question of course was, how to get dry: they had a consultation about this, and Alice hardly felt herself at all surprised at finding herself talking familiarly with the birds, as if she had known them all her life. Indeed, she had quite a long argument with the Lory, who at last turned sulky, and would only say 'I am older than you, and must know best', and this Alice would not admit without knowing how old the Lory was, and as the Lory positively refused to tell its age, there was nothing more to be said.

At last the mouse, who seemed to have some authority among them [proceeded to give the history lesson, as in the published version, as 'the driest thing I know'; but Alice was forced to admit that] 'it doesn't seem to dry me at all.'

'In that case,' said the Dodo solemnly, rising to his feet, 'I move that the meeting adjourn, for immediate adoption of more energetic remedies—'

'Speak English!' said the Duck, 'I don't know the meaning of half those long words, and what's more, I don't believe you do either!' And the Duck quacked a comfortable laugh to itself. Some of the other birds tittered audibly.

'I only meant to say,' said the Dodo in rather an offended tone, 'that I know of a house near here, where we could get the young lady and the rest of the party dried, and then we could listen comfortably to the story which I think you were good enough to promise to tell us,' bowing gravely to the mouse.

The mouse made no objection to this, and the whole party moved along the river bank (for the pool had by this time begun to flow out of the hall, and the edge of it was fringed with rushes and forget-me-nots), in a slow procession, the Dodo leading the way. After a time the Dodo became impatient, and, leaving the Duck to bring up the rest of the party, moved on at a quicker pace with Alice, the Lory and the Eaglet, and soon brought them to a little cottage, and there they sat snugly by the fire, wrapped up in blankets, until the rest of the party had arrived, and they were all dry again.

And when, at the mention of Dinah, all the creatures have departed in a hurry (p. 30 line 3), Alice—

. . . began talking to herself again as usual: 'I do wish some of them had stayed a little longer! and I was getting to be such friends with them—really the Lory and I were almost like sisters! and so was the dear little Eaglet! And then the Duck and the Dodo! How nicely the Duck sang to us as we came along through the water: and if the Dodo hadn't known the way to that nice little cottage, I don't know when we should have got dry again . . .'

As the Lory and the Eaglet were obviously her sisters Lorina and Edith, this passage must have delighted Alice, just as the other references reminded her how Duckworth would sing such songs as 'Beautiful Star' and 'Sally Come Up' for their entertainment, and how Dodgson had been able to guide them to the cottage in Sandford.

Such obviously personal references as these were naturally altered or removed when Dodgson revised the book for publication; but many slighter references and background suggestions remain in both *Alice* and *Through the Looking-Glass*, and these, whenever they can be identified, are discussed in the Notes to the present edition.

Having promised to write out the story for Alice Liddell, Dodgson proceeded to do so at odd times, apparently including several stories told later in the year (for example he notes in his *Diary* for 6 August 1862 that, during another river trip that day, 'I had to go on with my interminable fairy-tale of *Alice's Adventures*')—sometimes with a slightly clumsy link, as at the point where the Duchess's predecessor and the Queen of Hearts are combined when the White Rabbit meets Alice at the Croquet Party (p. 73 line 16):

'Where's the Marchioness?' [asked Alice].

'Hush, hush!' said the rabbit in a low voice, 'she'll hear you. The Queen's the Marchioness: didn't you know that?'

'No, I didn't,' said Alice, 'what of?'

'Queen of Hearts,' said the rabbit in a whisper, putting its mouth close to her ear, 'and Marchioness of Mock Turtles.'

'What are *they*?' said Alice, but there was no time for the answer, for they had reached the croquet-ground, and the game began instantly.[1]

Dodgson noted in his *Diary* for 13 November 1862: 'Began writing the fairy-tale for Alice, which I told them July 4, going to Godstow—I hope to finish it by Christmas.' He finished it, however, only 'before Feb: 10, 1863', and probably gave it to Alice on the 16th when he dined at the Deanery and 'the children remained through the whole evening'. But apparently he had not completed the illustrations, for he noted later: 'Pictures in M.S. finished Sept: 13, 1864', and 'M.S. finally sent to Alice, Nov: 26, 1864'.

But the copy which was finished in February 1863 (whether the final copy, but with incomplete illustrations, or his own rougher copy, no longer extant and never mentioned) 'used often to be seen on the drawing-room table at the Deanery', according to Duckworth. 'One day Henry Kingsley, when on a visit to the Dean, took up the MS., and read it through with the greatest delight, urging Mrs. Liddell to persuade the author to publish it.'[2] Dodgson consulted Duckworth, who felt certain the book would be a success if only some well-known artist could be engaged to illustrate it, and suggested John Tenniel, already popular for his *Punch* cartoons and known from his edition of *Æsop's Fables* (1848) to be a skilled delineator of animals in unnatural or fantastic settings and positions.

---

[1] The three extracts from *Alice's Adventures Underground* are from pp. 24–7, 32, and 74 of the facsimile published by Macmillan in 1886. The original MS. is in the British Museum.   [2] *The Lewis Carroll Picture Book* (1899), p. 360.

To be quite certain, Dodgson lent the manuscript to George MacDonald, who took it home to try on his own children: 'Accordingly my mother read the story to us', records Greville MacDonald. 'When she came to the end I, being aged six, exclaimed that there ought to be sixty thousand volumes of it. Certainly it was our enthusiasm that persuaded our Uncle Dodgson, as we called him, to present the English-speaking world with one of its future classics, *Alice in Wonderland*.'[1]

Having finally decided to publish the book, Dodgson prepared his text by omitting or altering the passages quoted above and adding, from stories told on other occasions, the chapters 'Pig and Pepper', 'A Mad Tea-Party', 'Who Stole the Tarts?', and 'Alice's Evidence', the two latter expanding the trial which in the original occupied less than a page. He also replaced the 'Mouse's Tail' and one other parody by better ones and considerably lengthened the discussion on lessons with the Mock Turtle. Finally he substituted the second, third, and fourth paragraphs of the epilogue (pp. 110–11) for the single paragraph of the original, which again had referred too specifically to the origin of the stories:

She saw an ancient city, and a quiet river winding near it along the plain, and up the stream went slowly gliding a boat with a merry party of children on board—she could hear their voices and laughter like music over the water—and among them was another little Alice, who sat listening with bright eager eyes to a tale that was being told, and she listened for the words of the tale, and lo! it was the dream of her own little sister. So the boat wound slowly along, beneath the bright summer day, with its merry crew and its music of voices and laughter, till it passed round one of the many turnings of the stream, and she saw it no more.[2]

On 25 January 1864, presumably with the book completed, Dodgson called on Tenniel (having obtained an introduction from their mutual friend Tom Taylor the dramatist). Tenniel read the book and agreed on 5 April to illustrate it. Dodgson

---

[1] Greville MacDonald, *George MacDonald and his Wife* (1924), p. 342.
[2] *Alice's Adventures Underground* (1886), pp. 89–90.

paid for the illustrations, about which he seems to have been extremely dictatorial—using Tenniel almost as an amanuensis to give visible form to what he could see in his own mind but lacked the skill to reproduce on paper—with the result that they have never been surpassed or superseded, and are probably more a part of the two *Alices* than the illustrations are to any other book.

Dodgson also paid for the printing, Macmillan merely publishing on commission, and was forced to withdraw the first edition on account of bad reproduction (mainly of the illustrations) and to have it done again by another printer. He received the first copy of this new edition on 9 November 1865, and the book was published later that month, though dated 1866.

By August 1866 Dodgson was considering a sequel, based on the rest of the stories told to the Liddell children which he could remember—notably that telling of the Garden of Live Flowers and the remarkable railway journey following it, based on a visit in April 1863 to the Liddells at Charlton Kings near Cheltenham and on a journey back to Oxford from Gloucester at the end of their holiday. The result, *Through the Looking-Glass and What Alice Found There*, grew more slowly than its predecessor, but was ready for publication with illustrations by Tenniel (obtaining these delayed Dodgson for some time) in December 1871—though it was dated 1872.

By this time *Wonderland* was in its twenty-ninth thousand, and, after a slow start, was already beginning to take its place as a nursery classic.

Its earliest reviews were not, on the whole, encouraging: 'Mr. Carroll has laboured hard to heap together strange adventures and heterogenous combinations—and we acknowledge the hard labour', said the *Athenaeum*, 'a stiff, overwrought story.'[1] 'Too extravagantly absurd to produce more diversion than disappointment and irritation', said the *Illustrated Times*. 'The reader looks in vain for any immediate

[1] *Athenaeum*, 16 December 1865.

B

reason why Alice should have dreamt such a dream or for any very edifying result arising from it.'[1] *The Times* praised Tenniel's drawings but dismissed the book in one line: '[it] may best be described as an excellent piece of nonsense'.[2] The *Pall Mall Gazette*, however, declared that 'This delightful little book is a children's feast and triumph of nonsense; it is nonsense with bon-bons, flags and music; never inhuman, never inelegant, never tedious';[3] and the *Spectator*, while condemning some of Tenniel's illustrations (probably because it took the Mad Hatter to be a caricature of Gladstone—which was never intended [see note 2 to p. 59]), declared that 'this is the book for little folks, and big folks who take it home to their little folks will find themselves reading more than they intended, and laughing more than they had any right to expect'.[4]

Before the end of the century *Alice* (counting both books as a single entity) had become not only a classic but part of nursery folklore. By 1894 Charlotte in *The Golden Age* can tell the story of Alice's adventures to her dolls as if it were *Cinderella* or *Puss in Boots*, the author assuming that every reader would know the book intimately without further explanation.[5] It had also captured the imagination of older readers, as is shown by Kipling in *Stalky & Co.* (1899) where his schoolboys (aged fifteen to eighteen) quote from it frequently, almost certainly reflecting the actual practice at the United Services College when he was a boy there between 1878 and 1882.

A census carried out by the *Academy* (2 July 1898) shows that *Alice* was well at the top of the list of favourite children's books by the time Dodgson died on 14 January 1898, and its influence was in full swing—though it only produced satisfactory results when the spirit of the book rather than its outward form was being followed. '*Alice* is always being imitated!'

---

[1] *Illustrated Times*, 16 December 1865.   [2] *The Times*, 26 December 1865.
[3] *Pall Mall Gazette*, 23 December 1865.   [4] *Spectator*, 23 December 1865.
[5] Kenneth Grahame, 'Sawdust and Sin', in the *National Observer* (25 August 1894); collected in his *The Golden Age* (1895), pp. 52-60.

complained Andrew Lang in 1895.[1] And Harvey Darton as late as 1932 noted: 'The fault of the many imitators of Lewis Carroll—who are to this day a permanent plague to all editors and publishers of literature for children—is that they force the transition from one nature to another; they invent, but they have not the logic.'[2]

Certainly Dodgson's use of logic is the most obvious source of his particular turn of humour and one of the most important tools with which he constructed his masterpiece. It was his training in formal logic—as Peter Alexander, himself a professional logician, points out—which enabled him to build 'a setting within which inconsistency would appear inevitable, and so convincing; or, more precisely, showed him how to *use* a common fairy tale setting to contain more than any normal fairy tale ever contained'. The purely logical sequence of reasoning from an illogical premiss—usually a phrase in popular use but used loosely—is well exemplified by the conversation between Alice and the Cheshire Cat on 'getting somewhere' (p. 57), or by her discussion with the White King on eating hay (p. 201).

Professor Alexander goes on to point out how wrong Alexander Woollcott was in talking of a discrepancy between 'the man who wrote the most enchanting nonsense in the English language' and the 'puttering, fussy, fastidious, didactic, old bachelor',[3] and comments:

For the will to escape was joined with the ability to escape; an ability which depended on a detailed knowledge of, and interest in, logic. Without Dodgson the pedantic logician, Carroll the artist would have been of considerably less importance; there was no discrepancy. [4]

But with the logic went the exceptional knowledge and

---

[1] Andrew Lang, 'Literary Fairy Tales', as Introduction to Frederick Van Eeden's *Little Johannes* (1895), p. xv.

[2] F. J. Harvey Darton, *Children's Books in England* (1932), p. 269.

[3] Alexander Woollcott, Introduction to *The Complete Works of Lewis Carroll* (1937), p. 5.

[4] Peter Alexander, 'Logic and the Humour of Lewis Carroll', in *Proceedings of the Leeds Philosophical Society*, VI, Part viii, 551 and 555 (May 1951).

understanding of the child-mind which seems never to have been so completely achieved by any other author, though from time to time writers as various as John Habberton, Kenneth Grahame, Mrs. Molesworth, and Edith Nesbit have drawn near to it. In Dodgson's case this knowledge and understanding came fortuitously. As the eldest son in a large family, with five sisters and three brothers younger than himself (there were two older sisters), living very much isolated in the country first at Daresbury in Cheshire and then at Croft near Richmond in Yorkshire, he was accustomed from the beginning to the society of children. And from an early age he was the family entertainer, inventing games, giving marionette and conjuring shows, and writing by far the largest share of the numerous family magazines.

This was not in itself an unusual background for a member of a large family in the Victorian period: Julian Horatia Gatty (Mrs. Ewing), nine years his junior, fulfilled much the same functions in a similarly large family at another lonely Yorkshire vicarage—though her juvenile writings seem not to have survived, and her subsequent adult writings for children are on a lower level than Dodgson's. That Edith Nesbit introduced a family magazine made by the children in *The Treasure Seekers* (1899) without any apology or explanation suggests that the average child reader would not have found anything unusual in this.

Dodgson, however, continued entertaining the youngest members of his family with nonsense letters even when he had just become a lecturer at Christ Church; and there was little or no gap before he had begun entertaining the children of his friends, and then making friends with children rather than with their parents. Tennyson's two small sons, George MacDonald's large family, and the occasional child on the beach preceded Dean Liddell's children or overlapped with the beginning of the friendship that started with Harry Liddell, the eldest, in March 1856, and extended to Rhoda in 1864. After this, disagreement with both the Dean and Mrs. Liddell over Christ Church matters put an end to his close relationship with the family. But by this time he was making other friendships with children, which increased in importance to him, until about 1888 he could confess in an unusual moment of candour to an undergraduate friend, Arthur Richey Girdlestone, that 'they are three-fourths of my life!'[1]

Greville MacDonald, looking back to his own childhood in the 1860s, wrote of Dodgson: 'Debarred from clerical work by an incurable stammer, it was instantly effaced when surrounded by children';[2] and Isa Bowman, one of the half-dozen later child-friends who were almost as dear to him as Alice Liddell, remembered how Dodgson took her to the Panorama of the Niagara Falls in London on 11 July 1888 and told her a long and amusing story about a little dog in the foreground, without any sign of hesitation. But 'suddenly he began to stammer, and looking round in some alarm I saw a dozen grown-ups and children had gathered around and were listening'.[3]

It seems to have been this life-long stammer which led Dodgson into the society of children and so was indirectly one of the main causes of his unusually deep knowledge of their modes of thought and imagination. Others who have stammered have found the same freedom in the society of children, and those who have not suffered from this affliction cannot imagine the glorious sense of freedom and escape of being suddenly able to speak for a while as easily and naturally as the rest of us. Even those who have later overcome their disability know how strong the craving for the society of children becomes (and the freedom is far greater in the society of girls than of boys—for the latter are apt to be a reminder of what the stammerer has suffered at school). More and more time and thought is given to how he may entertain them (or perhaps, but certainly subconsciously, ingratiate himself with them), and in so doing life, in their company at least, comes

---

[1] Quoted in Isa Bowman's *The Story of Lewis Carroll* (1899), p. 60.
[2] Greville MacDonald, *Reminiscences of a Specialist* (1932), p. 15.
[3] Isa Bowman, in Langford Reed's *Lewis Carroll* (1932), p. 75.

xxii   INTRODUCTION

more and more to be viewed through their eyes—and their apparently free and happy world to be more and more desired. Dodgson at the age of twenty-one wrote:

> I'd give all wealth that years have piled,
>   The slow result of Life's decay,
> To be once more a little child
>   For one bright summer-day.[1]

When writing *Alice's Adventures* and *Through the Looking-Glass* Dodgson held the balance perfectly between his recaptured child-self and the literary skill and logical judgement of the clever adult. But by the time he reached *Sylvie and Bruno* (1889) the balance had tilted, and he was using the actual sayings and fantasies of his child-friends unfiltered through the limbeck of mature skill and selection.

'Since childhood remained in him entire, he could do what no one else has ever been able to do—he could return to that world, he could recreate it, so that we too become children again', wrote Virginia Woolf. 'It is for this reason that the two *Alices* are not books for children; they are the only books in which we become children.'[2] If Mrs. Woolf's paradox is to be accepted at its face value, it follows that none of the great children's books are books for children—for to enjoy them fully we must to some extent become children again as we read, and whenever this happens (if we follow her dictum) the book—and there are others besides *Alice*—ceases *ipso facto* to be a book for children: 'which is absurd.' But, although she presents another version of the common attempt to excuse the enjoyment of a children's book by trying to prove that it was really intended for adults, Mrs. Woolf gets as near as may be to the secret of Lewis Carroll—the circumstances which made him able to write the greatest of all children's books and, in so doing, to exercise the greatest influence on subsequent children's books that any writer has ever had.

---

[1] 'Solitude' (written 15 March 1853), first published in *The Train*, i. 154-5, March 1856 (over the first use of the pseudonym 'Lewis Carroll'), and collected in *Phantasmagoria* (1889), pp. 181-3.

[2] Virginia Woolf, *The Moment, and Other Essays* (1948), p. 83.

'The directness of such a work was a revolution in its sphere', wrote Harvey Darton:

It was the coming to the surface, powerfully and permanently, the first unapologetic, undocumented appearance in print, for readers who sorely needed it, of liberty of thought in children's books. Henceforth fear had gone, and with it shy disquiet. There was to be in hours of pleasure no more dread about the moral value, the ponderable, measured quality and extent of the pleasure itself. It was to be enjoyed and even promoted with neither forethought nor remorse. . . . The *Alices* are pure invention. . . . Yet they fell then and still fall into the category of 'fairy-tales'; and as Dodgson himself once thought of calling the Wonderland book *Alice's Hour in Elfland*, that is perhaps justifiable, though neither fairy nor. elf appears from one end to the other. There is simply magic, and even that is treated as just an extension of the natural—'curiouser and curiouser'. The essence of the story is the translation of the ordinary into the extraordinary in a plausible way—not as a conjuring trick (a white rabbit out of a madman's hat, so to speak), but as an almost logical extension of properties inherent in this or that person or animal.[1]

Yet *Alice* was not born quite without ancestors. Some freedom and a little excellent nonsense had been introduced into the nursery in 1839 by Catherine Sinclair with her immensely popular *Holiday House*; nonsense pure and simple with Edward Lear's little book of limericks in 1846, with enlarged editions in '61, '62, and '63; light fairyland burlesque, though still with too much of a moral, by F. E. Paget in *The Hope of the Katzekopfs* in 1844, and a real classic in the same genre but with scarcely any but an implied moral in Thackeray's *The Rose and the Ring* (1855). Dodgson must have known all these well, and also Norman MacLeod's *The Gold Thread* (1861) which, in spite of the heavy allegory, is moving towards Wonderland; and he seems to have read George MacDonald's nonsense-fairy-tale, *The Light Princess*, in manuscript early in 1862, before its publication in *Adela Cathcart* two years later. Kingsley's amalgam of charming

---

[1] F. J. Harvey Darton, op. cit., pp. 268-9.

fantasy and nauseous avuncularism, *The Water Babies*, appeared in 1863 between the writing and the publication of *Alice's Adventures in Wonderland*, and W. B. Rands's *Lilliput Levée* the following year.

The first obvious influence of *Alice* on a book still read today came in 1869 with the publication of Jean Ingelow's *Mopsa the Fairy*. Dodgson's cousins Menella Smedley and her sister Mrs. Hart acknowledge their debt in their volume of verse, *Child-World*, published in the same year; and the effect of the book begins at once to spread as influence with the better writers and imitation with the lesser ones—Mrs. Ewing and Mrs. Craik, for example, on the one side, and E. Knatchbull-Huggessen and Tom Hood on the other. But to follow further would be to write another history of children's literature; and to investigate *Alice's* relationship to Lang's *Prince Prigio* or Nesbit's *Unlikely Tales*, to *Just So Stories*, *The Wind in the Willows*, or *Winnie-the-Pooh* would demand a full-length critical study.

There is probably no definite answer to the mystery of *Alice's* success. As in the case of the Mad Hatter's riddle any answer is no more than an afterthought: 'The Riddle, as originally invented, had no answer at all.' We can give no mathematically exact solution to the problem of why these two little books should have been so dearly loved by most readers for a century, why they are among the most frequently quoted works in the English language—and have been translated into nearly every foreign tongue; why scholars and critics have spent so much time studying the books and their author and writing more about him than he himself ever wrote in his whole life; why he has been celebrated with collections and exhibitions in many parts of the world and a Lewis Carroll Society founded in his honour.

Perhaps we can do no better than end by accepting Dodgson's admission when questioned about *The Hunting of the Snark*:

I'm very much afraid I didn't mean anything but nonsense! Still, you know, words mean more than we mean to express when we use them; so a whole book ought to mean a great deal more than the writer meant. So, whatever good meanings are in the book, I'm very glad to accept as the meaning of the book.[1]

And certainly the best way to enjoy the book itself is to follow the advice of the King of Hearts: 'Begin at the beginning, and go on till you come to the end: then stop.'

[1] *A Selection from the Letters of Lewis Carroll to his Child-Friends*, ed. Evelyn M. Hatch (1933), p. 243.

NOTE ON THE TEXT

THE text is printed from the revised editions of 1897 which contain Dodgson's final corrections and additions. He made these corrections in copies of the 1882 *Alice's Adventures* and the 1880 *Through the Looking-Glass*, bound in one volume, which he borrowed from his young friend May Barber (later Mrs. H. T. Stretton). After Dodgson's death in January 1898 she retrieved them from Macmillans, and they were still in her possession in 1958 when Mr. Stanley Godman transcribed the corrections from manuscript and published them in *The Times Literary Supplement* (2 May). Dodgson made the corrections in the autumn of 1896 and included in the volumes two more or less new Prefaces, both dated Christmas 1896.

The first edition of *Alice's Adventures in Wonderland* was printed by Oxford University Press in 1865 and was cancelled, probably before any copies had been sold, owing to bad printing of the illustrations, to which Tenniel objected. About forty-eight copies are known to have been bound, which Dodgson gave away to friends. When the edition was cancelled, he asked for these to be returned, and gave away all that came back to him to children's hospitals. Of this edition twenty copies are known to have survived (two of them are now lost), and also a proof copy bound up by the printer who set the type. The original edition was of 2,000, and the remaining sheets were sold to the American firm of Appleton and Co. with a specially printed title-page dated 1866.

Meanwhile Dodgson had the book reprinted by Richard Clay and Sons, with virtually no alteration to the text, and published in December 1865 (dated 1866). In this edition he made a number of small corrections, most of which appeared in the 1867 reprints. The copy of the 1866 edition bearing his autograph corrections is in the Parrish Collection at Princeton University, U.S.A.

From time to time Dodgson noticed misprints, which were sometimes corrected, and in 1886 he added a short Preface and expanded one poem from six to sixteen lines.

Through the Looking-Glass and What Alice Found There was published in December 1871 (dated 1872). No corrections, except for misprints, were made until he prepared the 1897 editions of both books. I have followed the texts of these final editions, making only one correction (deleting the full-stop at the end of Chapter III, which is not found in any of the earlier editions). All substantive variations between the edition used and the earlier editions, and changes of emphasis, are listed in the Textual Notes (pp. 250-2).

SELECT BIBLIOGRAPHY

THERE have been editions without number of both *Alice* books, both with the Tenniel illustrations and with illustrations by dozens of other artists. Editions with Introductions of interest include: *Wonderland*—Sir Henry Newbolt (Nelson, 1910); Guy N. Pocock (Dent and Dutton, 1930); Hugh Walpole (Macmillan, 1932); Kathleen Norris (Doubleday, N.Y., 1942); Eleanor Graham (Puffins, 1946). *Looking-Glass*—Florence Milner (Rand, Chicago, 1917); Eleanor Graham (Puffins, 1948). *Wonderland* and *Looking-Glass* together—Ernest Rhys (Dent, Everyman's Library, 1929); May L. Becker (World Pub. C., N.Y., 1945); Martin Gardner (*The Annotated Alice*, Clarkson N. Potter, N.Y., 1960; Anthony Blond [1962]; World Pub. Co., N.Y., 1963); Roger Lancelyn Green (Dent, Everyman's Library, 1965).

COLLECTED EDITIONS. There is no complete edition of Lewis Carroll, even excluding the mathematical works. Random House, N.Y., produced a volume called *The Complete Works of Lewis Carroll* in 1937 with an introduction by Alexander Woollcott; this was reprinted in England by the Nonesuch Press in 1939 and 1949. A much more nearly complete edition was published by Paul Hamlyn in 1965 as *The Works of Lewis Carroll*, edited and with an introduction by Roger Lancelyn Green: its main omissions are the juvenilia and *Symbolic Logic*.

BIBLIOGRAPHY. S. H. Williams, *A Bibliography of the Writings of Lewis Carroll* (1924); largely superseded by S. H. Williams and Falconer Madan, *A Handbook of the Literature of Rev. C. L. Dodgson* (1931), with *Supplement* by Madan (1935); this was revised and brought down to 1960 (but with some sections omitted) by Roger Lancelyn Green as *The Lewis Carroll Handbook* (1962), reprinted with corrections 1970. Warren Weaver's *Alice in Many Tongues* (Wisconsin, 1964) lists all known translations. For the suppression of the 1865 *Alice* see W. H. Bond in *Harvard Library Bulletin*, x (1956), 306–24; a monograph on the subject by Warren Weaver describing all known copies will shortly be published.

BIOGRAPHY AND CRITICISM. The primary sources are S. D. Collingwood's *Life and Letters of Lewis Carroll* (1898) and *The Diaries of Lewis Carroll* (2 vols.), edited and supplemented by Roger Lancelyn Green (1953). The *Collected Letters*, edited by Morton N. Cohen and Roger Lancelyn Green, should be published in 1973. Other books on Lewis Carroll include: Walter de la Mare, *Lewis Carroll* (1932), an essay reprinted from *The Eighteen-Eighties* (1930); Langford Reed, *The Life of Lewis Carroll* (1932); Florence Becker Lennon, *Victoria through the Looking-Glass: the Life of Lewis Carroll* (N.Y. 1945, London 1947), reprinted in a revised edition as *The Life of Lewis Carroll* (N.Y. 1962); Helmut Gernsheim, *Lewis Carroll, Photographer* (1949); Elizabeth Sewell, *The Field of Nonsense* (1952); Alexander L. Taylor, *The White Knight: A Study of C. L. Dodgson* (1952); Derek Hudson, *Lewis Carroll* (1954) and his British Council pamphlet (1958); Phyllis Greenacre, *Swift and Carroll: A Psycho-analytical Study of Two Lives* (N.Y. 1955); Roger Lancelyn Green, *Lewis Carroll* (1960); Robert D. Sutherland, *Language and Lewis Carroll* (The Hague, 1970); Jean Gattegno, *Lewis Carroll* (Paris 1970).

A CHRONOLOGY OF
'LEWIS CARROLL'

C

ALICE'S ADVENTURES
IN WONDERLAND

All in the golden afternoon
  Full leisurely we glide;
For both our oars, with little skill,
  By little arms are plied,
While little hands make vain pretence
  Our wanderings to guide.

Ah, cruel Three! In such an hour,
  Beneath such dreamy weather,
To beg a tale of breath too weak
  To stir the tiniest feather!
Yet what can one poor voice avail
  Against three tongues together?

Imperious Prima flashes forth
  Her edict 'to begin it':
In gentler tones Secunda hopes
  'There will be nonsense in it!'
While Tertia[1] interrupts the tale
  Not *more* than once a minute.

Anon, to sudden silence won,
  In fancy they pursue
The dream-child moving through a land
  Of wonders wild and new,
In friendly chat with bird or beast—
  And half believe it true.

And ever, as the story drained
  The wells of fancy dry,
And faintly strove that weary one
  To put the subject by,
'The rest next time—' 'It *is* next time!'
  The happy voices cry.

Thus grew the tale of Wonderland:
  Thus slowly, one by one,
Its quaint events were hammered out—
  And now the tale is done,
And home we steer, a merry crew,
  Beneath the setting sun.

Alice! A childish story take,
  And, with a gentle hand,
Lay it where Childhood's dreams are twined
  In Memory's mystic band,
Like pilgrim's wither'd wreath of flowers
  Pluck'd in a far-off land.

PREFACE TO THE
SEVENTY-NINTH THOUSAND

As Alice is about to appear on the Stage,[1] and as the lines beginning: ' 'Tis the voice of the Lobster' were found to be too fragmentary for dramatic purposes four lines have been added to the first stanza and six to the second, while the Oyster[2] has been developed into a Panther.

Christmas, 1886

PREFACE TO THE
EIGHTY-SIXTH THOUSAND
OF THE 6/- EDITION

ENQUIRIES have been so often addressed to me, as to whether any answer to the Hatter's Riddle (see p. 60) can be imagined, that I may as well put on record here what seems to me to be a fairly appropriate answer, viz. 'Because it can produce a few notes, though they are *very* flat; and it is never put with the wrong end in front!' This, however, is merely an afterthought: the Riddle, as originally invented, had no answer at all.

For this eighty-sixth thousand, fresh electrotypes have been taken from the wood-blocks (which, never having been used for printing from, are in as good condition as when first cut in 1865), and the whole book has been set up afresh with new type. If the artistic qualities of this re-issue fall short, in any particular, of those possessed by the original issue, it will not be for want of painstaking on the part of author, publisher, or printer.

I take this opportunity of announcing that the Nursery 'Alice,'[1] hitherto priced at four shillings, net, is now to be had on the same terms as the ordinary shilling picture-books—although I feel sure that it is, in every quality (except the *text* itself, on which I am not qualified to pronounce), greatly superior to them. Four shillings was a perfectly reasonable price to charge, considering the very heavy initial outlay I had incurred: still, as the Public have practically said 'We will *not* give more than a shilling for a picture-book, however artistically got-up', I am content to reckon my outlay on the book as so much dead loss, and, rather than let the little ones, for whom it was written, go without it, I am selling it at a price which is, to me, much the same thing as *giving* it away.

Christmas, 1896

CONTENTS

CHAPTER I

DOWN THE RABBIT-HOLE

ALICE was beginning to get very tired of sitting by her sister on the bank, and of having nothing to do: once or twice she had peeped into the book her sister was reading, but it had no pictures or conversations in it, 'and what is the use of a book,' thought Alice, 'without pictures or conversations?'

So she was considering, in her own mind (as well as she could, for the hot day made her feel very sleepy and stupid), whether the pleasure of making a daisy-chain would be worth the trouble of getting up and picking the daisies, when suddenly a White Rabbit with pink eyes ran close by her.

There was nothing so *very* remarkable in that; nor did Alice think it so *very* much out of the way to hear the Rabbit say to itself 'Oh dear! Oh dear! I shall be too late!' (when she thought it over afterwards, it occurred to her that she ought to have wondered at this, but at the time it all seemed quite natural); but, when the Rabbit actually *took a watch out of its waistcoat-pocket*, and looked at it, and then hurried on, Alice started to her feet, for it flashed across her mind that she had never before seen a rabbit with either a waistcoat-pocket, or a watch to take out of it, and, burning with curiosity, she ran across the field after it, and was just in time to see it pop down a large rabbit-hole under the hedge.

In another moment down went Alice after it, never once considering how in the world she was to get out again.

The rabbit-hole went straight on like a tunnel for some way, and then dipped suddenly down, so suddenly that Alice had not a moment to think about stopping herself before she found herself falling down what seemed to be a very deep well.

Either the well was very deep, or she fell very slowly, for she had plenty of time as she went down to look about her, and to wonder what was going to happen next. First, she tried to look down and make out what she was coming to, but it was too dark to see anything: then she looked at the sides of the well, and noticed that they were filled with cupboards and book-shelves: here and there she saw maps and pictures hung upon pegs. She took down a jar from one of the shelves as she passed: it was labeled 'ORANGE MARMALADE,'[1] but to her great disappointment it was empty: she did not like to drop the jar, for fear of killing somebody underneath, so managed to put it into one of the cupboards as she fell past it.

'Well!' thought Alice to herself. 'After such a fall as this, I shall think nothing of tumbling down-stairs! How brave they'll all think me at home! Why, I wouldn't say anything about it, even if I fell off the top of the house!' (Which was very likely true.)

Down, down, down. Would the fall *never* come to an end? 'I wonder how many miles I've fallen by this time?' she said aloud. 'I must be getting somewhere near the centre of the earth. Let me see: that would be four thousand miles down, I think—' (for, you see, Alice had learnt several things of this sort in her lessons in the school-room, and though this was not a *very* good opportunity for showing off her knowledge, as there was no one to listen to her, still it was good practice to say it over) '—yes, that's about the right distance—but then I wonder what Latitude or Longitude I've got to?' (Alice had not the slightest idea what Latitude was, or Longitude either, but she thought they were nice grand words to say.)

Presently she began again. 'I wonder if I shall fall right *through* the earth! How funny it'll seem to come out among the people that walk with their heads downwards! The antipathies, I think—' (she was rather glad there *was* no one listening, this time, as it didn't sound at all the right word) '—but I shall have to ask them what the name of the country is, you know. Please, Ma'am, is this New Zealand? Or Australia?' (and she tried to curtsey as she spoke—fancy, *curtseying* as you're fall-ing through the air! Do you think you could manage it?) 'And what an ignorant little girl she'll think me for asking! No, it'll never do to ask: perhaps I shall see it written up somewhere.'

Down, down, down. There was nothing else to do, so Alice soon began talking again. 'Dinah'll miss me very much to-night, I should think!' (Dinah[1] was the cat.) 'I hope they'll remember her saucer of milk at tea-time. Dinah, my dear! I wish you were down here with me! There are no mice in the air, I'm afraid, but you might catch a bat, and that's very like a mouse, you know. But do cats eat bats, I wonder?' And here Alice began to get rather sleepy, and went on saying to herself, in a dreamy sort of way, 'Do cats eat bats?[2] Do cats eat bats?' and sometimes 'Do bats eat cats?', for, you see, as she couldn't answer either question, it didn't much matter which way she put it. She felt that she was dozing off, and had just begun to dream that she was walking hand in hand with Dinah, and was saying to her, very earnestly, 'Now, Dinah, tell me the truth: did you ever eat a bat?', when suddenly, thump! thump! down she came upon a heap of sticks and dry leaves, and the fall was over.

Alice was not a bit hurt, and she jumped up on to her feet in a moment: she looked up, but it was all dark overhead:

before her was another long passage, and the White Rabbit was still in sight, hurrying down it. There was not a moment to be lost: away went Alice like the wind, and was just in time to hear it say, as it turned a corner, 'Oh my ears and whiskers, how late it's getting!' She was close behind it when she turned the corner, but the Rabbit was no longer to be seen: she found herself in a long, low hall, which was lit up by a row of lamps hanging from the roof.

There were doors all round the hall, but they were all locked; and when Alice had been all the way down one side and up the other, trying every door, she walked sadly down the middle, wondering how she was ever to get out again.

Suddenly she came upon a little three-legged table, all made of solid glass: there was nothing on it but a tiny golden key,[1] and Alice's first idea was that this might belong to one of the doors of the hall; but, alas! either the locks were too large, or the key was too small, but at any rate it would not open any of them. However, on the second time round, she came upon a low curtain she had not noticed before, and behind it was a little door about fifteen inches high: she tried the little golden key in the lock, and to her great delight it fitted!

Alice opened the door and found that it led into a small passage, not much larger than a rat-hole: she knelt down and looked along the passage into the loveliest garden you ever saw. How she longed to get out of that dark hall, and wander about among those beds of bright flowers[1] and those cool fountains, but she could not even get her head through the doorway; 'and even if my head *would* go through,' thought poor Alice, 'it would be of very little use without my shoulders. Oh, how I wish I could shut up like a telescope! I think I could, if I only knew how to begin.' For, you see, so many out-of-the-way things had happened lately, that Alice had begun to think that very few things indeed were really impossible.

There seemed to be no use in waiting by the little door, so she went back to the table, half hoping she might find another key on it, or at any rate a book of rules for shutting people up like telescopes: this time she found a little bottle on it ('which certainly was not here before,' said Alice), and tied round the neck of the bottle was a paper label, with the words 'DRINK ME' beautifully printed on it in large letters.

It was all very well to say 'Drink me,' but the wise little Alice was not going to do *that* in a hurry. 'No, I'll look first,' she said, 'and see whether it's marked "*poison*" or not'; for she had read several nice little stories[2] about children who had got burnt, and eaten up by wild beasts, and other unpleasant things, all because they *would* not remember the simple rules their friends had taught them: such as, that a red-hot poker will burn you if you hold it too long; and that, if you cut your finger *very* deeply with a knife, it usually bleeds; and she had never forgotten that, if you drink much from a bottle marked 'poison,' it is almost certain to disagree with you, sooner or later.

However, this bottle was *not* marked 'poison,' so Alice ventured to taste it, and, finding it very nice (it had, in fact, a sort of mixed flavour of cherry-tart, custard, pine-apple, roast turkey, toffy, and hot buttered toast), she very soon finished it off.

      *   *   *   *

         *   *   *

      *   *   *   *

'What a curious feeling!' said Alice. 'I must be shutting up like a telescope!'

And so it was indeed: she was now only ten inches high, and her face brightened up at the thought that she was now the right size for going through the little door into that lovely garden. First, however, she waited for a few minutes to see if she was going to shrink any further: she felt a little nervous about this; 'for it might end, you know,' said Alice to herself, 'in my going out altogether, like a candle. I wonder what I should be like then?' And she tried to fancy what the flame of a candle looks like after the candle is blown out, for she could not remember ever having seen such a thing.

After a while, finding that nothing more happened, she decided on going into the garden at once; but, alas for poor Alice! when she got to the door, she found she had forgotten the little golden key, and when she went back to the table for it, she found she could not possibly reach it: she could see it quite plainly through the glass, and she tried her best to climb up one of the legs of the table, but it was too slippery; and when she had tired herself out with trying, the poor little thing sat down and cried.

'Come, there's no use in crying like that!' said Alice to herself rather sharply. 'I advise you to leave off this minute!' She generally gave herself very good advice (though she very seldom followed it), and sometimes she scolded herself so severely as to bring tears into her eyes; and once she remembered trying to box her own ears for having cheated herself in a game of croquet she was playing against herself, for this curious child was very fond of pretending to be two people. 'But it's no use now,' thought poor Alice, 'to pretend to be two people! Why, there's hardly enough of me left to make *one* respectable person.'

Soon her eye fell on a little glass box that was lying under the table: she opened it, and found in it a very small cake, on which the words 'EAT ME' were beautifully marked in currants. 'Well, I'll eat it,' said Alice, 'and if it makes me grow larger, I can reach the key; and if it makes me grow smaller, I can creep under the door: so either way I'll get into the garden, and I don't care which happens!'

She ate a little bit, and said anxiously to herself 'Which way? Which way?', holding her hand on the top of her head to feel which way it was growing; and she was quite surprised to find that she remained the same size. To be sure, this is what generally happens when one eats cake; but Alice had got so much into the way of expecting nothing but out-of-the-way things to happen, that it seemed quite dull and stupid for life to go on in the common way.

So she set to work, and very soon finished off the cake.

       *   *   *   *

           *   *   *

       *   *   *   *

D

CHAPTER II

THE POOL OF TEARS

'CURIOUSER and curi-ouser!' cried Alice (she was so much surprised, that for the moment she quite forgot how to speak good English). 'Now I'm opening out like the lar-gest telescope that ever was! Good-bye, feet!' (for when she looked down at her feet, they seemed to be almost out of sight, they were get-ting so far off). 'Oh, my poor little feet, I wonder who will put on your shoes and stock-ings for you now, dears? I'm sure *I* sha'n't be able! I shall be a great deal too far off to trouble myself about you: you must manage the best way you can—but I must be kind to them,' thought Alice, 'or perhaps they wo'n't walk the way I want to go! Let me see. I'll give them a new pair of boots every Christmas.'

And she went on planning to herself how she would manage it. 'They must go by the carrier,' she thought; 'and how funny it'll seem, sending presents to one's own feet! And how odd the directions will look!

> *Alice's Right Foot, Esq.*
> *Hearthrug,*
> *near the Fender,*
> (*with Alice's love*).

Oh dear, what nonsense I'm talking!'

Just at this moment her head struck against the roof of the hall: in fact she was now rather more than nine feet high, and she at once took up the little golden key and hurried off to the garden door.

Poor Alice! It was as much as she could do, lying down on one side, to look through into the garden with one eye; but to get through was more hopeless than ever: she sat down and began to cry again.

'You ought to be ashamed of yourself,' said Alice, 'a great girl like you,' (she might well say this), 'to go on crying in this way! Stop this moment, I tell you!' But she went on all the same, shedding gallons of tears, until there was a large pool all round her, about four inches deep, and reaching half down the hall.

After a time she heard a little pattering of feet in the distance, and she hastily dried her eyes to see what was coming. It was the White Rabbit returning, splendidly dressed, with a pair of white kid-gloves in one hand and a large fan in the other: he came trotting along in a great hurry, muttering to himself, as he came, 'Oh! The Duchess, the Duchess! Oh! *Wo'n't* she be savage if I've kept her waiting!' Alice felt so desperate that she was ready to ask help of any one: so, when the Rabbit came near her, she began, in a low, timid voice, 'If you please, Sir——' The Rabbit started violently, dropped the white kid-gloves and the fan, and skurried away into the darkness as hard as he could go.

Alice took up the fan and gloves, and, as the hall was very hot, she kept fanning herself all the time she went on talking. 'Dear, dear! How queer everything is to-day! And yesterday

things went on just as usual. I wonder if I've been changed in the night? Let me think: *was* I the same when I got up this morning? I almost think I can remember feeling a little different. But if I'm not the same, the next question is "Who in the world am I?" Ah, *that*'s the great puzzle!' And she began thinking over all the children she knew that were of the same age as herself, to see if she could have been changed for any of them.

'I'm sure I'm not Ada,' she said, 'for her hair goes in such long ringlets, and mine doesn't go in ringlets at all; and I'm sure I ca'n't be Mabel,[1] for I know all sorts of things, and she, oh, she knows such a very little! Besides, *she*'s she, and *I'm* I, and—oh dear, how puzzling it all is! I'll try if I know all the things I used to know. Let me see: four times five is twelve, and four times six is thirteen, and four times seven is—oh dear! I shall never get to twenty at that rate![1] However, the Multiplication-Table doesn't signify: let's try Geography. London is the capital of Paris, and Paris is the capital of Rome, and Rome—no, *that's* all wrong, I'm certain! I must have been changed for Mabel! I'll try and say "*How doth the little*—",' and she crossed her hands on her lap, as if she were saying lessons, and began to repeat it, but her voice sounded hoarse and strange, and the words did not come the same as they used to do:—

'*How doth the little crocodile*[2]
Improve his shining tail,
And pour the waters of the Nile
On every golden scale!

'*How cheerfully he seems to grin,*
How neatly spreads his claws,
And welcomes little fishes in,
With gently smiling jaws!'

'I'm sure those are not the right words,' said poor Alice, and her eyes filled with tears again as she went on, 'I must be Mabel after all, and I shall have to go and live in that poky little house, and have next to no toys to play with, and oh, ever so many lessons to learn! No, I've made up my mind about it: if I'm Mabel, I'll stay down here! It'll be no use their putting their heads down and saying "Come up again, dear!" I shall only look up and say "Who am I, then? Tell me that first, and then, if I like being that person, I'll come up: if not, I'll stay down here till I'm somebody else"—but, oh dear!' cried Alice, with a sudden burst of tears, 'I do wish they *would* put their heads down! I am so *very* tired of being all alone here!'

As she said this she looked down at her hands, and was surprised to see that she had put on one of the Rabbit's little white kid-gloves while she was talking. 'How *can* I have done that?' she thought. 'I must be growing small again.' She got up and went to the table to measure herself by it, and found that, as nearly as she could guess, she was now about two feet high, and was going on shrinking rapidly: she soon found out that the cause of this was the fan she was holding, and she dropped it hastily, just in time to save herself from shrinking away altogether.

'That *was* a narrow escape!' said Alice, a good deal frightened at the sudden change, but very glad to find herself still in existence. 'And now for the garden!' And she ran with all speed back to the little door; but, alas! the little door was shut again, and the little golden key was lying on the glass table as before, 'and things are worse than ever,' thought the poor child, 'for I never was so small as this before, never! And I declare it's too bad, that it is!'

As she said these words her foot slipped, and in another moment, splash! she was up to her chin in salt-water. Her first

idea was that she had somehow fallen into the sea, 'and in that case I can go back by railway,' she said to herself. (Alice had been to the seaside once in her life,[1] and had come to the general conclusion that, wherever you go to on the English coast, you find a number of bathing-machines[2] in the sea, some children digging in the sand with wooden spades, then a row of lodging-houses, and behind them a railway-station.) However, she soon made out that she was in the pool of tears which she had wept when she was nine feet high.

'I wish I hadn't cried so much!' said Alice, as she swam about, trying to find her way out. 'I shall be punished for it now, I suppose, by being drowned in my own tears! That *will* be a queer thing, to be sure! However, everything is queer to-day.'

Just then she heard something splashing about in the pool a little way off, and she swam nearer to make out what it was: at first she thought it must be a walrus or hippopotamus, but then she remembered how small she was now, and she soon made out that it was only a mouse, that had slipped in like herself.

'Would it be of any use, now,' thought Alice, 'to speak to this mouse? Everything is so out-of-the-way down here, that I should think very likely it can talk: at any rate, there's no harm in trying.' So she began: 'O Mouse, do you know the way out of this pool? I am very tired of swimming about here, O Mouse!' (Alice thought this must be the right way of speaking to a mouse: she had never done such a thing before, but she remembered having seen, in her brother's[1] Latin Grammar,[2] 'A mouse—of a mouse—to a mouse—a mouse—O mouse!') The mouse looked at her rather inquisitively, and seemed to her to wink with one of its little eyes, but it said nothing.

'Perhaps it doesn't understand English,' thought Alice. 'I daresay it's a French mouse, come over with William the Conqueror.' (For, with all her knowledge of history, Alice had no very clear notion how long ago anything had happened.) So she began again: 'Où est ma chatte?', which was the first sentence in her French lesson-book.[3] The Mouse gave a sudden leap out of the water, and seemed to quiver all over with fright. 'Oh, I beg your pardon!' cried Alice hastily, afraid that she had hurt the poor animal's feelings. 'I quite forgot you didn't like cats.'

'Not like cats!' cried the Mouse in a shrill, passionate voice. 'Would *you* like cats, if you were me?'

'Well, perhaps not,' said Alice in a soothing tone: 'don't be angry about it. And yet I wish I could show you our cat Dinah. I think you'd take a fancy to cats, if you could only see her. She is such a dear quiet thing,' Alice went on, half to herself, as she swam lazily about in the pool, 'and she sits purring so

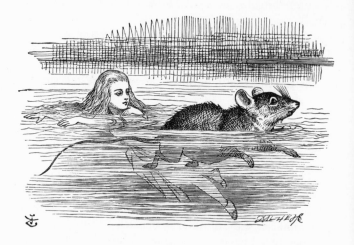

nicely by the fire, licking her paws and washing her face—and she is such a nice soft thing to nurse—and she's such a capital one for catching mice——oh, I beg your pardon!' cried Alice again, for this time the Mouse was bristling all over, and she felt certain it must be really offended. 'We wo'n't talk about her any more, if you'd rather not.'

'We, indeed!' cried the Mouse, who was trembling down to the end of its tail. 'As if *I* would talk on such a subject! Our family always *hated* cats: nasty, low, vulgar things! Don't let me hear the name again!'

'I wo'n't indeed!' said Alice, in a great hurry to change the subject of conversation. 'Are you—are you fond—of—of dogs?' The Mouse did not answer, so Alice went on eagerly: 'There is such a nice little dog, near our house, I should like to show you! A little bright-eyed terrier, you know, with oh, such long curly brown hair! And it'll fetch things when you throw them, and it'll sit up and beg for its dinner, and all sorts of things—I ca'n't remember half of them—and it belongs to a farmer, you know, and he says it's so useful, it's worth a hundred pounds! He says it kills all the rats and—oh dear!' cried Alice in a sorrowful tone. 'I'm afraid I've offended it again!' For the Mouse was swimming away from her as hard as it could go, and making quite a commotion in the pool as it went.

So she called softly after it, 'Mouse dear! Do come back again, and we wo'n't talk about cats, or dogs either, if you don't like them!' When the Mouse heard this, it turned round and swam slowly back to her: its face was quite pale (with passion, Alice thought), and it said, in a low trembling voice, 'Let us get to the shore, and then I'll tell you my history, and you'll understand why it is I hate cats and dogs.'[1]

It was high time to go, for the pool was getting quite crowded with the birds and animals that had fallen into it: there was a Duck and a Dodo, a Lory and an Eaglet, and several other curious creatures.[2] Alice led the way, and the whole party swam to the shore.

CHAPTER III

A CAUCUS-RACE AND A LONG TALE

THEY were indeed a queer-looking party that assembled on the bank—the birds with draggled feathers, the animals with their fur clinging close to them, and all dripping wet, cross, and uncomfortable.

The first question of course was, how to get dry again: they had a consultation about this, and after a few minutes it seemed quite natural to Alice to find herself talking familiarly with them, as if she had known them all her life. Indeed, she had quite a long argument with the Lory, who at last turned sulky, and would only say 'I'm older than you, and must know better.' And this Alice would not allow, without knowing how old it was, and, as the Lory positively refused to tell its age, there was no more to be said.

At last the Mouse,[1] who seemed to be a person of some authority among them, called out 'Sit down, all of you, and listen to me! *I'll* soon make you dry enough!' They all sat

down at once, in a large ring, with the Mouse in the middle.
Alice kept her eyes anxiously fixed on it, for she felt sure she
would catch a bad cold if she did not get dry very soon.

'Ahem!' said the Mouse with an important air. 'Are you
all ready? This is the driest thing I know. Silence all round,
if you please! "William the Conqueror, whose cause was
favoured by the pope, was soon submitted to by the English,
who wanted leaders, and had been of late much accustomed
to usurpation and conquest. Edwin and Morcar, the earls of
Mercia and Northumbria——"'

'Ugh!' said the Lory, with a shiver.

'I beg your pardon!' said the Mouse, frowning, but very
politely. 'Did you speak?'

'Not I!' said the Lory, hastily.

'I thought you did,' said the Mouse. 'I proceed. "Edwin
and Morcar, the earls of Mercia and Northumbria, declared
for him; and even Stigand, the patriotic archbishop of
Canterbury, found it advisable——"'

'Found *what?*' said the Duck.

'Found *it*,' the Mouse replied rather crossly: 'of course you
know what "it" means.'

'I know what "it" means well enough, when *I* find a thing,'
said the Duck: 'it's generally a frog, or a worm. The question
is, what did the archbishop find?'

The Mouse did not notice this question, but hurriedly went
on, '"—found it advisable to go with Edgar Atheling to meet
William and offer him the crown. William's conduct at first
was moderate. But the insolence of his Normans——"[1] How
are you getting on now, my dear?' it continued, turning to
Alice as it spoke.

'As wet as ever,' said Alice in a melancholy tone: 'it doesn't
seem to dry me at all.'

'In that case,' said the Dodo solemnly, rising to its feet,
'I move that the meeting adjourn, for the immediate adoption
of more energetic remedies——'

'Speak English!' said the Eaglet. 'I don't know the meaning
of half those long words, and, what's more, I don't believe you
do either!' And the Eaglet bent down its head to hide a smile:
some of the other birds tittered audibly.

'What I was going to say,' said the Dodo in an offended tone, 'was, that the best thing to get us dry would be a Caucus-race.'[1]

'What *is* a Caucus-race?' said Alice; not that she much wanted to know, but the Dodo had paused as if it thought that *somebody* ought to speak, and no one else seemed inclined to say anything.

'Why,' said the Dodo, 'the best way to explain it is to do it.' (And, as you might like to try the thing yourself, some winter-day. I will tell you how the Dodo managed it.)

First it marked out a race-course, in a sort of circle, ('the exact shape doesn't matter,' it said,) and then all the party were placed along the course, here and there. There was no 'One, two, three, and away!', but they began running when they liked, and left off when they liked, so that it was not easy to know when the race was over. However, when they had been running half an hour or so, and were quite dry again, the Dodo suddenly called out 'The race is over!', and they all crowded round it, panting, and asking 'But who has won?'

This question the Dodo could not answer without a great deal of thought, and it stood for a long time with one finger pressed upon its forehead (the position in which you usually see Shakespeare, in the pictures of him), while the rest waited in silence. At last the Dodo said '*Everybody* has won, and *all* must have prizes.'[2]

'But who is to give the prizes?' quite a chorus of voices asked.

'Why, *she*, of course,' said the Dodo, pointing to Alice with one finger; and the whole party at once crowded round her, calling out, in a confused way, 'Prizes! Prizes!'

Alice had no idea what to do, and in despair she put her hand in her pocket, and pulled out a box of comfits[3] (luckily the salt water had not got into it), and handed them round as prizes. There was exactly one a-piece, all round.

'But she must have a prize herself, you know,' said the Mouse.

'Of course,' the Dodo replied very gravely. 'What else have you got in your pocket?' it went on, turning to Alice.

'Only a thimble,' said Alice sadly.

'Hand it over here,' said the Dodo.

Then they all crowded round her once more, while the Dodo solemnly presented the thimble, saying 'We beg your acceptance of this elegant thimble'; and, when it had finished this short speech, they all cheered.

Alice thought the whole thing very absurd, but they all looked so grave that she did not dare to laugh; and, as she could not think of anything to say, she simply bowed, and took the thimble, looking as solemn as she could.

The next thing was to eat the comfits: this caused some noise and confusion, as the large birds complained that they could not taste theirs, and the small ones choked and had to be patted on the back. However, it was over at last, and they sat down again in a ring, and begged the Mouse to tell them something more.

'You promised to tell me your history, you know,' said

Alice, 'and why it is you hate—C and D,' she added in a whisper, half afraid that it would be offended again.

'Mine is a long and a sad tale!' said the Mouse, turning to Alice, and sighing.

'It *is* a long tail, certainly,' said Alice, looking down with wonder at the Mouse's tail; 'but why do you call it sad?' And she kept on puzzling about it while the Mouse was speaking, so that her idea of the tale was something like this:——

'Fury said to
a mouse, That
he met in the
house,   "Let
us both go
to law: *I*
will prose-
cute *you*.—
Come, I'll
take no de-
nial: We
must have
the trial;
For really
this morn-
ing I've
nothing
to do."
Said the
mouse to
the cur,
"Such   a
trial, dear
sir, With
no jury
or judge,
would
be wast-
ing our
breath."
"I'll be
judge,
I'll be
jury,"
said
cun-
ning
old
Fury:
"I'll
try
the
whole
cause,
and
con-
demn
you to
death".'

'You are not attending!' said the Mouse to Alice, severely. 'What are you thinking of?'

'I beg your pardon,' said Alice very humbly: 'you had got to the fifth bend, I think?'

'I had *not!*' cried the Mouse, sharply and very angrily.

'A knot!' said Alice, always ready to make herself useful, and looking anxiously about her 'Oh, do let me help to undo it!'

'I shall do nothing of the sort,' said the Mouse, getting up and walking away. 'You insult me by talking such nonsense!'

'I didn't mean it!' pleaded poor Alice. 'But you're so easily offended, you know!'

The Mouse only growled in reply.

'Please come back, and finish your story!' Alice called after it. And the others all joined in chorus 'Yes, please do!' But the Mouse only shook its head impatiently, and walked a little quicker.

'What a pity it wouldn't stay!' sighed the Lory, as soon as it was quite out of sight. And an old Crab took the opportunity of saying to her daughter 'Ah, my dear! Let this be a lesson to you never to lose *your* temper!' 'Hold your tongue, Ma!' said the young Crab, a little snappishly. 'You're enough to try the patience of an oyster!'

'I wish I had our Dinah here, I know I do!' said Alice aloud, addressing nobody in particular. '*She'd* soon fetch it back!'

'And who is Dinah, if I might venture to ask the question?' said the Lory.

Alice replied eagerly, for she was always ready to talk about her pet: 'Dinah's our cat. And she's such a capital one for catching mice, you ca'n't think! And oh, I wish you could see her after the birds! Why, she'll eat a little bird as soon as look at it!'

This speech caused a remarkable sensation among the party. Some of the birds hurried off at once: one old Magpie began wrapping itself up very carefully, remarking 'I really must be getting home: the night-air doesn't suit my throat!' And a Canary called out in a trembling voice, to its children, 'Come away, my dears! It's high time you were all in bed!' On various pretexts they all moved off, and Alice was soon left alone.

'I wish I hadn't mentioned Dinah!' she said to herself in a melancholy tone. 'Nobody seems to like her, down here, and I'm sure she's the best cat in the world! Oh, my dear Dinah! I wonder if I shall ever see you any more!' And here poor Alice began to cry again, for she felt very lonely and low-spirited. In a little while, however, she again heard a little pattering of footsteps in the distance, and she looked up eagerly, half hoping that the Mouse had changed his mind, and was coming back to finish his story.

CHAPTER IV

THE RABBIT SENDS IN A LITTLE BILL

IT was the White Rabbit, trotting slowly back again, and looking anxiously about as it went, as if it had lost something; and
she heard it muttering to itself, 'The Duchess! The Duchess!
Oh my dear paws! Oh my fur and whiskers! She'll get me
executed, as sure as ferrets are ferrets! Where *can* I have
dropped them, I wonder?' Alice guessed in a moment that
it was looking for the fan and the pair of white kid-gloves,
and she very good-naturedly began hunting about for them,
but they were nowhere to be seen—everything seemed to
have changed since her swim in the pool; and the great hall,
with the glass table and the little door, had vanished completely.

Very soon the Rabbit noticed Alice, as she went hunting
about, and called out to her, in an angry tone, 'Why, Mary
Ann,[1] what *are* you doing out here? Run home this moment,
and fetch me a pair of gloves and a fan! Quick, now!' And
Alice was so much frightened that she ran off at once in the
direction it pointed to, without trying to explain the mistake
that it had made.

'He took me for his housemaid,' she said to herself as she
ran. 'How surprised he'll be when he finds out who I am! But
I'd better take him his fan and gloves—that is, if I can find
them.' As she said this, she came upon a neat little house, on
the door of which was a bright brass plate with the name
'W. RABBIT' engraved upon it. She went in without knocking, and hurried upstairs, in great fear lest she should meet
the real Mary Ann, and be turned out of the house before she
had found the fan and gloves.

'How queer it seems,' Alice said to herself, 'to be going
messages for a rabbit! I suppose Dinah'll be sending me on

E

messages next!' And she began fancying the sort of thing that would happen: '"Miss Alice! Come here directly, and get ready for your walk!" "Coming in a minute, nurse! But I've got to watch this mouse-hole till Dinah comes back, and see that the mouse doesn't get out." Only I don't think,' Alice went on, 'that they'd let Dinah stop in the house if it began ordering people about like that!'

By this time she had found her way into a tidy little room with a table in the window, and on it (as she had hoped) a fan and two or three pairs of tiny white kid-gloves: she took up the fan and a pair of the gloves, and was just going to leave the room, when her eye fell upon a little bottle that stood near the looking-glass. There was no label this time with the words 'DRINK ME,' but nevertheless she uncorked it and put it to her lips. 'I know *something* interesting is sure to happen,' she said to herself, 'whenever I eat or drink anything: so I'll just see what this bottle does. I do hope it'll make me grow large again, for really I'm quite tired of being such a tiny little thing!'

It did so indeed, and much sooner than she had expected: before she had drunk half the bottle, she found her head pressing against the ceiling, and had to stoop to save her neck from being broken. She hastily put down the bottle, saying to herself 'That's quite enough—I hope I sha'n't grow any more—As it is, I ca'n't get out at the door—I do wish I hadn't drunk quite so much!'

Alas! It was too late to wish that! She went on growing, and growing, and very soon had to kneel down on the floor: in another minute there was not even room for this, and she tried the effect of lying down with one elbow against the door, and the other arm curled round her head. Still she went on growing, and, as a last resource, she put one arm out of the window, and one foot up the chimney, and said to herself 'Now I can do no more, whatever happens. What *will* become of me?'

Luckily for Alice, the little magic bottle had now had its full effect, and she grew no larger: still it was very uncom-

fortable, and, as there seemed to be no sort of chance of her ever getting out of the room again, no wonder she felt unhappy.

'It was much pleasanter at home,' thought poor Alice, 'when one wasn't always growing larger and smaller, and being ordered about by mice and rabbits. I almost wish I hadn't gone down that rabbit-hole—and yet—and yet—it's rather curious, you know, this sort of life! I do wonder what *can* have happened to me! When I used to read fairy tales, I fancied that kind of thing never happened, and now here I am in the middle of one! There ought to be a book written about me, that there ought! And when I grow up, I'll write one—but I'm grown up now,' she added in a sorrowful tone: 'at least there's no room to grow up any more *here*.'

'But then,' thought Alice, 'shall I *never* get any older than I am now? That'll be a comfort, one way—never to be an old woman—but then—always to have lessons to learn! Oh, I shouldn't like *that!*'

'Oh, you foolish Alice!' she answered herself. 'How can you learn lessons in here? Why, there's hardly room for *you*, and no room at all for any lesson-books!'

And so she went on, taking first one side and then the other, and making quite a conversation of it altogether; but after a few minutes she heard a voice outside, and stopped to listen.

'Mary Ann! Mary Ann!' said the voice. 'Fetch me my gloves this moment!' Then same a little pattering of feet on the stairs. Alice knew it was the Rabbit coming to look for her, and she trembled till she shook the house, quite forgetting that she was now about a thousand times as large as the Rabbit, and had no reason to be afraid of it.

Presently the Rabbit came up to the door, and tried to open it; but, as the door opened inwards, and Alice's elbow was pressed hard against it, that attempt proved a failure. Alice

heard it say to itself 'Then I'll go round and get in at the window.'

'*That* you wo'n't!' thought Alice, and, after waiting till she fancied she heard the Rabbit just under the window, she suddenly spread out her hand, and made a snatch in the air. She did not get hold of anything, but she heard a little shriek and a fall, and a crash of broken glass, from which she concluded that it was just possible it had fallen into a cucumber-frame, or something of the sort.

Next came an angry voice—the Rabbit's—'Pat! Pat! Where are you?' And then a voice she had never heard before, 'Sure then I'm here! Digging for apples, yer honour!'

'Digging for apples, indeed!' said the Rabbit angrily. 'Here!

Come and help me out of *this!*' (Sounds of more broken glass.)

'Now tell me, Pat, what's that in the window?'

'Sure, it's an arm, yer honour!' (He pronounced it 'arrum.')

'An arm, you goose! Who ever saw one that size? Why, it fills the whole window!'

'Sure, it does, yer honour: but it's an arm for all that.'

'Well, it's got no business there, at any rate: go and take it away!'

There was a long silence after this, and Alice could only hear whispers now and then; such as 'Sure, I don't like it, yer honour, at all, at all!' 'Do as I tell you, you coward!', and at last she spread out her hand again, and made another snatch in the air. This time there were *two* little shrieks, and more sounds of broken glass. 'What a number of cucumber-frames there must be!' thought Alice. 'I wonder what they'll do next! As for pulling me out of the window, I only wish they *could!* I'm sure *I* don't want to stay in here any longer!'

She waited for some time without hearing anything more: at last came a rumbling of little cart-wheels, and the sound of a good many voices all talking together: she made out the words: 'Where's the other ladder?—Why, I hadn't to bring but one. Bill's got the other—Bill! Fetch it here, lad!—Here, put 'em up at this corner—No, tie 'em together first—they don't reach half high enough yet—Oh, they'll do well enough. Don't be particular—Here, Bill! Catch hold of this rope—Will the roof bear?—Mind that loose slate—Oh, it's coming down! Heads below!' (a loud crash)—'Now, who did that? —It was Bill, I fancy—Who's to go down the chimney?— Nay, *I* sha'n't! *You* do it!—*That* I wo'n't, then!—Bill's got to go down—Here, Bill! The master says you've got to go down the chimney!'

'Oh! So Bill's got to come down the chimney, has he?' said Alice to herself. 'Why, they seem to put everything upon Bill! I wouldn't be in Bill's place for a good deal: this fireplace is narrow, to be sure; but I *think* I can kick a little!'

She drew her foot as far down the chimney as she could, and waited till she heard a little animal (she couldn't guess of what sort it was) scratching and scrambling about in the chimney close above her: then, saying to herself 'This is Bill', she gave one sharp kick, and waited to see what would happen next.

The first thing she heard was a general chorus of 'There goes Bill!' then the Rabbit's voice alone—'Catch him, you by the hedge!' then silence, and then another confusion of voices— 'Hold up his head—Brandy now—Don't choke him—How was it, old fellow? What happened to you? Tell us all about it!'

Last came a little feeble, squeaking voice ('That's Bill,' thought Alice), 'Well, I hardly know—No more, thank ye; I'm better now—but I'm a deal too flustered to tell you— all I know is, something comes at me like a Jack-in-the-box, and up I goes like a sky-rocket!'

'So you did, old fellow!' said the others.

'We must burn the house down!' said the Rabbit's voice. And Alice called out, as loud as she could, 'If you do, I'll set Dinah at you!'

There was a dead silence instantly, and Alice thought to herself 'I wonder what they *will* do next! If they had any sense, they'd take the roof off.' After a minute or two, they began moving about again, and Alice heard the Rabbit say 'A barrowful will do, to begin with.'

'A barrowful of *what?*' thought Alice. But she had not long to doubt, for the next moment a shower of little pebbles came rattling in at the window, and some of them hit her in the face. 'I'll put a stop to this,' she said to herself, and shouted out 'You'd better not do that again!', which produced another dead silence.

Alice noticed, with some surprise, that the pebbles were all turning into little cakes as they lay on the floor, and a bright idea came into her head. 'If I eat one of these cakes,' she thought, 'it's sure to make *some* change in my size; and, as it ca'n't possibly make me larger, it must make me smaller, I suppose.'

So she swallowed one of the cakes, and was delighted to find that she began shrinking directly. As soon as she was small enough to get through the door, she ran out of the house, and found quite a crowd of little animals[1] and birds waiting outside. The poor little Lizard, Bill, was in the middle, being held up by two guinea-pigs, who were giving it something out of a bottle. They all made a rush at Alice the moment she appeared; but she ran off as hard as she could, and soon found herself safe in a thick wood.

'The first thing I've got to do,' said Alice to herself, as she wandered about in the wood, 'is to grow to my right size again; and the second thing is to find my way into that lovely garden. I think that will be the best plan.'

It sounded an excellent plan, no doubt, and very neatly and simply arranged: the only difficulty was, that she had not the smallest idea how to set about it; and, while she was peering about anxiously among the trees, a little sharp bark just over her head made her look up in a great hurry.

An enormous puppy was looking down at her with large round eyes, and feebly stretching out one paw, trying to touch her. 'Poor little thing!' said Alice, in a coaxing tone, and she tried hard to whistle to it; but she was terribly frightened

all the time at the thought that it might be hungry, in which case it would be very likely to eat her up in spite of all her coaxing.

Hardly knowing what she did, she picked up a little bit of stick, and held it out to the puppy: whereupon the puppy jumped into the air off all its feet at once, with a yelp of delight, and rushed at the stick, and made believe to worry it: then Alice dodged behind a great thistle, to keep herself from being run over; and, the moment she appeared on the other side, the puppy made another rush at the stick, and tumbled head over heels in its hurry to get hold of it: then Alice, thinking it was very like having a game of play with a cart-horse, and expecting every moment to be trampled under its feet, ran round the thistle again: then the puppy began a series of short charges at the stick, running a very little way forwards each time and a long way back, and barking hoarsely all the while, till at last it sat down a good way off, panting, with its tongue hanging out of its mouth, and its great eyes half shut.

This seemed to Alice a good opportunity for making her escape: so she set off at once, and ran till she was quite tired and out of breath, and till the puppy's bark sounded quite faint in the distance.

'And yet what a dear little puppy it was!' said Alice, as she leant against a buttercup to rest herself, and fanned herself with one of the leaves. 'I should have liked teaching it tricks very much, if—if I'd only been the right size to do it! Oh dear! I'd nearly forgotten that I've got to grow up again! Let me see—how *is* it to be managed? I suppose I ought to eat or drink something or other; but the great question is "What?"'

The great question certainly was 'What?' Alice looked all round her at the flowers and the blades of grass, but she could not see anything that looked like the right thing to eat or drink under the circumstances. There was a large mushroom growing near her, about the same height as herself; and, when she had looked under it, and on both sides of it, and behind it, it occurred to her that she might as well look and see what was on the top of it.

She stretched herself up on tiptoe, and peeped over the edge of the mushroom, and her eyes immediately met those of a large blue caterpillar, that was sitting on the top, with its arms folded, quietly smoking a long hookah, and taking not the smallest notice of her or of anything else.

CHAPTER V

ADVICE FROM A CATERPILLAR

THE Caterpillar and Alice looked at each other for some time in silence: at last the Caterpillar took the hookah out of its mouth, and addressed her in a languid, sleepy voice.

'Who are *you?*' said the Caterpillar.

This was not an encouraging opening for a conversation. Alice replied, rather shyly, 'I—I hardly know, Sir, just at present—at least I know who I *was* when I got up this mornng, but I think I must have been changed several times since then.'

'What do you mean by that?' said the Caterpillar, sternly. Explain yourself!'

'I ca'n't explain *myself*, I'm afraid, Sir,' said Alice, 'because I'm not myself, you see.'

'I don't see,' said the Caterpillar.

'I'm afraid I ca'n't put it more clearly,' Alice replied, very politely, 'for I ca'n't understand it myself, to begin with; and being so many different sizes in a day is very confusing.'

'It isn't,' said the Caterpillar.

'Well, perhaps you haven't found it so yet,' said Alice; 'but when you have to turn into a chrysalis—you will some day, you know—and then after that into a butterfly, I should think you'll feel it a little queer, wo'n't you?'

'Not a bit,' said the Caterpillar.

'Well, perhaps *your* feelings may be different,' said Alice: 'all I know is, it would feel very queer to *me*.'

'You!' said the Caterpillar contemptuously. 'Who are *you?*'

Which brought them back again to the beginning of the conversation. Alice felt a little irritated at the Caterpillar's making such *very* short remarks, and she drew herself up and said, very gravely, 'I think you ought to tell me who *you* are, first.'

'Why?' said the Caterpillar.

Here was another puzzling question; and, as Alice could not think of any good reason, and the Caterpillar seemed to be in a *very* unpleasant state of mind, she turned away.

'Come back!' the Caterpillar called after her. 'I've something important to say!'

This sounded promising, certainly. Alice turned and came back again.

'Keep your temper,' said the Caterpillar.

'Is that all?' said Alice, swallowing down her anger as well as she could.

'No,' said the Caterpillar.

Alice thought she might as well wait, as she had nothing else to do, and perhaps after all it might tell her something worth hearing. For some minutes it puffed away without speaking; but at last it unfolded its arms, took the hookah out of its mouth again, and said 'So you think you're changed, do you?'

'I'm afraid I am, Sir,' said Alice. 'I ca'n't remember things as I used—and I don't keep the same size for ten minutes together!'

'Ca'n't remember *what* things?' said the Caterpillar.

'Well, I've tried to say "*How doth the little busy bee*," but it all came different!' Alice replied in a very melancholy voice.

'Repeat "*You are old, Father William*,"¹ said the Caterpillar.

Alice folded her hands, and began:—

'*You are old, Father William,*' the young man said,
   '*And your hair has become very white;*
And yet you incessantly stand on your head—
   Do you think, at your age, it is right?'

'*In my youth,*' Father William replied to his son,
   '*I feared it might injure the brain;*
But, now that I'm perfectly sure I have none,
   Why, I do it again and again.'

'*You are old,*' said the youth, '*as I mentioned before,*
   And have grown most uncommonly fat;
Yet you turned a back-somersault in at the door—
   Pray, what is the reason of that?'

'*In my youth,*' said the sage, as he shook his grey locks,
   '*I kept all my limbs very supple*
By the use of this ointment—one shilling the box—[1]
   Allow me to sell you a couple?'

'You are old,' said the youth, 'and your jaws are too weak
    For anything tougher than suet;
Yet you finished the goose, with the bones and the beak—
    Pray, how did you manage to do it?'

'In my youth,' said his father, 'I took to the law,
    And argued each case with my wife;
And the muscular strength, which it gave to my jaw
    Has lasted the rest of my life.'

'You are old,' said the youth, 'one would hardly suppose
    That your eye was as steady as ever;
Yet you balanced an eel on the end of your nose—
    What made you so awfully clever?'

'I have answered three questions, and that is enough,'
    Said his father. 'Don't give yourself airs!
Do you think I can listen all day to such stuff?
    Be off, or I'll kick you down-stairs!'

'That is not said right,' said the Caterpillar.

'Not *quite* right, I'm afraid,' said Alice, timidly: 'some of the words have got altered.'

'It is wrong from beginning to end,' said the Caterpillar, decidedly; and there was silence for some minutes.

The Caterpillar was the first to speak.

'What size do you want to be?' it asked.

'Oh, I'm not particular as to size,' Alice hastily replied; 'only one doesn't like changing so often, you know.'

'I *don't* know,' said the Caterpillar.

Alice said nothing: she had never been so much contradicted in all her life before, and she felt that she was losing her temper.

'Are you content now?' said the Caterpillar.

'Well, I should like to be a *little* larger, Sir, if you wouldn't mind,' said Alice: 'three inches is such a wretched height to be.'

'It is a very good height indeed!' said the Caterpillar angrily, rearing itself upright as it spoke (it was exactly three inches high).

'But I'm not used to it!' pleaded poor Alice in a piteous tone. And she thought to herself 'I wish the creatures wouldn't be so easily offended!'

'You'll get used to it in time,' said the Caterpillar; and it put the hookah into its mouth, and began smoking again.

This time Alice waited patiently until it chose to speak again. In a minute or two the Caterpillar took the hookah out of its mouth, and yawned once or twice, and shook itself. Then it got down off the mushroom, and crawled away into the grass, merely remarking, as it went, 'One side will make you grow taller, and the other side will make you grow shorter.'

'One side of *what*? The other side of *what*?' thought Alice to herself.

'Of the mushroom,' said the Caterpillar, just as if she had asked it aloud; and in another moment it was out of sight.

Alice remained looking thoughtfully at the mushroom for a minute, trying to make out which were the two sides of it; and, as it was perfectly round, she found this a very difficult question. However, at last she stretched her arms round it as far as they would go, and broke off a bit of the edge with each hand.

'And now which is which?' she said to herself, and nibbled a little of the right-hand bit to try the effect. The next moment she felt a violent blow underneath her chin: it had struck her foot!

She was a good deal frightened by this very sudden change, but she felt that there was no time to be lost, as she was shrinking rapidly: so she set to work at once to eat some of the other bit. Her chin was pressed so closely against her foot, that there was hardly room to open her mouth; but she did it at last, and managed to swallow a morsel of the left-hand bit.

  *   *   *   *   *

   *   *   *   *

  *   *   *   *   *

'Come, my head's free at last!' said Alice in a tone of delight, which changed into alarm in another moment, when she found that her shoulders were nowhere to be found: all she could see, when she looked down, was an immense length of neck, which seemed to rise like a stalk out of a sea of green leaves that lay far below her.

'What *can* all that green stuff be?' said Alice. 'And where *have* my shoulders got to? And oh, my poor hands, how is it I ca'n't see you?' She was moving them about, as she spoke, but no result seemed to follow, except a little shaking among the distant green leaves.

As there seemed to be no chance of getting her hands up to her head, she tried to get her head down to *them*, and was delighted to find that her neck would bend about easily in any direction, like a serpent. She had just succeeded in curving it down into a graceful zigzag, and was going to dive in among the leaves, which she found to be nothing but the tops of the trees under which she had been wandering, when a sharp hiss made her draw back in a hurry: a large pigeon had flown into her face, and was beating her violently with its wings.

'Serpent!' screamed the Pigeon.

'I'm *not* a serpent!' said Alice indignantly. 'Let me alone!'

'Serpent, I say again!' repeated the Pigeon, but in a more subdued tone, and added, with a kind of sob, 'I've tried every way, but nothing seems to suit them!'

'I haven't the least idea what you're talking about,' said Alice.

'I've tried the roots of trees, and I've tried banks, and I've tried hedges,' the Pigeon went on, without attending to her; 'but those serpents! There's no pleasing them!'

Alice was more and more puzzled, but she thought there was no use in saying anything more till the Pigeon had finished.

'As if it wasn't trouble enough hatching the eggs,' said the Pigeon; 'but I must be on the look-out for serpents, night and day! Why, I haven't had a wink of sleep these three weeks!'

'I'm very sorry you've been annoyed,' said Alice, who was beginning to see its meaning.

F

'And just as I'd taken the highest tree in the wood,' continued the Pigeon, raising its voice to a shriek, 'and just as I was thinking I should be free of them at last, they must needs come wriggling down from the sky! Ugh, Serpent!'

'But I'm *not* a serpent, I tell you!' said Alice. 'I'm a——I'm a——'

'Well! *What* are you?' said the Pigeon. 'I can see you're trying to invent something!'

'I—I'm a little girl,' said Alice, rather doubtfully, as she remembered the number of changes she had gone through, that day.

'A likely story indeed!' said the Pigeon, in a tone of the deepest contempt. 'I've seen a good many little girls in my time, but never *one* with such a neck as that! No, no! You're a serpent; and there's no use denying it. I suppose you'll be telling me next that you never tasted an egg!'

'I *have* tasted eggs, certainly,' said Alice, who was a very truthful child; 'but little girls eat eggs quite as much as serpents do, you know.'

'I don't believe it,' said the Pigeon; 'but if they do, why, then they're a kind of serpent: that's all I can say.'

This was such a new idea to Alice, that she was quite silent for a minute or two, which gave the Pigeon the opportunity of adding 'You're looking for eggs, I know *that* well enough; and what does it matter to me whether you're a little girl or a serpent?'

'It matters a good deal to *me*,' said Alice hastily; 'but I'm not looking for eggs, as it happens; and, if I was, I shouldn't want *yours*: I don't like them raw.'

'Well, be off, then!' said the Pigeon in a sulky tone, as it settled down again into its nest. Alice crouched down among the trees as well as she could, for her neck kept getting entangled among the branches, and every now and then she had to stop and untwist it. After a while she remembered that she still held the pieces of mushroom in her hands, and she set to work very carefully, nibbling first at one and then at the other, and growing sometimes taller, and sometimes

shorter, until she had succeeded in bringing herself down to
her usual height.

It was so long since she had been anything near the right
size, that it felt quite strange at first; but she got used to it in
a few minutes, and began talking to herself, as usual, 'Come,
there's half my plan done now! How puzzling all these changes
are! I'm never sure what I'm going to be, from one minute to
another! However, I've got back to my right size: the next
thing is, to get into that beautiful garden—how *is* that to be
done, I wonder?' As she said this,[1] she came suddenly upon
an open place, with a little house in it about four feet high.
'Whoever lives there,' thought Alice, 'it'll never do to come
upon them *this* size: why, I should frighten them out of their
wits!' So she began nibbling at the right-hand bit again, and
did not venture to go near the house till she had brought herself down to nine inches high.

CHAPTER VI

PIG AND PEPPER

FOR a minute or two she stood looking at the house, and
wondering what to do next, when suddenly a footman in
livery came running out of the wood—(she considered him to
be a footman because he was in livery: otherwise, judging by his
face only, she would have called him a fish)—and rapped
loudly at the door with his knuckles. It was opened by another
footman in livery, with a round face, and large eyes like a frog;
and both footmen, Alice noticed, had powdered hair that curled
all over their heads. She felt very curious to know what it was
all about, and crept a little way out of the wood to listen.

The Fish-Footman began by producing from under his arm a great letter, nearly as large as himself, and this he handed over to the other, saying, in a solemn tone, 'For the Duchess. An invitation from the Queen to play croquet.' The Frog-Footman repeated, in the same solemn tone, only changing the order of the words a little, 'From the Queen. An invitation for the Duchess to play croquet.'

Then they both bowed low, and their curls got entangled together.

Alice laughed so much at this, that she had to run back into the wood for fear of their hearing her; and, when she next peeped out, the Fish-Footman was gone, and the other was sitting on the ground near the door, staring stupidly up into the sky.

Alice went timidly up to the door, and knocked.

'There's no sort of use in knocking,' said the Footman, 'and that for two reasons. First, because I'm on the same side of the door as you are: secondly, because they're making such a noise inside, no one could possibly hear you.' And certainly there *was* a most extraordinary noise going on within—a constant howling and sneezing, and every now and then a great crash, as if a dish or kettle had been broken to pieces.

'Please, then,' said Alice, 'how am I to get in?'

'There might be some sense in your knocking,' the Footman went on, without attending to her, 'if we had the door between us. For instance, if you were *inside*, you might knock, and I could let you out, you know.' He was looking up into the sky all the time he was speaking, and this Alice thought decidedly uncivil. 'But perhaps he ca'n't help it,' she said to herself; 'his eyes are so *very* nearly at the top of his head. But at any rate he might answer questions.—How am I to get in?' she repeated, aloud.

'I shall sit here,' the Footman remarked, 'till to-morrow——'

At this moment the door of the house opened, and a large plate came skimming out, straight at the Footman's head: it just grazed his nose, and broke to pieces against one of the trees behind him.

'——or next day, maybe,' the Footman continued in the same tone, exactly as if nothing had happened.

'How am I to get in?' asked Alice again, in a louder tone.

'*Are* you to get in at all?' said the Footman. 'That's the first question, you know.'

It was, no doubt: only Alice did not like to be told so. 'It's really dreadful,' she muttered to herself, 'the way all the creatures argue. It's enough to drive one crazy!'

The Footman seemed to think this a good opportunity for repeating his remark, with variations. 'I shall sit here,' he said, 'on and off, for days and days.'

'But what am *I* to do?' said Alice.

'Anything you like,' said the Footman, and began whistling.

'Oh, there's no use in talking to him,' said Alice desperately: 'he's perfectly idiotic!' And she opened the door and went in.

The door led right into a large kitchen, which was full of smoke from one end to the other: the Duchess was sitting on a three-legged stool in the middle, nursing a baby: the cook

was leaning over the fire, stirring a large cauldron which seemed to be full of soup.

'There's certainly too much pepper in that soup!' Alice said to herself, as well as she could for sneezing.

There was certainly too much of it in the *air*. Even the Duchess sneezed occasionally; and as for the baby, it was sneezing and howling alternately without a moment's pause. The only two creatures in the kitchen, that did *not* sneeze, were the cook, and a large cat, which was lying on the hearth and grinning from ear to ear.

'Please would you tell me,' said Alice, a little timidly, for she was not quite sure whether it was good manners for her to speak first, 'why your cat grins like that?'

'It's a Cheshire-Cat,'[1] said the Duchess, 'and that's why. Pig!'

She said the last word with such sudden violence that Alice quite jumped; but she saw in another moment that it was addressed to the baby, and not to her, so she took courage, and went on again:—

'I didn't know that Cheshire-Cats always grinned; in fact, I didn't know that cats *could* grin.'

'They all can,' said the Duchess; 'and most of 'em do.'

'I don't know of any that do,' Alice said very politely, feeling quite pleased to have got into a conversation.

'You don't know much,' said the Duchess; 'and that's a fact.'

Alice did not at all like the tone of this remark, and thought it would be as well to introduce some other subject of conversation. While she was trying to fix on one, the cook took the cauldron of soup off the fire, and at once set to work throwing everything within her reach at the Duchess and the baby—the fire-irons came first; then followed a shower of saucepans, plates, and dishes. The Duchess took no notice of them even when they hit her; and the baby was howling so much already, that it was quite impossible to say whether the blows hurt it or not.

'Oh, *please* mind what you're doing!' cried Alice, jumping up and down in an agony of terror. 'Oh, there goes his *precious* nose!', as an unusually large saucepan flew close by it, and very nearly carried it off.

'If everybody minded their own business,' the Duchess said, in a hoarse growl, 'the world would go round a deal faster than it does.'

'Which would *not* be an advantage,' said Alice, who felt very glad to get an opportunity of showing off a little of her knowledge. 'Just think what work it would make with the day and night! You see the earth takes twenty-four hours to turn round on its axis——'

'Talking of axes,' said the Duchess, 'chop off her head!'

Alice glanced rather anxiously at the cook, to see if she meant to take the hint; but the cook was busily stirring the soup, and seemed not to be listening, so she went on again: 'Twenty-four hours, I *think*; or is it twelve? I——'

'Oh, don't bother *me!*' said the Duchess. 'I never could abide figures!' And with that she began nursing her child again, singing a sort of lullaby to it as she did so, and giving it a violent shake at the end of every line:—

> '*Speak roughly to your little boy*,[1]
> *And beat him when he sneezes*:
> *He only does it to annoy*,
> *Because he knows it teases.*'

CHORUS

(in which the cook and the baby joined):—

> '*Wow! wow! wow!*'

While the Duchess sang the second verse of the song, she kept tossing the baby violently up and down, and the poor little thing howled so, that Alice could hardly hear the words:—

'I speak severely to my boy,
  I beat him when he sneezes;
For he can thoroughly enjoy
  The pepper when he pleases!'

CHORUS

'Wow! wow! wow!'

'Here! You may nurse it a bit, if you like!' the Duchess said to Alice, flinging the baby at her as she spoke. 'I must go and get ready to play croquet with the Queen,' and she hurried out of the room. The cook threw a frying-pan after her as she went, but it just missed her.

Alice caught the baby with some difficulty, as it was a queer-shaped little creature, and held out its arms and legs in all directions, 'just like a star-fish,' thought Alice. The poor little thing was snorting like a steam-engine when she caught it, and kept doubling itself up and straightening itself out again, so that altogether, for the first minute or two, it was as much as she could do to hold it.

As soon as she had made out the proper way of nursing it (which was to twist it up into a sort of knot, and then keep tight hold of its right ear and left foot, so as to prevent its undoing itself), she carried it out into the open air. 'If I don't take this child away with me,' thought Alice, 'they're sure to kill it in a day or two. Wouldn't it be murder to leave it behind?' She said the last words out loud, and the little thing grunted in reply (it had left off sneezing by this time). 'Don't grunt,' said Alice; 'that's not at all a proper way of expressing yourself.'

The baby grunted again, and Alice looked very anxiously into its face to see what was the matter with it. There could be no doubt that it had a *very* turn-up nose, much more like a snout than a real nose: also its eyes were getting extremely small for a baby: altogether Alice did not like the look of the thing at all. 'But perhaps it was only sobbing,' she thought, and looked into its eyes again, to see if there were any tears.

No, there were no tears. 'If you're going to turn into a pig, my dear,' said Alice, seriously, 'I'll have nothing more to do with you. Mind now!' The poor little thing sobbed again (or grunted, it was impossible to say which), and they went on for some while in silence.

Alice was just beginning to think to herself, 'Now, what am I to do with this creature, when I get it home?' when it grunted

again, so violently, that she looked down into its face in some alarm. This time there could be *no* mistake about it: it was neither more nor less than a pig,[1] and she felt that it would be quite absurd for her to carry it any further.

So she set the little creature down, and felt quite relieved to see it trot away quietly into the wood. 'If it had grown up,' she said to herself, 'it would have made a dreadfully ugly child : but it makes rather a handsome pig, I think.' And she began thinking over other children she knew, who might do very well as pigs, and was just saying to herself 'if one only knew the right way to change them——' when she was a little startled by seeing the Cheshire-Cat sitting on a bough of a tree a few yards off.

The Cat only grinned when it saw Alice. It looked good-natured, she thought: still it had *very* long claws and a great many teeth, so she felt that it ought to be treated with respect.

'Cheshire-Puss,' she began, rather timidly, as she did not at all know whether it would like the name: however, it only

grinned a little wider. 'Come, it's pleased so far,' thought Alice, and she went on. 'Would you tell me, please, which way I ought to go from here?'

'That depends a good deal on where you want to get to,' said the Cat.

'I don't much care where——' said Alice.

'Then it doesn't matter which way you go,' said the Cat.

'——so long as I get *some-where*,' Alice added as an explanation.

'Oh, you're sure to do that,' said the Cat, 'if you only walk long enough.'

Alice felt that this could not be denied, so she tried another question. 'What sort of people live about here?'

'In *that* direction,' the Cat said, waving its right paw round, 'lives a Hatter: and in *that* direction,' waving the other paw, 'lives a March Hare. Visit either you like: they're both mad.'[1]

'But I don't want to go among mad people,' Alice remarked.

'Oh, you ca'n't help that,' said the Cat: 'we're all mad here. I'm mad. You're mad.'

'How do you know I'm mad?' said Alice.

'You must be,' said the Cat, 'or you wouldn't have come here.'[1]

Alice didn't think that proved it at all: however, she went on: 'And how do you know that you're mad?'

'To begin with,' said the Cat, 'a dog's not mad. You grant that?'

'I suppose so,' said Alice.

'Well, then,' the Cat went on, 'you see a dog growls when it's angry, and wags its tail when it's pleased. Now *I* growl when I'm pleased, and wag my tail when I'm angry. There-fore I'm mad.'

'*I* call it purring, not growling,' said Alice.

'Call it what you like,' said the Cat. 'Do you play croquet with the Queen to-day?'

'I should like it very much,' said Alice, 'but I haven't been invited yet.'

'You'll see me there,' said the Cat, and vanished.

Alice was not much surprised at this, she was getting so well used to queer things happening. While she was still looking at the place where it had been, it suddenly appeared again.

'By-the-bye, what became of the baby?' said the Cat. 'I'd nearly forgotten to ask.'

'It turned into a pig,' Alice answered very quietly, just as if the Cat had come back in a natural way.

'I thought it would,' said the Cat, and vanished again.

Alice waited a little, half expecting to see it again, but it did not appear, and after a minute or two she walked on in the direction in which the March Hare was said to live. 'I've seen hatters before,' she said to herself: 'the March Hare will be much the most interesting, and perhaps, as this is May, it wo'n't be raving mad—at least not so mad as it was in March.'

As she said this, she looked up, and there was the Cat again, sitting on a branch of a tree.

'Did you say "pig", or "fig"?' said the Cat.

'I said "pig",' replied Alice; 'and I wish you wouldn't keep appearing and vanishing so suddenly: you make one quite giddy!'

'All right,' said the Cat; and this time it vanished quite slowly, beginning with the end of the tail, and ending with the grin, which remained some time after the rest of it had gone.

'Well! I've often seen a cat without a grin,' thought Alice; 'but a grin without a cat![1] It's the most curious thing I ever saw in all my life!'

She had not gone much farther before she came in sight of the house of the March Hare: she thought it must be the right house, because the chimneys were shaped like ears and the roof was thatched with fur. It was so large a house, that she did not like to go nearer till she had nibbled some more of the left-hand bit of mushroom, and raised herself to about two feet high: even then she walked up towards it rather timidly, saying to herself 'Suppose it should be raving mad after all! I almost wish I'd gone to see the Hatter[2] instead!'

CHAPTER VII

A MAD TEA-PARTY

THERE was a table set out under a tree in front of the house, and the March Hare and the Hatter were having tea at it: a Dormouse was sitting between them, fast asleep, and the other two were using it as a cushion, resting their elbows on it, and talking over its head. 'Very uncomfortable for the Dormouse,' thought Alice; 'only as it's asleep, I suppose it doesn't mind.'

The table was a large one, but the three were all crowded together at one corner of it. 'No room! No room!' they cried out when they saw Alice coming. 'There's *plenty* of room!' said Alice indignantly, and she sat down in a large arm-chair at one end of the table.

'Have some wine,' the March Hare said in an encouraging tone.

Alice looked all round the table, but there was nothing on it but tea. 'I don't see any wine,' she remarked.

'There isn't any,' said the March Hare.

'Then it wasn't very civil of you to offer it,' said Alice angrily.

'It wasn't very civil of you to sit down without being invited,' said the March Hare.

'I didn't know it was *your* table,' said Alice: 'it's laid for a great many more than three.'

'Your hair wants cutting,' said the Hatter. He had been looking at Alice for some time with great curiosity, and this was his first speech.

'You should learn not to make personal remarks,' Alice said with some severity: 'it's very rude.'

The Hatter opened his eyes very wide on hearing this; but all he *said* was 'Why is a raven like a writing-desk?'[1]

'Come, we shall have some fun now!' thought Alice. 'I'm glad they've begun asking riddles—I believe I can guess that,' she added aloud.

'Do you mean that you think you can find out the answer to it?' said the March Hare.

'Exactly so,' said Alice.

'Then you should say what you mean,' the March Hare went on.

'I do,' Alice hastily replied; 'at least—at least I mean what I say—that's the same thing, you know.'

'Not the same thing a bit!' said the Hatter. 'Why, you might just as well say that "I see what I eat" is the same thing as "I eat what I see"!'

'You might just as well say,' added the March Hare, 'that "I like what I get" is the same thing as "I get what I like"!'

'You might just as well say,' added the Dormouse, which seemed to be talking in its sleep, 'that "I breathe when I sleep" is the same thing as "I sleep when I breathe"!'

'It *is* the same thing with you,' said the Hatter, and here the conversation dropped, and the party sat silent for a minute, while Alice thought over all she could remember about ravens and writing-desks, which wasn't much.

The Hatter was the first to break the silence. 'What day of the month is it?'[1] he said, turning to Alice: he had taken his watch out of his pocket, and was looking at it uneasily, shaking it every now and then, and holding it to his ear.

Alice considered a little, and then said 'The fourth.'

'Two days wrong!'[2] sighed the Hatter. 'I told you butter wouldn't suit the works!' he added, looking angrily at the March Hare.

'It was the *best* butter,' the March Hare meekly replied.

'Yes, but some crumbs must have got in as well,' the Hatter grumbled: 'you shouldn't have put it in with the bread-knife.'

The March Hare took the watch and looked at it gloomily: then he dipped it into his cup of tea, and looked at it again: but he could think of nothing better to say than his first remark, 'It was the *best* butter, you know.'

Alice had been looking over his shoulder with some curiosity. 'What a funny watch!' she remarked. 'It tells the day of the month, and doesn't tell what o'clock it is!'

'Why should it?' muttered the Hatter. 'Does *your* watch tell you what year it is?'

'Of course not,' Alice replied very readily: 'but that's because it stays the same year for such a long time together.'

'Which is just the case with *mine*,' said the Hatter.

Alice felt dreadfully puzzled. The Hatter's remark seemed to her to have no sort of meaning in it, and yet it was certainly English. 'I don't quite understand you,' she said, as politely as she could.

'The Dormouse is asleep again,' said the Hatter, and he poured a little hot tea upon its nose.

The Dormouse shook its head impatiently, and said, without opening its eyes, 'Of course, of course: just what I was going to remark myself.'

'Have you guessed the riddle yet?' the Hatter said, turning to Alice again.

'No, I give it up,' Alice replied. 'What's the answer?'

'I haven't the slightest idea,' said the Hatter.

'Nor I,' said the March Hare.

Alice sighed wearily. 'I think you might do something better with the time,' she said, 'than wasting it in asking riddles that have no answers.'

'If you knew Time as well as I do,' said the Hatter, 'you wouldn't talk about wasting *it*. It's *him*.'

'I don't know what you mean,' said Alice.

'Of course you don't!' the Hatter said, tossing his head contemptuously. 'I dare say you never even spoke to Time!'

'Perhaps not,' Alice cautiously replied; 'but I know I have to beat time when I learn music.'

'Ah! That accounts for it,' said the Hatter. 'He wo'n't stand beating. Now, if you only kept on good terms with him, he'd do almost anything you liked with the clock. For instance, suppose it were nine o'clock in the morning, just time to begin lessons: you'd only have to whisper a hint to Time, and round goes the clock in a twinkling! Half-past one, time for dinner!'

('I only wish it was,' the March Hare said to itself in a whisper.)

'That would be grand, certainly,' said Alice thoughtfully; 'but then—I shouldn't be hungry for it, you know.'

'Not at first, perhaps,' said the Hatter: 'but you could keep it to half-past one as long as you liked.'

'Is that the way *you* manage?' Alice asked.

The Hatter shook his head mournfully. 'Not I!' he replied. 'We quarreled last March—— just before *he* went mad, you know——' (pointing with his teaspoon at the March Hare,) '——it was at the great concert given by the Queen of Hearts, and I had to sing

> "*Twinkle, twinkle, little bat!*[1]
> *How I wonder what you're at!*"

You know the song, perhaps?'

'I've heard something like it,' said Alice.

G

'It goes on, you know,' the Hatter continued, 'in this way:—

> *"Up above the world you fly*
> *Like a tea-tray in the sky.*
> *Twinkle, twinkle——"'*

Here the Dormouse shook itself, and began singing in its sleep '*Twinkle, twinkle, twinkle, twinkle——*' and went on so long that they had to pinch it to make it stop.

'Well, I'd hardly finished the first verse,' said the Hatter, 'when the Queen bawled out "He's murdering the time![1] Off with his head!"'

'How dreadfully savage!' exclaimed Alice.

'And ever since that,' the Hatter went on in a mournful tone, 'he wo'n't do a thing I ask! It's always six o'clock now.'

A bright idea came into Alice's head. 'Is that the reason so many tea-things are put out here?' she asked.

'Yes, that's it,' said the Hatter with a sigh: 'it's always tea-time,[2] and we've no time to wash the things between whiles.'

'Then you keep moving round, I suppose?' said Alice.

'Exactly so,' said the Hatter: 'as the things get used up.'

'But what happens when you come to the beginning again?' Alice ventured to ask.

'Suppose we change the subject,' the March Hare interrupted, yawning. 'I'm getting tired of this. I vote the young lady tells us a story.'

'I'm afraid I don't know one,' said Alice, rather alarmed at the proposal.

'Then the Dormouse shall!' they both cried. 'Wake up, Dormouse!' And they pinched it on both sides at once.

The Dormouse slowly opened its eyes. 'I wasn't asleep,' it said in a hoarse, feeble voice, 'I heard every word you fellows were saying.'

'Tell us a story!' said the March Hare.

'Yes, please do!' pleaded Alice.

'And be quick about it,' added the Hatter, 'or you'll be asleep again before it's done.'

'Once upon a time there were three little sisters,' the Dormouse began in a great hurry; 'and their names were Elsie, Lacie, and Tillie;[1] and they lived at the bottom of a well——'

'What did they live on?' said Alice, who always took a great interest in questions of eating and drinking.

'They lived on treacle,' said the Dormouse, after thinking a minute or two.

'They couldn't have done that, you know,' Alice gently remarked. 'They'd have been ill.'

'So they were,' said the Dormouse; '*very* ill.'

Alice tried a little to fancy to herself what such an extra-ordinary way of living would be like, but it puzzled her too much: so she went on: 'But why did they live at the bottom of a well?'

'Take some more tea,' the March Hare said to Alice, very earnestly.

'I've had nothing yet,' Alice replied in an offended tone: 'so I ca'n't take more.'

'You mean you ca'n't take *less*,' said the Hatter: 'it's very easy to take *more* than nothing.'

'Nobody asked *your* opinion,' said Alice.

'Who's making personal remarks now?' the Hatter asked triumphantly.

Alice did not quite know what to say to this: so she helped

herself to some tea and bread-and-butter, and then turned to the Dormouse, and repeated her question. 'Why did they live at the bottom of a well?'

The Dormouse again took a minute or two to think about it, and then said 'It was a treacle-well.'[1]

'There's no such thing!' Alice was beginning very angrily, but the Hatter and the March Hare went 'Sh! Sh!' and the Dormouse sulkily remarked 'If you ca'n't be civil, you'd better finish the story for yourself.'

'No, please go on!' Alice said very humbly. 'I wo'n't interrupt you again. I dare say there may be *one*.'

'One, indeed!' said the Dormouse indignantly. However, he consented to go on. 'And so these three little sisters—they were learning to draw, you know——'

'What did they draw?' said Alice, quite forgetting her promise.

'Treacle,' said the Dormouse, without considering at all, this time.

'I want a clean cup,' interrupted the Hatter: 'let's all move one place on.'

He moved on as he spoke, and the Dormouse followed him: the March Hare moved into the Dormouse's place, and Alice rather unwillingly took the place of the March Hare. The Hatter was the only one who got any advantage from the change; and Alice was a good deal worse off than before, as the March Hare had just upset the milk-jug into his plate.

Alice did not wish to offend the Dormouse again, so she began very cautiously: 'But I don't understand. Where did they draw the treacle from?'

'You can draw water out of a water-well,' said the Hatter; 'so I should think you could draw treacle out of a treacle-well —eh, stupid?'

'But they were *in* the well,' Alice said to the Dormouse, not choosing to notice this last remark.

'Of course they were,' said the Dormouse: 'well in.'

This answer so confused poor Alice, that she let the Dormouse go on for some time without interrupting it.

'They were learning to draw,' the Dormouse went on,
yawning and rubbing its eyes, for it was getting very sleepy;
'and they drew all manner of things—everything that begins
with an M——'

'Why with an M?' said Alice.

'Why not?' said the March Hare.

Alice was silent.

The Dormouse had closed its eyes by this time, and was
going off into a doze; but, on being pinched by the Hatter, it
woke up again with a little shriek, and went on: '——that
begins with an M, such as mouse-traps, and the moon, and
memory, and muchness—you know you say things are "much
of a muchness"—did you ever see such a thing as a drawing of
a muchness!'

'Really, now you ask me,' said Alice, very much confused,
'I don't think——'

'Then you shouldn't talk,' said the Hatter.

This piece of rudeness was more than Alice could bear: she
got up in great disgust, and walked off: the Dormouse fell
asleep instantly, and neither of the others took the least notice
of her going, though she looked back once or twice, half
hoping that they would call after her: the last time she saw
them, they were trying to put the Dormouse into the teapot.[1]

'At any rate I'll never go *there* again!' said Alice, as she picked her way through the wood. 'It's the stupidest tea-party I ever was at in all my life!'

Just as she said this,[1] she noticed that one of the trees had a door leading right into it. 'That's very curious!' she thought. 'But everything's curious to-day. I think I may as well go in at once.' And in she went.

Once more she found herself in the long hall, and close to the little glass table. 'Now, I'll manage better this time,' she said to herself, and began by taking the little golden key, and unlocking the door that led into the garden. Then she set to work nibbling at the mushroom (she had kept a piece of it in her pocket) till she was about a foot high: then she walked down the little passage: and *then*—she found herself at last in the beautiful garden, among the bright flower-beds and the cool fountains.

CHAPTER VIII

THE QUEEN'S CROQUET-GROUND

A LARGE rose-tree stood near the entrance of the garden: the roses growing on it were white, but there were three gardeners at it, busily painting them red.[1] Alice thought this a very curious thing, and she went nearer to watch them, and, just as she came up to them, she heard one of them say 'Look out now, Five! Don't go splashing paint over me like that!'

'I couldn't help it,' said Five, in a sulky tone. 'Seven jogged my elbow.'

On which Seven looked up and said 'That's right, Five! Always lay the blame on others!'

'*You'd* better not talk!' said Five. 'I heard the Queen say only yesterday you deserved to be beheaded.'

'What for?' said the one who had spoken first.

'That's none of *your* business, Two!' said Seven.

'Yes, it *is* his business!' said Five. 'And I'll tell him—it was for bringing the cook tulip-roots instead of onions.'

Seven flung down his brush, and had just begun 'Well, of

all the unjust things—' when his eye chanced to fall upon
Alice, as she stood watching them, and he checked himself
suddenly: the others looked round also, and all of them
bowed low.

'Would you tell me, please,' said Alice, a little timidly, 'why
you are painting those roses?'

Five and Seven said nothing, but looked at Two. Two
began, in a low voice, 'Why, the fact is, you see, Miss, this
here ought to have been a *red* rose-tree, and we put a white one
in by mistake; and, if the Queen was to find it out, we should
all have our heads cut off, you know. So you see, Miss, we're
doing our best, afore she comes, to—' At this moment, Five,
who had been anxiously looking across the garden, called out
'The Queen! The Queen!', and the three gardeners instantly
threw themselves flat upon their faces. There was a sound of
many footsteps, and Alice looked round, eager to see the
Queen.

First came ten soldiers carrying clubs: these were all
shaped like the three gardeners, oblong and flat, with their
hands and feet at the corners: next the ten courtiers: these
were ornamented all over with diamonds, and walked two and
two, as the soldiers did. After these came the royal children:
there were ten of them, and the little dears came jumping
merrily along, hand in hand, in couples: they were all ornamented with hearts. Next came the guests, mostly Kings and
Queens, and among them Alice recognised the White Rabbit:
it was talking in a hurried nervous manner, smiling at everything that was said, and went by without noticing her. Then
followed the Knave of Hearts, carrying the King's crown
on a crimson velvet cushion; and, last of all this grand procession,[1] came THE KING AND THE QUEEN OF
HEARTS.

Alice was rather doubtful whether she ought not to lie
down on her face like the three gardeners, but she could not
remember ever having heard of such a rule at processions;
'and besides, what would be the use of a procession,' thought
she, 'if people had all to lie down on their faces, so that

they couldn't see it?' So she stood where she was, and waited.

When the procession came opposite to Alice, they all stopped and looked at her, and the Queen said, severely, 'Who is this?' She said it to the Knave of Hearts, who only bowed and smiled in reply.

'Idiot!' said the Queen, tossing her head impatiently; and, turning to Alice, she went on: 'What's your name, child?'

'My name is Alice, so please your Majesty,' said Alice very

politely; but she added, to herself, 'Why, they're only a pack
of cards, after all. I needn't be afraid of them!'

'And who are *these*?' said the Queen, pointing to the three
gardeners who were lying round the rose-tree; for, you see,
as they were lying on their faces, and the pattern on their backs
was the same as the rest of the pack, she could not tell whether
they were gardeners, or soldiers, or courtiers, or three of her
own children.

'How should *I* know?' said Alice, surprised at her own
courage. 'It's no business of *mine*.'

The Queen turned crimson with fury, and, after glaring at
her for a moment like a wild beast, began screaming 'Off with
her head![1] Off with——'

'Nonsense!' said Alice, very loudly and decidedly, and the
Queen was silent.

The King laid his hand upon her arm, and timidly said
'Consider, my dear: she is only a child!'

The Queen turned angrily away from him, and said to the
Knave 'Turn them over!'

The Knave did so, very carefully, with one foot.

'Get up!' said the Queen in a shrill, loud voice, and
the three gardeners instantly jumped up, and began bowing
to the King, the Queen, the royal children, and everybody
else.

'Leave off that!' screamed the Queen. 'You make me giddy.'
And then, turning to the rose-tree, she went on 'What *have*
you been doing here?'

'May it please your Majesty,' said Two, in a very humble
tone, going down on one knee as he spoke, 'we were
trying——'

'*I* see!' said the Queen, who had meanwhile been examin-
ing the roses. 'Off with their heads!' and the procession
moved on, three of the soldiers remaining behind to execute
the unfortunate gardeners, who ran to Alice for protec-
tion.

'You sha'n't be beheaded!' said Alice, and she put them
into a large flower-pot that stood near. The three soldiers

wandered about for a minute or two, looking for them, and then quietly marched off after the others.

'Are their heads off?' shouted the Queen.

'Their heads are gone, if it please your Majesty!' the soldiers shouted in reply.

'That's right!' shouted the Queen. 'Can you play croquet?'

The soldiers were silent, and looked at Alice, as the question was evidently meant for her.

'Yes!' shouted Alice.

'Come on, then!' roared the Queen, and Alice joined the procession, wondering very much what would happen next.

'It's—it's a very fine day!' said a timid voice at her side. She was walking by the White Rabbit, who was peeping anxiously into her face.

'Very,' said Alice. 'Where's the Duchess?'

'Hush! Hush!' said the Rabbit in a low hurried tone. He looked anxiously over his shoulder as he spoke, and then raised himself upon tiptoe, put his mouth close to her ear, and whispered 'She's under sentence of execution.'

'What for?' said Alice.

'Did you say "What a pity!"?' the Rabbit asked.

'No, I didn't,' said Alice. 'I don't think it's at all a pity. I said "What for?"'

'She boxed the Queen's ears—' the Rabbit began. Alice gave a little scream of laughter. 'Oh, hush!' the Rabbit whispered in a frightened tone. 'The Queen will hear you! You see she came rather late, and the Queen said—'

'Get to your places!' shouted the Queen in a voice of thunder, and people began running about in all directions, tumbling up against each other: however, they got settled down in a minute or two, and the game began.

Alice thought she had never seen such a curious croquet-ground[1] in her life: it was all ridges and furrows: the croquet balls were live hedgehogs, and the mallets live flamingoes,[2] and the soldiers had to double themselves up and stand on their hands and feet, to make the arches.

The chief difficulty Alice found at first was in managing her flamingo: she succeeded in getting its body tucked away, comfortably enough, under her arm, with its legs hanging down, but generally, just as she had got its neck nicely straightened out, and was going to give the hedgehog a blow

with its head, it *would* twist itself round and look up in her face, with such a puzzled expression that she could not help bursting out laughing; and, when she had got its head down, and was going to begin again, it was very provoking to find that the hedgehog had unrolled itself, and was in the act of crawling away: besides all this, there was generally a ridge or a furrow in the way wherever she wanted to send the hedgehog to, and, as the doubled-up soldiers were always getting up and walking off to other parts of the ground, Alice soon came to the conclusion that it was a very difficult game indeed.

The players all played at once, without waiting for turns, quarrelling all the while, and fighting for the hedgehogs; and in a very short time the Queen was in a furious passion, and went stamping about, and shouting 'Off with his head!' or 'Off with her head!' about once in a minute.[1]

Alice began to feel very uneasy: to be sure, she had not as yet had any dispute with the Queen, but she knew that it might happen any minute, 'and then,' thought she, 'what would become of me? They're dreadfully fond of beheading people here: the great wonder is, that there's any one left alive!'

She was looking about for some way of escape, and wondering whether she could get away without being seen, when she noticed a curious appearance in the air: it puzzled her very much at first, but after watching it a minute or two she made it out to be a grin, and she said to herself 'It's the Cheshire-Cat: now I shall have somebody to talk to.'

'How are you getting on?' said the Cat, as soon as there was mouth enough for it to speak with.

Alice waited till the eyes appeared, and then nodded. 'It's no use speaking to it,' she thought, 'till its ears have come, or at least one of them.' In another minute the whole head appeared, and then Alice put down her flamingo, and began an account of the game, feeling very glad she had some one to listen to her. The Cat seemed to think that there was enough of it now in sight, and no more of it appeared.

'I don't think they play at all fairly,' Alice began, in rather a complaining tone, 'and they all quarrel so dreadfully one ca'n't hear oneself speak—and they don't seem to have any rules in particular: at least, if there are, nobody attends to them—and you've no idea how confusing it is all the things being alive: for instance, there's the arch I've got to go through next walking about at the other end of the ground—and I should have croqueted the Queen's hedgehog just now, only it ran away when it saw mine coming!'

'How do you like the Queen?' said the Cat in a low voice.

'Not at all,' said Alice: 'she's so extremely—' Just then she noticed that the Queen was close behind her, listening: so she went on '—likely to win, that it's hardly worth while finishing the game.'

The Queen smiled and passed on.

'Who *are* you talking to?' said the King, coming up to Alice, and looking at the Cat's head with great curiosity.

'It's a friend of mine—a Cheshire-Cat,' said Alice: 'allow me to introduce it.'

'I don't like the look of it at all,' said the King: 'however, it may kiss my hand, if it likes.'

'I'd rather not,' the Cat remarked.

'Don't be impertinent,' said the King, 'and don't look at me like that!' He got behind Alice as he spoke.

'A cat may look at a king,'[1] said Alice. 'I've read that in some book, but I don't remember where.'

'Well, it must be removed,' said the King very decidedly; and he called to the Queen, who was passing at the moment, 'My dear! I wish you would have this cat removed!'

The Queen had only one way of settling all difficulties, great or small. 'Off with his head!' she said without even looking round.

'I'll fetch the executioner myself,' said the King eagerly, and he hurried off.

Alice thought she might as well go back and see how the game was going on, as she heard the Queen's voice in the distance, screaming with passion. She had already heard her sentence three of the players to be executed for having missed their turns, and she did not like the look of things at all, as the game was in such confusion that she never knew whether it was her turn or not. So she went off in search of her hedgehog.

The hedgehog was engaged in a fight with another hedgehog, which seemed to Alice an excellent opportunity for croqueting one of them with the other: the only difficulty was, that her flamingo was gone across to the other side of the garden, where Alice could see it trying in a helpless sort of way to fly up into a tree.

By the time she had caught the flamingo and brought it back, the fight was over, and both the hedgehogs were out of sight: 'but it doesn't matter much,' thought Alice, 'as all the arches are gone from this side of the ground.' So she tucked it away under her arm, that it might not escape again, and went back to have a little more conversation with her friend.

When she got back to the Cheshire-Cat, she was surprised to find quite a large crowd collected round it: there was a dispute going on between the executioner, the King, and the Queen, who were all talking at once, while all the rest were quite silent, and looked very uncomfortable.

The moment Alice appeared, she was appealed to by all

three to settle the question, and they repeated their arguments to her, though, as they all spoke at once, she found it very hard to make out exactly what they said.

The executioner's argument was, that you couldn't cut off a head unless there was a body to cut it off from: that he had never had to do such a thing before, and he wasn't going to begin at *his* time of life.

The King's argument was that anything that had a head could be beheaded, and that you weren't to talk nonsense.

The Queen's argument was that, if something wasn't done about it in less than no time, she'd have everybody executed, all round. (It was this last remark that had made the whole party look so grave and anxious.)

Alice could think of nothing else to say but 'It belongs to the Duchess: you'd better ask *her* about it.'

'She's in prison,' the Queen said to the executioner: 'fetch her here.' And the executioner went off like an arrow.

The Cat's head began fading away the moment he was gone, and, by the time he had come back with the Duchess, it had entirely disappeared: so the King and the executioner ran wildly up and down, looking for it, while the rest of the party went back to the game.

CHAPTER IX

THE MOCK TURTLE'S STORY

'You ca'n't think how glad I am to see you again, you dear old thing!' said the Duchess, as she tucked her arm affectionately into Alice's, and they walked off together.

Alice was very glad to find her in such a pleasant temper, and thought to herself that perhaps it was only the pepper that had made her so savage when they met in the kitchen.

'When *I'm* a Duchess,' she said to herself (not in a very hopeful tone, though), 'I wo'n't have any pepper in my kitchen *at all*. Soup does very well without—Maybe it's always pepper that makes people hot-tempered,' she went on, very much pleased at having found out a new kind of rule, 'and vinegar that makes them sour—and camomile[1] that makes them bitter—and—and barley-sugar and such things that make children sweet-tempered. I only wish people knew *that*: then they wouldn't be so stingy about it, you know——'

She had quite forgotten the Duchess by this time, and was a little startled when she heard her voice close to her ear. 'You're thinking about something, my dear, and that makes you forget to talk. I ca'n't tell you just now what the moral of that is, but I shall remember it in a bit.'

'Perhaps it hasn't one,' Alice ventured to remark.

'Tut, tut, child!' said the Duchess. 'Every thing's got a moral, if only you can find it.' And she squeezed herself up closer to Alice's side as she spoke.

Alice did not much like her keeping so close to her: first, because the Duchess was *very* ugly; and secondly, because she was exactly the right height to rest her chin on Alice's

H

shoulder, and it was an uncomfortably sharp chin. However, she did not like to be rude: so she bore it as well as she could.

'The game's going on rather better now,' she said, by way of keeping up the conversation a little.

''Tis so,' said the Duchess: 'and the moral of that is—"Oh, 'tis love, 'tis love, that makes the world go round!"'[1]

'Somebody said,' Alice whispered, 'that it's done by everybody minding their own business!'[2]

'Ah, well! It means much the same thing,' said the Duchess, digging her sharp little chin into Alice's shoulder as she added 'and the moral of *that* is—"Take care of the sense, and the sounds will take care of themselves."'[3]

'How fond she is of finding morals in things!' Alice thought to herself.

'I dare say you're wondering why I don't put my arm round your waist,' the Duchess said, after a pause: 'the reason is, that I'm doubtful about the temper of your flamingo. Shall I try the experiment?'

'He might bite,' Alice cautiously replied, not feeling at all anxious to have the experiment tried.

'Very true,' said the Duchess: 'flamingoes and mustard both bite. And the moral of that is—"Birds of a feather flock together."'[4]

'Only mustard isn't a bird,' Alice remarked.

'Right, as usual,' said the Duchess: 'what a clear way you have of putting things!'

'It's a mineral, I *think*,' said Alice.

'Of course it is,' said the Duchess, who seemed ready to agree to everything that Alice said: 'there's a large mustard-mine near here. And the moral of that is—"The more there is of mine, the less there is of yours."'

'Oh, I know!' exclaimed Alice, who had not attended to this last remark. 'It's a vegetable. It doesn't look like one, but it is.'

'I quite agree with you,' said the Duchess; 'and the moral of that is—"Be what you would seem to be"[1]—or, if you'd like it put more simply—"Never imagine yourself not to be otherwise than what it might appear to others that what you were or might have been was not otherwise than what you had been would have appeared to them to be otherwise."'

'I think I should understand that better,' Alice said very politely, 'if I had it written down: but I ca'n't quite follow it as you say it.'

'That's nothing to what I could say if I chose,' the Duchess replied, in a pleased tone.

'Pray don't trouble yourself to say it any longer than that,' said Alice.

'Oh, don't talk about trouble!' said the Duchess. 'I make you a present of everything I've said as yet.'

'A cheap sort of present!' thought Alice. 'I'm glad people don't give birthday-presents like that!' But she did not venture to say it out loud.

'Thinking again?' the Duchess asked, with another dig of her sharp little chin.

'I've a right to think,' said Alice sharply, for she was beginning to feel a little worried.

'Just about as much right,' said the Duchess, 'as pigs have to fly;[2] and the m——'

But here, to Alice's great surprise, the Duchess's voice died away, even in the middle of her favourite word "moral," and the arm that was linked into hers began to tremble. Alice looked up, and there stood the Queen in front of them, with her arms folded, frowning like a thunderstorm.

'A fine day, your Majesty!' the Duchess began in a low, weak voice.

'Now, I give you fair warning,' shouted the Queen, stamping on the ground as she spoke; 'either you or your head must be off, and that in about half no time! Take your choice!'

The Duchess took her choice, and was gone in a moment.

'Let's go on with the game,' the Queen said to Alice; and Alice was too much frightened to say a word, but slowly followed her back to the croquet-ground.

The other guests had taken advantage of the Queen's absence, and were resting in the shade: however, the moment they saw her, they hurried back to the game, the Queen merely remarking that a moment's delay would cost them their lives.

All the time they were playing the Queen never left off quarreling with the other players, and shouting 'Off with his head!' or 'Off with her head!' Those whom she sentenced were taken into custody by the soldiers, who of course had to leave off being arches to do this, so that, by the end of half an hour or so, there were no arches left, and all the players, except the King, the Queen, and Alice, were in custody and under sentence of execution.

Then the Queen left off, quite out of breath, and said to Alice 'Have you seen the Mock Turtle yet?'

'No,' said Alice. 'I don't even know what a Mock Turtle is.'

'It's the thing Mock Turtle Soup[1] is made from,' said the Queen.

'I never saw one, or heard of one,' said Alice.

'Come on, then,' said the Queen, 'and he shall tell you his history.'

As they walked off together, Alice heard the King say in a low voice, to the company generally, 'You are all pardoned.' 'Come, *that's* a good thing!' she said to herself, for she had felt quite unhappy at the number of executions the Queen had ordered.

They very soon came upon a Gryphon,[1] lying fast asleep in the sun. (If you don't know what a Gryphon is, look at the picture.) 'Up, lazy thing!' said the Queen, 'and take this young lady to see the Mock Turtle, and to hear his history. I must go back and see after some executions I have ordered;' and she walked off, leaving Alice alone with the Gryphon. Alice did not quite like the look of the creature, but on the whole she thought it would be quite as safe to stay with it as to go after that savage Queen: so she waited.

The Gryphon sat up and rubbed its eyes: then it watched the Queen till she was out of sight: then it chuckled. 'What fun!' said the Gryphon, half to itself, half to Alice.

'What *is* the fun?' said Alice.

'Why, *she*,' said the Gryphon. 'It's all her fancy, that: they never executes nobody, you know. Come on!'

'Everybody says "come on!" here,' thought Alice, as she went slowly after it: 'I never was so ordered about before, in all my life, never!'

They had not gone far before they saw the Mock Turtle in the distance, sitting sad and lonely on a little ledge of rock, and, as they came nearer, Alice could hear him sighing as if his heart would break. She pitied him deeply. 'What is his sorrow?' she asked the Gryphon. And the Gryphon answered, very nearly in the same words as before, 'It's all his fancy, that: he hasn't got no sorrow, you know. Come on!'

So they went up to the Mock Turtle, who looked at them with large eyes full of tears, but said nothing.

'This here young lady,' said the Gryphon, 'she wants for to know your history, she do.'

'I'll tell it her,' said the Mock Turtle in a deep, hollow tone. 'Sit down, both of you, and don't speak a word till I've finished.'

So they sat down, and nobody spoke for some minutes. Alice thought to herself 'I don't see how he can *ever* finish, if he doesn't begin.' But she waited patiently.

'Once,' said the Mock Turtle at last, with a deep sigh, 'I was a real Turtle.'

These words were followed by a very long silence, broken only by an occasional exclamation of 'Hjckrrh!' from the Gryphon, and the constant heavy sobbing of the Mock Turtle. Alice was very nearly getting up and saying 'Thank you, Sir, for your interesting story,' but she could not help thinking there *must* be more to come, so she sat still and said nothing.

'When we were little,' the Mock Turtle went on at last, more calmly, though still sobbing a little now and then, 'we went to school in the sea. The master was an old Turtle—we used to call him Tortoise——'

'Why did you call him Tortoise, if he wasn't one?' Alice asked.

'We called him Tortoise because he taught us,' said the Mock Turtle angrily. 'Really you are very dull!'

'You ought to be ashamed of yourself for asking such a simple question,' added the Gryphon; and then they both sat silent and looked at poor Alice, who felt ready to sink into the earth. At last the Gryphon said to the Mock Turtle 'Drive on, old fellow! Don't be all day about it!', and he went on in these words:—

'Yes, we went to school in the sea, though you mayn't believe it——'

'I never said I didn't!' interrupted Alice.

'You did,' said the Mock Turtle.

'Hold your tongue!' added the Gryphon, before Alice could speak again. The Mock Turtle went on.

'We had the best of educations—in fact, we went to school every day——'

'*I've* been to a day-school, too,' said Alice. 'You needn't be so proud as all that.'

'With extras?' asked the Mock Turtle, a little anxiously.

'Yes,' said Alice: 'we learned French and music.'

'And washing?' said the Mock Turtle.

'Certainly not!' said Alice indignantly.

'Ah! Then yours wasn't a really good school,' said the Mock Turtle in a tone of great relief. 'Now, at *ours*, they had, at the end of the bill, "French, music, *and washing*—extra."'

'You couldn't have wanted it much,' said Alice; 'living at the bottom of the sea.'

'I couldn't afford to learn it,' said the Mock Turtle, with a sigh. 'I only took the regular course.'

'What was that?' inquired Alice.

'Reeling and Writhing,¹ of course, to begin with,' the Mock Turtle replied; 'and then the different branches of Arithmetic—Ambition, Distraction, Uglification, and Derision.'

'I never heard of "Uglification,"' Alice ventured to say. 'What is it?'

The Gryphon lifted up both its paws in surprise. 'Never heard of uglifying!' it exclaimed. 'You know what to beautify is, I suppose?'

'Yes,' said Alice doubtfully: 'it means—to—make—anything—prettier.'

'Well, then,' the Gryphon went on, 'if you don't know what to uglify is, you *are* a simpleton.'

Alice did not feel encouraged to ask any more questions about it: so she turned to the Mock Turtle, and said 'What else had you to learn?'

'Well, there was Mystery,' the Mock Turtle replied, counting off the subjects on his flappers,—'Mystery, ancient and modern, with Seaography: then Drawling—the Drawling-master² was an old conger-eel, that used to come once a week: *he* taught us Drawling, Stretching, and Fainting in Coils.'

'What was *that* like?' said Alice.

'Well, I ca'n't show it you, myself,' the Mock Turtle said: 'I'm too stiff. And the Gryphon never learnt it.'

'Hadn't time,' said the Gryphon: 'I went to the Classical master, though. He was an old crab, *he* was.'

'I never went to him,' the Mock Turtle said with a sigh. 'He taught Laughing and Grief, they used to say.'

'So he did, so he did,' said the Gryphon, sighing in his turn; and both creatures hid their faces in their paws.

'And how many hours a day did you do lessons?' said Alice, in a hurry to change the subject.

'Ten hours the first day,' said the Mock Turtle: 'nine the next, and so on.'

'What a curious plan!' exclaimed Alice.

'That's the reason they're called lessons,' the Gryphon remarked: 'because they lessen from day to day.'

This was quite a new idea to Alice, and she thought it over a little before she made her next remark. 'Then the eleventh day must have been a holiday?'

'Of course it was,' said the Mock Turtle.

'And how did you manage on the twelfth?' Alice went on eagerly.

'That's enough about lessons,' the Gryphon interrupted in a very decided tone. 'Tell her something about the games now.'

CHAPTER X

THE LOBSTER-QUADRILLE

The Mock Turtle sighed deeply, and drew the back of one flapper across his eyes. He looked at Alice and tried to speak, but, for a minute or two, sobs choked his voice. 'Same as if he had a bone in his throat,' said the Gryphon; and it set to work shaking him and punching him in the back. At last the Mock Turtle recovered his voice, and, with tears running down his cheeks, he went on again:—

'You may not have lived much under the sea—' ('I haven't,' said Alice)—'and perhaps you were never even introduced to a lobster—' (Alice began to say 'I once tasted——' but checked herself hastily, and said 'No, never') '——so you can have no idea what a delightful thing a Lobster-Quadrille¹ is!'

'No, indeed,' said Alice. 'What sort of a dance is it?'

'Why,' said the Gryphon, 'you first form into a line along the sea-shore——'

'Two lines!' cried the Mock Turtle. 'Seals, turtles, salmon, and so on: then, when you've cleared all the jelly-fish out of the way——'

'*That* generally takes some time,' interrupted the Gryphon.

'—you advance twice——'

'Each with a lobster as a partner!' cried the Gryphon.

'Of course,' the Mock Turtle said: 'advance twice, set to partners——'

'—change lobsters, and retire in same order,' continued the Gryphon.

'Then, you know,' the Mock Turtle went on, 'you throw the——'

'The lobsters!' shouted the Gryphon, with a bound into the air.

'—as far out to sea as you can——'

'Swim after them!' screamed the Gryphon.

'Turn a somersault in the sea!' cried the Mock Turtle, capering wildly about.

'Change lobsters again!' yelled the Gryphon at the top of its voice.

'Back to land again, and—that's all the first figure,' said the Mock Turtle, suddenly dropping his voice; and the two creatures, who had been jumping about like mad things all this time, sat down again very sadly and quietly, and looked at Alice.

'It must be a very pretty dance,' said Alice timidly.

'Would you like to see a little of it?' said the Mock Turtle.

'Very much indeed,' said Alice.

'Come, let's try the first figure!' said the Mock Turtle to the Gryphon. 'We can do it without lobsters, you know. Which shall sing?'

'Oh, *you* sing,' said the Gryphon. 'I've forgotten the words.'

So they began solemnly dancing round and round Alice, every now and then treading on her toes when they passed too close, and waving their fore-paws to mark the time, while the Mock Turtle sang this, very slowly and sadly:—

'Will you walk a little faster?'[1] *said a whiting to a snail,*
'There's a porpoise close behind us, and he's treading on my tail.
See how eagerly the lobsters and the turtles all advance!
They are waiting on the shingle—will you come and join the
dance?
  Will you, wo'n't you, will you, wo'n't you, will you join the
  dance?
  Will you, wo'n't you, will you, wo'n't you, wo'n't you join the
  dance?

'You can really have no notion how delightful it will be
When they take us up and throw us, with the lobsters, out to sea!'
But the snail replied 'Too far, too far!', and gave a look
askance—
Said he thanked the whiting kindly, but he would not join the
dance.
  Would not, could not, would not, could not, would not join the
  dance.
  Would not, could not, would not, could not, could not join the
  dance.

'What matters it how far we go?' his scaly friend replied.
'There is another shore, you know, upon the other side.
The further off from England the nearer is to France—
Then turn not pale, beloved snail, but come and join the dance.
  Will you, wo'n't you, will you, wo'n't you, will you join the
  dance?
  Will you, wo'n't you, will you, wo'n't you, wo'n't you join the
  dance?'

'Thank you, it's a very interesting dance to watch,' said Alice, feeling very glad that it was over at last: 'and I do so like that curious song about the whiting!'

'Oh, as to the whiting,' said the Mock Turtle, 'they—you've seen them, of course?'

'Yes,' said Alice, 'I've often seen them at dinn——' she checked herself hastily.

'I don't know where Dinn may be,' said the Mock Turtle; 'but, if you've seen them so often, of course you know what they're like?'

'I believe so,' Alice replied thoughtfully. 'They have their tails in their mouths¹—and they're all over crumbs.'

'You're wrong about the crumbs,' said the Mock Turtle: 'crumbs would all wash off in the sea. But they *have* their tails in their mouths; and the reason is—' here the Mock Turtle yawned and shut his eyes. 'Tell her about the reason and all that,' he said to the Gryphon.

'The reason is,' said the Gryphon, 'that they *would* go with the lobsters to the dance. So they got thrown out to sea. So they had to fall a long way. So they got their tails fast in their mouths. So they couldn't get them out again. That's all.'

'Thank you,' said Alice, 'it's very interesting. I never knew so much about a whiting before.'

'I can tell you more than that, if you like,' said the Gryphon. 'Do you know why it's called a whiting?'

'I never thought about it,' said Alice. 'Why?'

'*It does the boots and shoes,*' the Gryphon replied very solemnly.

Alice was thoroughly puzzled. 'Does the boots and shoes!' she repeated in a wondering tone.

'Why, what are *your* shoes done with?' said the Gryphon. 'I mean, what makes them so shiny?'

Alice looked down at them, and considered a little before she gave her answer. 'They're done with blacking, I believe.'

'Boots and shoes under the sea,' the Gryphon went on in a deep voice, 'are done with whiting. Now you know.'

'And what are they made of?' Alice asked in a tone of great curiosity.

'Soles and eels, of course,' the Gryphon replied, rather impatiently: 'any shrimp could have told you that.'

'If I'd been the whiting,' said Alice, whose thoughts were still running on the song, 'I'd have said to the porpoise "Keep back, please! We don't want *you* with us!"'

'They were obliged to have him with them,' the Mock Turtle said. 'No wise fish would go anywhere without a porpoise.'

'Wouldn't it, really?' said Alice, in a tone of great surprise.

'Of course not,' said the Mock Turtle. 'Why, if a fish came to *me*, and told me he was going a journey, I should say "With what porpoise?"'

'Don't you mean "purpose"?' said Alice.

'I mean what I say,' the Mock Turtle replied, in an offended tone. And the Gryphon added 'Come, let's hear some of *your* adventures.'

'I could tell you my adventures—beginning from this morning,' said Alice a little timidly; 'but it's no use going back to yesterday, because I was a different person then.'

'Explain all that,' said the Mock Turtle.

'No, no! The adventures first,' said the Gryphon in an impatient tone: 'explanations take such a dreadful time.'

So Alice began telling them her adventures from the time when she first saw the White Rabbit. She was a little nervous about it, just at first, the two creatures got so close to her, one on each side, and opened their eyes and mouths so *very* wide; but she gained courage as she went on. Her listeners were perfectly quiet till she got to the part about her repeating '*You are old, Father William*,' to the Caterpillar, and the words all coming different, and then the Mock Turtle drew a long breath, and said 'That's very curious!'

'It's all about as curious as it can be,' said the Gryphon.

'It all came different!' the Mock Turtle repeated thoughtfully. 'I should like to hear her try and repeat something now.

Tell her to begin.' He looked at the Gryphon as if he thought it had some kind of authority over Alice.

'Stand up and repeat "'*Tis the voice of the sluggard*,"' said the Gryphon.

'How the creatures order one about, and make one repeat lessons!' thought Alice. 'I might just as well be at school at once.' However, she got up, and began to repeat it, but her head was so full of the Lobster-Quadrille, that she hardly knew what she was saying; and the words came very queer indeed:—

''*Tis the voice of the Lobster:*[1] *I heard him declare*
"*You have baked me too brown, I must sugar my hair.*"
As a duck with its eyelids, so he with his nose
Trims his belt and his buttons, and turns out his toes.
When the sands are all dry, he is gay as a lark,
And will talk in contemptuous tones of the Shark:
But, when the tide rises and sharks are around,
His voice has a timid and tremulous sound.'

'That's different from what *I* used to say when I was a child,' said the Gryphon.

'Well, *I* never heard it before,' said the Mock Turtle; 'but it sounds uncommon nonsense.'

Alice said nothing: she had sat down with her face in her

hands, wondering if anything would *ever* happen in a natural way again.

'I should like to have it explained,' said the Mock Turtle.

'She ca'n't explain it,' said the Gryphon hastily. 'Go on with the next verse.'

'But about his toes?' the Mock Turtle persisted. 'How *could* he turn them out with his nose, you know?'

'It's the first position in dancing,' Alice said; but she was dreadfully puzzled by the whole thing, and longed to change the subject.

'Go on with the next verse,' the Gryphon repeated: 'it begins "*I passed by his garden.*"'

Alice did not dare to disobey, though she felt sure it would all come wrong, and she went on in a trembling voice:—

> '*I passed by his garden,*[1] *and marked, with one eye,*
> *How the Owl and the Panther were sharing a pie:*
> *The Panther took pie-crust, and gravy, and meat,*
> *While the Owl had the dish as its share of the treat.*
> *When the pie was all finished, the Owl, as a boon,*
> *Was kindly permitted to pocket the spoon:*
> *While the Panther received knife and fork with a growl,*
> *And concluded the banquet by——*'

'What *is* the use of repeating all that stuff?' the Mock Turtle interrupted, 'if you don't explain it as you go on? It's by far the most confusing thing *I* ever heard!'

'Yes, I think you'd better leave off,' said the Gryphon, and Alice was only too glad to do so.

'Shall we try another figure of the Lobster-Quadrille?' the Gryphon went on. 'Or would you like the Mock Turtle to sing you another song?'

'Oh, a song, please, if the Mock Turtle would be so kind,' Alice replied, so eagerly that the Gryphon said, in a rather offended tone, 'Hm! No accounting for tastes! Sing her "*Turtle Soup*,"[2] will you, old fellow?'

The Mock Turtle sighed deeply, and began, in a voice choked with sobs, to sing this:—

> *'Beautiful Soup, so rich and green,*
> *Waiting in a hot tureen!*
> *Who for such dainties would not stoop?*
> *Soup of the evening, beautiful Soup!*
> *Soup of the evening, beautiful Soup!*
>   *Beau—ootiful Soo—oop!*
>   *Beau—ootiful Soo—oop!*
> *Soo—oop of the e—e—evening,*
>   *Beautiful, beautiful Soup!*

> *'Beautiful Soup! Who cares for fish,*[1]
> *Game, or any other dish?*
> *Who would not give all else for two p*
> *ennyworth only of beautiful Soup?*
> *Pennyworth only of beautiful soup?*
>   *Beau—ootiful Soo—oop!*
>   *Beau—ootiful Soo—oop!*
> *Soo—oop of the e—e—evening,*
>   *Beautiful, beauti—FUL SOUP!'*

'Chorus again!' cried the Gryphon, and the Mock Turtle had just begun to repeat it, when a cry of 'The trial's beginning!' was heard in the distance.

'Come on!' cried the Gryphon, and, taking Alice by the hand, it hurried off, without waiting for the end of the song.

'What trial is it?' Alice panted as she ran; but the Gryphon only answered 'Come on!' and ran the faster, while more and more faintly came, carried on the breeze that followed them, the melancholy words:—

> *'Soo—oop of the e—e—evening,*
>   *Beautiful, beautiful Soup!'*

I

CHAPTER XI

THE King and Queen of Hearts were seated on their throne when they arrived, with a great crowd assembled about them —all sorts of little birds and beasts, as well as the whole pack of cards: the Knave was standing before them, in chains, with a soldier on each side to guard him; and near the King was the White Rabbit, with a trumpet in one hand, and a scroll of parchment in the other. In the very middle of the court was a table, with a large dish of tarts upon it: they looked so good, that it made Alice quite hungry to look at them—'I wish they'd get the trial done,' she thought, 'and hand round the refreshments!' But there seemed to be no chance of this; so she began looking at everything about her to pass away the time.

Alice had never been in a court of justice before,[1] but she had read about them in books, and she was quite pleased to find that she knew the name of nearly everything there. 'That's the judge,' she said to herself, 'because of his great wig.'

The judge, by the way, was the King; and, as he wore his crown over the wig (look at the frontispiece if you want to see how he did it), he did not look at all comfortable, and it was certainly not becoming.

'And that's the jury-box,' thought Alice; 'and those twelve creatures,' (she was obliged to say 'creatures,' you see, because some of them were animals, and some were birds,) 'I suppose they are the jurors.' She said this last word two or three times over to herself, being rather proud of it: for she thought, and rightly too, that very few little girls of her age knew the meaning of it at all. However, 'jurymen' would have done just as well.

The twelve jurors were all writing very busily on slates. 'What are they doing?' Alice whispered to the Gryphon.

'They ca'n't have anything to put down yet, before the trial's begun.'

'They're putting down their names,' the Gryphon whispered in reply, 'for fear they should forget them before the end of the trial.'

'Stupid things!' Alice began in a loud indignant voice; but she stopped herself hastily, for the White Rabbit cried out 'Silence in the court!', and the King put on his spectacles and looked anxiously round, to make out who was talking.

Alice could see, as well as if she were looking over their shoulders, that all the jurors were writing down 'Stupid things!' on their slates, and she could even make out that one of them didn't know how to spell 'stupid,' and that he had to ask his neighbour to tell him. 'A nice muddle their slates'll be in, before the trial's over!' thought Alice.

One of the jurors had a pencil that squeaked. This, of course, Alice could *not* stand, and she went round the court and got behind him, and very soon found an opportunity of taking it away. She did it so quickly that the poor little juror (it was Bill, the Lizard) could not make out at all what had become of it; so, after hunting all about for it, he was obliged to write with one finger for the rest of the day; and this was of very little use, as it left no mark on the slate.

'Herald, read the accusation!' said the King.

On this the White Rabbit blew three blasts on the trumpet,

and then unrolled the parchment-scroll, and read as follows:—

> '*The Queen of Hearts, she made some tarts,*[1]
> *All on a summer day:*
> *The Knave of Hearts, he stole those tarts*
> *And took them quite away!*'

'Consider your verdict,' the King said to the jury.

'Not yet, not yet!' the Rabbit hastily interrupted. 'There's a great deal to come before that!'

'Call the first witness,' said the King; and the White Rabbit blew three blasts on the trumpet, and called out 'First witness!'

The first witness was the Hatter. He came in with a teacup in one hand and a piece of bread-and-butter in the other. 'I beg pardon, your Majesty,' he began, 'for bringing these in; but I hadn't quite finished my tea when I was sent for.'

'You ought to have finished,' said the King. 'When did you begin?'

The Hatter looked at the March Hare, who had followed him into the court, arm-in-arm with the Dormouse. 'Fourteenth of March,[2] I *think* it was,' he said.

'Fifteenth,' said the March Hare.

'Sixteenth,' said the Dormouse.

'Write that down,' the King said to the jury; and the jury eagerly wrote down all three dates on their slates, and then added them up, and reduced the answer to shillings and pence.

'Take off your hat,' the King said to the Hatter.

'It isn't mine,' said the Hatter.

'*Stolen!*' the King exclaimed, turning to the jury, who instantly made a memorandum of the fact.

'I keep them to sell,' the Hatter added as an explanation. 'I've none of my own. I'm a hatter.'

Here the Queen put on her spectacles, and began staring hard at the Hatter, who turned pale and fidgeted.

'Give your evidence,' said the King; 'and don't be nervous, or I'll have you executed on the spot.'

This did not seem to encourage the witness at all: he kept shifting from one foot to the other, looking uneasily at the Queen, and in his confusion he bit a large piece out of his tea-cup instead of the bread-and-butter.

Just at this moment Alice felt a very curious sensation, which puzzled her a good deal until she made out what it was: she was beginning to grow larger again, and she thought at first she would get up and leave the court; but on second thoughts she decided to remain where she was as long as there was room for her.

'I wish you wouldn't squeeze so,' said the Dormouse, who was sitting next to her. 'I can hardly breathe.'

'I ca'n't help it,' said Alice very meekly: 'I'm growing.'

'You've no right to grow *here*,' said the Dormouse.

'Don't talk nonsense,' said Alice more boldly: 'you know you're growing too.'

'Yes, but *I* grow at a reasonable pace,' said the Dormouse: 'not in that ridiculous fashion.' And he got up very sulkily and crossed over to the other side of the court.

All this time the Queen had never left off staring at the Hatter, and, just as the Dormouse crossed the court, she said, to one of the offi-cers of the court, 'Bring me the list of the singers in the last concert!' on which the wretched Hatter trembled so, that he shook off both his shoes.

'Give your evidence,' the King repeated angrily, 'or I'll have you executed, whether you're nervous or not.'

'I'm a poor man, your Majesty,' the Hatter began, in a trembling voice, 'and I hadn't begun my tea—not above a week or so—and what with the bread-and-butter getting so thin— and the twinkling of the tea——'

'The twinkling of *what?*' said the King.

'It *began* with the tea,' the Hatter replied.

'Of course twinkling *begins* with a T!' said the King sharply. 'Do you take me for a dunce? Go on!'

'I'm a poor man,' the Hatter went on, 'and most things twinkled after that—only the March Hare said——'

'I didn't!' the March Hare interrupted in a great hurry.

'You did!' said the Hatter.

'I deny it!' said the March Hare.

'He denies it,' said the King: 'leave out that part.'

'Well, at any rate, the Dormouse said——' the Hatter went on, looking anxiously round to see if he would deny it too; but the Dormouse denied nothing, being fast asleep.

'After that,' continued the Hatter, 'I cut some more bread-and-butter——'

'But what did the Dormouse say?' one of the jury asked.

'That I ca'n't remember,' said the Hatter.

'You *must* remember,' remarked the King, 'or I'll have you executed.'

The miserable Hatter dropped his teacup and bread-and-butter, and went down on one knee. 'I'm a poor man, your Majesty,' he began.

'You're a *very* poor *speaker*,' said the King.

Here one of the guinea-pigs cheered, and was immediately suppressed by the officers of the court. (As that is rather a hard word, I will just explain to you how it was done. They had a large canvas bag, which tied up at the mouth with strings: into this they slipped the guinea-pig, head first, and then sat upon it.)

'I'm glad I've seen that done,' thought Alice. 'I've so often read in the newspapers, at the end of trials, "There was some attempt at applause, which was immediately suppressed by the officers of the court," and I never understood what it meant till now.'

'If that's all you know about it, you may stand down,' continued the King.

'I ca'n't go no lower,' said the Hatter: 'I'm on the floor, as it is.'

'Then you may *sit* down,' the King replied.

Here the other guinea-pig cheered, and was suppressed.

'Come, that finishes the guinea-pigs!' thought Alice. 'Now we shall get on better.'

'I'd rather finish my tea,' said the Hatter, with an anxious look at the Queen, who was reading the list of singers.

'You may go,' said the King, and the Hatter hurriedly left the court, without even waiting to put his shoes on.

'——and just take his head off outside,' the Queen added to one of the officers; but the Hatter was out of sight before the officer could get to the door.

'Call the next witness!' said the King.

The next witness was the Duchess's cook. She carried the pepper-box in her hand, and Alice guessed who it was, even before she got into the court, by the way the people near the door began sneezing all at once.

'Give your evidence,' said the King.

'Sha'n't,' said the cook.

The King looked anxiously at the White Rabbit, who said, in a low voice, 'Your Majesty must cross-examine *this* witness.'

'Well, if I must, I must,' the King said with a melancholy air, and, after folding his arms and frowning at the cook till his eyes were nearly out of sight, he said, in a deep voice, 'What are tarts made of?'

'Pepper, mostly,' said the cook.

'Treacle,' said a sleepy voice behind her.

'Collar that Dormouse!' the Queen shrieked out. 'Behead that Dormouse! Turn that Dormouse out of court! Suppress him! Pinch him! Off with his whiskers!'

For some minutes the whole court was in confusion, getting the Dormouse turned out, and, by the time they had settled down again, the cook had disappeared.

'Never mind!' said the King, with an air of great relief. 'Call the next witness.' And, he added, in an under-tone to the Queen, 'Really, my dear, *you* must cross-examine the next witness. It quite makes my forehead ache!'

Alice watched the White Rabbit as he fumbled over the list, feeling very curious to see what the next witness would be like, '—for they haven't got much evidence *yet*,' she said to herself. Imagine her surprise, when the White Rabbit read out, at the top of his shrill little voice, the name 'Alice!'

CHAPTER XII

ALICE'S EVIDENCE

'HERE!' cried Alice, quite forgetting in the flurry of the moment how large she had grown in the last few minutes, and she jumped up in such a hurry that she tipped over the jury-box with the edge of her skirt, upsetting all the jurymen on to the heads of the crowd below, and there they lay sprawling about, reminding her very much of a globe of gold-fish she had accidentally upset the week before.

'Oh, I *beg* your pardon!' she exclaimed in a tone of great dismay, and began picking them up again as quickly as she could for the accident of the gold-fish kept running in her head, and she had a vague sort of idea that they must be collected at once and put back into the jury-box, or they would die.

'The trial cannot proceed,' said the King, in a very grave voice, 'until all the jurymen are back in their proper places—*all*,' he repeated with great emphasis, looking hard at Alice as he said so.

Alice looked at the jury-box, and saw that, in her haste, she had put the Lizard in head downwards, and the poor little thing was waving its tail about in a melancholy way, being quite unable to move. She soon got it out again, and put it right; 'not that it signifies much,' she said to herself; 'I should think it would be *quite* as much use in the trial one way up as the other.'

As soon as the jury had a little recovered from the shock of being upset, and their slates and pencils had been found and handed back to them, they set to work very diligently to write out a history of the accident, all except the Lizard, who seemed too much overcome to do anything but sit with its mouth open, gazing up into the roof of the court.

'What do you know about this business?' the King said to Alice.

'Nothing,' said Alice.

'Nothing *whatever?*' persisted the King.

'Nothing whatever,' said Alice.

'That's very important,' the King said, turning to the jury. They were just beginning to write this down on their slates, when the White Rabbit interrupted: '*Un*important, your Majesty means, of course,' he said, in a very respectful tone, but frowning and making faces at him as he spoke.

'*Un*important, of course, I meant,' the King hastily said, and went on to himself in an undertone, 'important—unimportant—unimportant—important——' as if he were trying which word sounded best.

Some of the jury wrote it down 'important,' and some

unimportant.' Alice could see this, as she was near enough to look over their slates; 'but it doesn't matter a bit,' she thought to herself.

At this moment the King, who had been for some time busily writing in his note-book, called out 'Silence!', and read out from his book, 'Rule Forty-two.[1] *All persons more than a mile high to leave the court.*'

Everybody looked at Alice.

'*I'm* not a mile high,' said Alice.

'You are,' said the King.

'Nearly two miles high,' added the Queen.

'Well, I sha'n't go, at any rate,' said Alice: 'besides, that's not a regular rule: you invented it just now.'

'It's the oldest rule in the book,' said the King.

'Then it ought to be Number One,' said Alice.

The King turned pale, and shut his note-book hastily. 'Consider your verdict,' he said to the jury, in a low trembling voice.

'There's more evidence to come yet, please your Majesty,' said the White Rabbit, jumping up in a great hurry: 'this paper has just been picked up.'

'What's in it?' said the Queen.

'I haven't opened it yet,' said the White Rabbit; 'but it seems to be a letter, written by the prisoner to—to somebody.'

'It must have been that,' said the King, 'unless it was written to nobody, which isn't usual, you know.'

'Who is it directed to?' said one of the jurymen.

'It isn't directed at all,' said the White Rabbit: 'in fact, there's nothing written on the *outside*.' He unfolded the paper as he spoke, and added 'It isn't a letter, after all: it's a set of verses.'

'Are they in the prisoner's handwriting?' asked another of the jurymen.

'No, they're not,' said the White Rabbit, 'and that's the queerest thing about it.' (The jury all looked puzzled.)

'He must have imitated somebody else's hand,' said the King. (The jury all brightened up again.)

'Please your Majesty,' said the Knave, 'I didn't write it, and
they ca'n't prove that I did: there's no name signed at the end.'

'If you didn't sign it,' said the King, 'that only makes the
matter worse. You *must* have meant some mischief, or else
you'd have signed your name like an honest man.'

There was a general clapping of hands at this: it was the
first really clever thing the King had said that day.

'That *proves* his guilt, of course,' said the Queen: 'so
off with——.'

'It doesn't prove anything of the sort!' said Alice. 'Why
you don't even know what they're about!'

'Read them,' said the King.

The White Rabbit put on his spectacles. 'Where shall
I begin, please your Majesty?' he asked.

'Begin at the beginning,' the King said, very gravely, 'and
go on till you come to the end: then stop.'

There was dead silence in the court, whilst the White
Rabbit read out these verses:—

> *'They told me you had been to her,*[1]
> *And mentioned me to him:*
> *She gave me a good character,*
> *But said I could not swim.*
>
> *He sent them word I had not gone*
> *(We know it to be true):*
> *If she should push the matter on,*
> *What would become of you?*
>
> *I gave her one, they gave him two,*
> *You gave us three or more;*
> *They all returned from him to you,*
> *Though they were mine before.*
>
> *If I or she should chance to be*
> *Involved in this affair,*
> *He trusts to you to set them free,*
> *Exactly as we were.*

My notion was that you had been
    (Before she had this fit)
An obstacle that came between
    Him, and ourselves, and it.

Don't let him know she liked them best,
    For this must ever be
A secret, kept from all the rest,
    Between yourself and me.'

'That's the most important piece of evidence we've heard yet,' said the King, rubbing his hands; 'so now let the jury——'

'If any one of them can explain it,' said Alice, (she had grown so large in the last few minutes that she wasn't a bit afraid of interrupting him,) 'I'll give him sixpence. *I* don't believe there's an atom of meaning in it.'

The jury all wrote down, on their slates, '*She* doesn't believe there's an atom of meaning in it,' but none of them attempted to explain the paper.

'If there's no meaning in it,' said the King, 'that saves a world of trouble, you know, as we needn't try to find any. And yet I don't know,' he went on, spreading out the verses on his knee, and looking at them with one eye; 'I seem to see some meaning in them, after all. "*—said I could not swim—*" you ca'n't swim, can you?' he added, turning to the Knave.

The Knave shook his head sadly. 'Do I look like it?' he said. (Which he certainly did *not*, being made entirely of cardboard.)

'All right, so far,' said the King; and he went on muttering over the verses to himself: '"*We know it to be true*"— that's the jury, of course—"*If she should push the matter on*" —that must be the Queen—"*What would become of you?*"— What, indeed!—"*I gave her one, they gave him two*"—why, that must be what he did with the tarts, you know——'

'But it goes on "*they all returned from him to you,*"' said Alice.

'Why, there they are?' said
the King triumphantly, pointing to the tarts on the table.
'Nothing can be clearer than
that. Then again—"*before she
had this fit*"—you never had
fits, my dear, I think?' he said
to the Queen.

'Never!' said the Queen,
furiously, throwing an inkstand
at the Lizard as she spoke.
(The unfortunate little Bill
had left off writing on his slate
with one finger, as he found it
made no mark; but he now
hastily began again, using the
ink, that was trickling down his
face, as long as it lasted.)

'Then the words don't *fit* you,' said the King, looking round
the court with a smile. There was a dead silence.

'It's a pun!' the King added in an angry tone, and everybody laughed. 'Let the jury consider their verdict,' the King
said, for about the twentieth time that day.

'No, no!' said the Queen. 'Sentence first—verdict afterwards.'

'Stuff and nonsense!' said Alice loudly. 'The idea of having
the sentence first!'

'Hold your tongue!' said the Queen, turning purple.

'I wo'n't!' said Alice.

'Off with her head!' the Queen shouted at the top of her voice. Nobody moved.

'Who cares for *you?*' said Alice (she had grown to her full size by this time). 'You're nothing but a pack of cards!'

At this the whole pack rose up into the air, and came flying down upon her; she gave a little scream, half of fright and half of anger, and tried to beat them off, and found herself lying

on the bank, with her head in the lap of her sister, who was
gently brushing away some dead leaves that had fluttered
down from the trees upon her face.

'Wake up, Alice dear!' said her sister. 'Why, what a long
sleep you've had!'

'Oh, I've had such a curious dream!' said Alice. And she
told her sister, as well as she could remember them, all these
strange Adventures of hers that you have just been reading
about; and, when she had finished, her sister kissed her, and
said 'It *was* a curious dream, dear, certainly; but now run in
to your tea: it's getting late.' So Alice got up and ran off,
thinking while she ran, as well she might, what a wonderful
dream it had been.

But her sister sat still just as she left her, leaning her head on
her hand, watching the setting sun, and thinking of little
Alice and all her wonderful Adventures, till she too began
dreaming after a fashion, and this was her dream:—

First, she dreamed about little Alice herself: once again the
tiny hands were clasped upon her knee, and the bright eager
eyes were looking up into hers—she could hear the very tones
of her voice, and see that queer little toss of her head to keep
back the wandering hair that *would* always get into her eyes—
and still as she listened, or seemed to listen, the whole place
around her became alive with the strange creatures of her
little sister's dream.

The long grass rustled at her feet as the White Rabbit
hurried by—the frightened Mouse splashed his way through
the neighbouring pool—she could hear the rattle of the teacups as the March Hare and his friends shared their never-
ending meal, and the shrill voice of the Queen ordering off
her unfortunate guests to execution—once more the pig-baby
was sneezing on the Duchess' knee, while plates and dishes
crashed around it—once more the shriek of the Gryphon, the
squeaking of the Lizard's slate-pencil, and the choking of the

suppressed guinea-pigs, filled the air, mixed up with the distant sob of the miserable Mock Turtle.

So she sat on, with closed eyes, and half believed herself in
Wonderland, though she knew she had but to open them
again, and all would change to dull reality—the grass would be
only rustling in the wind, and the pool rippling to the waving
of the reeds—the rattling teacups would change to tinkling
sheep-bells, and the Queen's shrill cries to the voice of the
shepherd-boy—and the sneeze of the baby, the shriek of the
Gryphon, and all the other queer noises, would change (she
knew) to the confused clamour of the busy farm-yard—while
the lowing of the cattle in the distance would take the place of
the Mock Turtle's heavy sobs.

Lastly, she pictured to herself how this same little sister of
hers would, in the after-time, be herself a grown woman; and
how she would keep, through all her riper years, the simple
and loving heart of her childhood; and how she would gather
about her other little children, and make *their* eyes bright and
eager with many a strange tale, perhaps even with the dream
of Wonderland of long ago; and how she would feel with all
their simple sorrows, and find a pleasure in all their simple
joys, remembering her own child-life, and the happy summer days.

THE END

K

THROUGH THE
LOOKING-GLASS
AND WHAT ALICE
FOUND THERE

RED.

WHITE.

White Pawn (Alice) to play, and win in eleven moves

CHILD of the pure unclouded brow
    And dreaming eyes of wonder!
Though time be fleet, and I and thou
    Are half a life asunder,
Thy loving smile will surely hail
The love-gift of a fairy-tale.

I have not seen thy sunny face,
    Nor heard thy silver laughter:
No thought of me shall find a place
    In thy young life's hereafter—
Enough that now thou wilt not fail
To listen to my fairy-tale.

A tale begun in other days,
    When summer suns were glowing—
A simple chime, that served to time
    The rhythm of our rowing—
Whose echoes live in memory yet,
Though envious years would say 'forget.'

Come, hearken then, ere voice of dread,
    With bitter tidings laden,
Shall summon to unwelcome bed
    A melancholy maiden!
We are but older children, dear,
Who fret to find our bedtime near.

Without, the frost, the blinding snow,
    The storm-wind's moody madness—
Within, the firelight's ruddy glow,
    And childhood's nest of gladness.
The magic words shall hold thee fast:
Thou shalt not heed the raving blast.

And, though the shadow of a sigh
    May tremble through the story,
For 'happy summer days'[1] gone by,
    And vanish'd summer glory—
It shall not touch, with breath of bale,
The pleasance[2] of our fairy-tale.

ADVERTISEMENT[1]

F OR over 25 years, I have made it my chief object, with regard to my books, that they should be of the best workmanship attainable for the price. And I am deeply annoyed to find that the last issue of 'Through the Looking-Glass,' consisting of the Sixtieth Thousand, has been put on sale without its being noticed that most of the pictures have failed so much, in the printing, as to make the book not worth buying. I request all holders of copies to send them to Messrs. Macmillan & Co., 29 Bedford Street, Covent Garden, with their names and addresses; and copies of the next issue shall be sent them in exchange.

Instead, however, of destroying the unsold copies, I propose to utilise them by giving them away, to Mechanics' Institutes, Village Reading-Rooms, and similar institutions, where the means for purchasing such books are scanty. Accordingly I invite applications for such gifts, addressed to me, 'care of Messrs. Macmillan.' Every such application should be signed by some responsible person, and should state how far they are able to buy books for themselves, and what is the average number of readers.

I take this opportunity of announcing that, if at any future time I should wish to communicate anything to my Readers, I will do so by advertising, in the 'Agony' Column of some of the Daily Papers, *on the first Tuesday in the month.*

L EWIS C ARROLL

Christmas, 1893

PREFACE TO
SIXTY-FIRST THOUSAND

As the chess-problem,[1] given on a previous page, has puzzled some of my readers, it may be well to explain that it is correctly worked out, so far as the *moves* are concerned. The *alternation* of Red and White is perhaps not so strictly observed as it might be, and the 'castling' of the three Queens is merely a way of saying that they entered the palace: but the 'check' of the White King at move 6, the capture of the Red Knight at move 7, and the final 'checkmate' of the Red King, will be found, by any one who will take the trouble to set the pieces and play the moves as directed, to be strictly in accordance with the laws of the game.

The new words, in the poem 'Jabberwocky' (see p. 134), have given rise to some differences of opinion as to their pronunciation: so it may be well to give instructions on *that* point also. Pronounce 'slithy' as if it were the two words 'sly, the': make the 'g' *hard* in 'gyre' and 'gimble': and pronounce 'rath' to rhyme with 'bath.'

For this sixty-first thousand, fresh electrotypes have been taken from the wood-blocks (which, never having been used for printing from, are in as good condition as when first cut in 1871), and the whole book has been set up afresh with new type. If the artistic qualities of this re-issue fall short, in any particular, of those possessed by the original issue, it will not be for want of painstaking on the part of author, publisher, or printer.

I take this opportunity of announcing that the Nursery 'Alice,' hitherto priced at four shillings, net, is now to be had on the same terms as the ordinary shilling picture-books— although I feel sure that it is, in every quality (except the *text* itself, on which I am not qualified to pronounce), greatly superior to them. Four shillings was a perfectly reasonable price to charge, considering the very heavy initial outlay I had incurred: still, as the Public have practically said 'We will *not* give more than a shilling for a picture-book, however artistically got-up,' I am content to reckon my outlay on the book as so much dead loss, and, rather than let the little ones, for whom it was written, go without it, I am selling it at a price which is, to me, much the same thing as *giving* it away.

Christmas, 1896

CONTENTS

CHAPTER I

LOOKING-GLASS HOUSE

ONE thing was certain, that the *white* kitten had had nothing to do with it[1]—it was the black kitten's fault entirely. For the white kitten had been having its face washed by the old cat for the last quarter of an hour (and bearing it pretty well, considering): so you see that it *couldn't* have had any hand in the mischief.

The way Dinah washed her children's faces was this: first she held the poor thing down by its ear with one paw, and then with the other paw she rubbed its face all over, the wrong way, beginning at the nose: and just now, as I said, she was hard at work on the white kitten, which was lying quite still and trying to purr—no doubt feeling that it was all meant for its good.

But the black kitten had been finished with earlier in the afternoon, and so, while Alice was sitting curled up in a corner of the great arm-chair, half talking to herself and half asleep, the kitten had been having a grand game of romps with the ball of worsted Alice had been trying to wind up, and had been rolling it up and down till it had all come undone again; and there it was, spread over the hearth-rug, all knots and tangles, with the kitten running after its own tail in the middle.

'Oh, you wicked wicked little thing!' cried Alice, catching up the kitten, and giving it a little kiss to make it understand that it was in disgrace. 'Really, Dinah ought to have taught you better manners! You *ought*, Dinah, you know you ought!' she added, looking reproachfully at the old cat, and speaking in as cross a voice as she could manage—and then she scrambled back into the arm-chair, taking the kitten and the worsted with her, and began winding up the ball again. But she didn't get on very fast, as she was talking all the time, some-times to the kitten, and sometimes to herself. Kitty sat very demurely on her knee, pretending to watch the progress of the winding, and now and then putting out one paw

and gently touching the ball, as if it would be glad to help if it might.

'Do you know what to-morrow is,¹ Kitty?' Alice began. 'You'd have guessed if you'd been up in the window with me —only Dinah was making you tidy, so you couldn't. I was watching the boys getting in sticks for the bonfire—and it wants plenty of sticks, Kitty! Only it got so cold, and it snowed so, they had to leave off. Never mind, Kitty, we'll go and see the bonfire to-morrow.' Here Alice wound two or three turns of the worsted round the kitten's neck, just to see how it would look: this led to a scramble, in which the ball rolled down upon the floor, and yards and yards of it got unwound again.

'Do you know, I was so angry, Kitty,' Alice went on, as soon as they were comfortably settled again, 'when I saw all the mischief you had been doing, I was very nearly opening the window, and putting you out into the snow! And you'd have deserved it, you little mischievous darling! What have you got to say for yourself? Now don't interrupt me!' she went on, holding up one finger. 'I'm going to tell you all your faults. Number one: you squeaked twice while Dinah was washing your face this morning. Now you ca'n't deny it, Kitty: I heard you! What's that you say?' (pretending that the kitten was speaking). 'Her paw went into your eye? Well, that's *your* fault, for keeping your eyes open—if you'd shut them tight up, it wouldn't have happened. Now don't make any more excuses, but listen! Number two: you pulled Snow-drop² away by the tail just as I had put down the saucer of milk before her! What, you were thirsty, were you? How do you know she wasn't thirsty too? Now for number three: you unwound every bit of the worsted while I wasn't looking!

'That's three faults, Kitty, and you've not been punished for any of them yet. You know I'm saving up all your punish-ments for Wednesday week—Suppose they had saved up all *my* punishments?' she went on, talking more to herself than the kitten. 'What *would* they do at the end of a year? I should be sent to prison, I suppose, when the day came. Or—let me see—suppose each punishment was to be going without a dinner: then, when the miserable day came, I should have to go without fifty dinners at once! Well, I shouldn't mind *that* much! I'd far rather go without them than eat them!

'Do you hear the snow against the window-panes, Kitty? How nice and soft it sounds! Just as if some one was kissing the window all over outside. I wonder if the snow *loves* the trees and fields, that it kisses them so gently? And then it covers them up snug, you know, with a white quilt; and perhaps it says "Go to sleep, darlings, till the summer comes again." And when they wake up in the summer, Kitty, they dress themselves all in green, and dance about—whenever the wind blows—oh, that's very pretty!' cried Alice, dropping the ball of worsted to clap her hands. 'And I do so *wish* it was true! I'm sure the woods look sleepy in the autumn, when the leaves are getting brown.

'Kitty, can you play chess? Now, don't smile, my dear, I'm asking it seriously. Because, when we were playing just now, you watched just as if you understood it: and when I said "Check!" you purred! Well, it *was* a nice check, Kitty, and really I might have won, if it hadn't been for that nasty Knight, that came wriggling down among my pieces. Kitty, dear, let's pretend——' And here I wish I could tell you half the things Alice used to say, beginning with her favourite phrase 'Let's pretend.' She had had quite a long argument with her sister only the day before—all because Alice had begun with 'Let's pretend we're kings and queens;' and her sister, who liked being very exact, had argued that they couldn't, because there were only two of them, and Alice had been reduced at last to say 'Well, *you* can be one of them, then, and *I'll* be all the rest.' And once she had really frightened her old nurse by shouting suddenly in her ear, 'Nurse! Do let's pretend that I'm a hungry hyæna, and you're a bone!'

But this is taking us away from Alice's speech to the kitten.

'Let's pretend that you're the Red Queen, Kitty! Do you know, I think if you sat up and folded your arms, you'd look exactly like her. Now do try, there's a dear!' And Alice got the Red Queen off the table, and set it up before the kitten as a model for it to imitate: however, the thing didn't succeed, principally, Alice said, because the kitten wouldn't fold its arms properly. So, to punish it, she held it up to the Looking-glass, that it might see how sulky it was, '—and if you're not good directly,' she added, 'I'll put you through into Looking-glass House. How would you like *that*?

'Now, if you'll only attend, Kitty, and not talk so much, I'll tell you all my ideas about Looking-glass House. First, there's the room you can see through the glass—that's just the same as our drawing-room, only the things go the other way. I can see all of it when I get upon a chair—all but the bit just behind the fireplace. Oh! I do so wish I could see *that* bit! I want so much to know whether they've a fire in the winter: you never *can* tell, you know, unless our fire smokes, and then smoke comes up in that room too—but that may be only pretence, just to make it look as if they had a fire. Well then, the books are something like our books, only the words go the wrong way: I know *that*, because I've held up one of our books to the glass, and then they hold up one in the other room.

'How would you like to live in Looking-glass House, Kitty? I wonder if they'd give you milk in there? Perhaps Looking-glass milk isn't good to drink—but oh, Kitty! now we come to the passage. You can just see a little *peep* of the passage in Looking-glass House, if you leave the door of our drawing-room wide open: and it's very like our passage as far as you can see, only you know it may be quite different on beyond. Oh, Kitty, how nice it would be if we could only get through into Looking-glass House! I'm sure it's got, oh! such beautiful things in it! Let's pretend there's a way of getting through into it, somehow, Kitty. Let's pretend the glass has got all soft like gauze, so that we can get through. Why, it's turning into a sort of mist now, I declare! It'll be easy enough to get

L

through——' She was up on the chimney-piece while she said this, though she hardly knew how she had got there. And certainly the glass *was* beginning to melt away, just like a bright silvery mist.

In another moment Alice was through the glass, and had jumped lightly down into the Looking-glass room. The very first thing she did was to look whether there was a fire in the fireplace, and she was quite pleased to find that there was a real one, blazing away as brightly as the one she had left behind. 'So I shall be as warm here as I was in the old room,' thought Alice: 'warmer, in fact, because there'll be no one

here to scold me away from the fire. Oh, what fun it'll be, when they see me through the glass in here, and ca'n't get at me!'

Then she began looking about, and noticed that what could be seen from the old room was quite common and uninteresting, but that all the rest was as different as possible. For instance, the pictures on the wall next the fire seemed to be all alive, and the very clock on the chimney-piece (you know you can only see the back of it in the Looking-glass) had got the face of a little old man, and grinned at her.

'They don't keep this room so tidy as the other,' Alice thought to herself, as she noticed several of the chessmen down in the hearth among the cinders; but in another moment, with a little 'Oh!' of surprise, she was down on her hands and knees watching them. The chessmen were walking about, two and two!

'Here are the Red King and the Red Queen,' Alice said (in a whisper, for fear of frightening them), 'and there are the White King and the White Queen sitting on the edge of the shovel—and here are two Castles walking arm in arm—I don't think they can hear me,' she went on, as she put her head closer down, 'and I'm nearly sure they ca'n't see me. I feel somehow as if I was getting invisible——'

Here something began squeaking on the table behind Alice, and made her turn her head just in time to see one of the White Pawns roll over and begin kicking: she watched it with great curiosity to see what would happen next.

'It is the voice of my child!' the White Queen cried out, as she rushed past the King, so violently that she knocked him over among the cinders. 'My precious Lily! My imperial kitten!' and she began scrambling wildly up the side of the fender.

'Imperial fiddlestick!' said the King, rubbing his nose, which had been hurt by the fall. He had a right to be a *little* annoyed with the Queen, for he was covered with ashes from head to foot.

Alice was very anxious to be of use, and, as the poor little Lily was nearly screaming herself into a fit, she hastily picked up the Queen and set her on the table by the side of her noisy little daughter.

The Queen gasped, and sat down: the rapid journey through the air had quite taken away her breath, and for a minute or two she could do nothing but hug the little Lily in silence. As soon as she had recovered her breath a little, she called out to the White King, who was sitting sulkily among the ashes, 'Mind the volcano!'

'What volcano?' said the King, looking up anxiously into the fire, as if he thought that was the most likely place to find one.

'Blew—me—up,' panted the Queen, who was still a little out of breath. 'Mind you come up—the regular way—don't get blown up!'

Alice watched the White King as he slowly struggled up from bar to bar, till at last she said 'Why, you'll be hours and hours getting to the table, at that rate. I'd far better help you, hadn't I?' But the King took no notice of the question: it was quite clear that he could neither hear her nor see her.

So Alice picked him up very gently, and lifted him across more slowly than she had lifted the Queen, that she mightn't take his breath away; but, before she put him on the table, she thought she might as well dust him a little, he was so covered with ashes.

She said afterwards that she had never seen in all her life

such a face as the King made, when he found himself held in the air by an invisible hand, and being dusted: he was far too much astonished to cry out, but his eyes and his mouth went on getting larger and larger, and rounder and rounder, till her hand shook so with laughing that she nearly let him drop upon the floor.

'Oh! *please* don't make such faces, my dear!' she cried out, quite forgetting that the King couldn't hear her. 'You make me laugh so that I can hardly hold you! And don't keep your mouth so wide open! All the ashes will get into it—there, now I think you're tidy enough!' she added, as she smoothed his hair, and set him upon the table near the Queen.

The King immediately fell flat on his back, and lay perfectly still; and Alice was a little alarmed at what she had done, and went round the room to see if she could find any water to throw over him. However, she could find nothing but a bottle of ink, and when she got back with it she found he had recovered, and he and the Queen were talking together in a frightened whisper—so low, that Alice could hardly hear what they said.

The King was saying 'I assure you, my dear, I turned cold to the very ends of my whiskers!'

To which the Queen replied 'You haven't got any whiskers.'

'The horror of that moment,' the King went on, 'I shall never, *never* forget!'

'You will, though,' the Queen said, 'if you don't make a memorandum of it.'

Alice looked on with great interest as the King took an enormous memorandum-book out of his pocket, and began writing. A sudden thought struck her, and she took hold of the end of the pencil, which came some way over his shoulder, and began writing for him.

The poor King looked puzzled and unhappy, and struggled with the pencil for some time without saying anything; but Alice was too strong for him, and at last he panted out 'My dear! I really *must* get a thinner pencil. I ca'n't manage this one a bit: it writes all manner of things that I don't intend——'

'What manner of things?' said the Queen, looking over the book (in which Alice had put "*The White Knight is sliding down the poker. He balances very badly*"). 'That's not a memorandum of *your* feelings!'

There was a book lying near Alice on the table, and while she sat watching the White King (for she was still a little anxious about him, and had the ink all ready to throw over him, in case he fainted again), she turned over the leaves, to find some part that she could read, '—for it's all in some language I don't know,' she said to herself.

It was like this.

JABBERWOCKY.

'Twas brillig, and the slithy toves
Did gyre and gimble in the wabe:
All mimsy were the borogoves,
And the mome raths outgrabe.

She puzzled over this for some time, but at last a bright thought struck her. 'Why, it's a Looking-glass book, of course! And, if I hold it up to a glass, the words will all go the right way again.'

This was the poem that Alice read.

JABBERWOCKY.[1]

> 'Twas brillig, and the slithy toves
>   Did gyre and gimble in the wabe:
> All mimsy were the borogoves,
>   And the mome raths outgrabe.

> 'Beware the Jabberwock, my son!
>   The jaws that bite, the claws that catch!
> Beware the Jubjub bird, and shun
>   The frumious Bandersnatch!'

> He took his vorpal sword in hand:
>   Long time the manxome foe he sought—
> So rested he by the Tumtum tree,
>   And stood awhile in thought.

> And, as in uffish thought he stood,
>   The Jabberwock, with eyes of flame,
> Came whiffling through the tulgey wood,
>   And burbled as it came!

> *One, two! One, two! And through and through*
>   *The vorpal blade went snicker-snack!*
> *He left it dead, and with its head*
>   *He went galumphing back.*
>
> *'And hast thou slain the Jabberwock?*
>   *Come to my arms, my beamish boy!*
> *O frabjous day! Callooh! Callay!'*
>   *He chortled in his joy.*
>
> *'Twas brillig, and the slithy toves*
>   *Did gyre and gimble in the wabe:*
> *All mimsy were the borogoves,*
>   *And the mome raths outgrabe.*

'It seems very pretty,' she said when she had finished it, 'but it's *rather* hard to understand!' (You see she didn't like to confess, even to herself, that she couldn't make it out at all.) 'Somehow it seems to fill my head with ideas—only I don't exactly know what they are! However, *somebody* killed *something*: that's clear, at any rate——'

'But oh!' thought Alice, suddenly jumping up, 'if I don't make haste, I shall have to go back through the Looking-glass, before I've seen what the rest of the house is like! Let's have a look at the garden first!' She was out of the room in a moment, and ran down stairs—or, at least, it wasn't exactly running, but a new invention for getting down stairs quickly and easily, as Alice said to herself. She just kept the tips of her fingers on the hand-rail, and floated gently down without even touching the stairs with her feet: then she floated on through the hall, and would have gone straight out at the door in the same way, if she hadn't caught hold of the door-post. She was getting a little giddy with so much floating in the air, and was rather glad to find herself walking again in the natural way.

CHAPTER II

THE GARDEN OF LIVE FLOWERS[1]

'I SHOULD see the garden far better,' said Alice to herself, 'if I could get to the top of that hill: and here's a path that leads straight to it—at least, no, it doesn't do *that*——' (after going a few yards along the path, and turning several sharp corners), 'but I suppose it will at last. But how curiously it twists! It's more like a corkscrew than a path! Well, *this* turn goes to the hill, I suppose—no, it doesn't! This goes straight back to the house! Well then, I'll try it the other way.'

And so she did: wandering up and down, and trying turn after turn, but always coming back to the house, do what she would. Indeed, once, when she turned a corner rather more quickly than usual, she ran against it before she could stop herself.

'It's no use talking about it,' Alice said, looking up at the house and pretending it was arguing with her. 'I'm *not* going in again yet. I know I should have to get through the Looking-glass again—back into the old room—and there'd be an end of all my adventures!'

So, resolutely turning her back upon the house, she set out once more down the path, determined to keep straight on till she got to the hill. For a few minutes all went on well, and she was just saying 'I really *shall* do it this time——' when the path gave a sudden twist and shook itself (as she described it afterwards), and the next moment she found herself actually walking in at the door.

'Oh, it's too bad!' she cried. 'I never saw such a house for getting in the way! Never!'

However, there was the hill full in sight, so there was nothing to be done but start again. This time she came upon

a large flower-bed, with a border of daisies, and a willow-tree growing in the middle. ‘

‘O Tiger-lily!’¹ said Alice, addressing herself to one that was waving gracefully about in the wind, ‘I *wish* you could talk!’

‘We *can* talk,’ said the Tiger-lily, ‘when there’s anybody worth talking to.’

Alice was so astonished that she couldn’t speak for a minute: it quite seemed to take her breath away. At length, as the Tiger-lily only went on waving about, she spoke again, in a timid voice—almost in a whisper. 'And can *all* the flowers talk?'

'As well as *you* can,' said the Tiger-lily. 'And a great deal louder.'

'It isn't manners for us to begin, you know,' said the Rose,[1] 'and I really was wondering when you'd speak! Said I to myself, "Her face has got *some* sense in it, though it's not a clever one!" Still, you're the right colour, and that goes a long way.'

'I don't care about the colour,' the Tiger-lily remarked. 'If only her petals curled up a little more, she'd be all right.'

Alice didn't like being criticized, so she began asking questions. 'Aren't you sometimes frightened at being planted out here, with nobody to take care of you?'

'There's the tree in the middle,' said the Rose. 'What else is it good for?'

'But what could it do, if any danger came?' Alice asked.

'It could bark,' said the Rose.

'It says "Bough-wough!"' cried a Daisy. 'That's why its branches are called boughs!'

'Didn't you know *that?*' cried another Daisy. And here they all began shouting together, till the air seemed quite full of little shrill voices. 'Silence, every one of you!' cried the Tiger-lily, waving itself passionately from side to side, and trembling with excitement. 'They know I ca'n't get at them!' it panted, bending its quivering head towards Alice, 'or they wouldn't dare to do it!'

'Never mind!' Alice said in a soothing tone, and, stooping down to the daisies, who were just beginning again, she whispered 'If you don't hold your tongues, I'll pick you!'

There was silence in a moment, and several of the pink daisies turned white.

'That's right!' said the Tiger-lily. 'The daisies are worst of all. When one speaks, they all begin together, and it's enough to make one wither to hear the way they go on!'

'How is it you can all talk so nicely?' Alice said, hoping to get it into a better temper by a compliment. 'I've been in many gardens before, but none of the flowers could talk.'

'Put your hand down, and feel the ground,' said the Tiger-lily. 'Then you'll know why.'

Alice did so. 'It's very hard,' she said; 'but I don't see what that has to do with it.'

'In most gardens,' the Tiger-lily said, 'they make the beds too soft—so that the flowers are always asleep.'

This sounded a very good reason, and Alice was quite pleased to know it. 'I never thought of that before!' she said.

'It's *my* opinion that you never think *at all*,' the Rose said, in a rather severe tone.

'I never saw anybody that looked stupider,' a Violet[1] said, so suddenly, that Alice quite jumped; for it hadn't spoken before.

'Hold *your* tongue!' cried the Tiger-lily. 'As if *you* ever saw anybody! You keep your head under the leaves, and snore away there, till you know no more what's going on in the world, than if you were a bud!'

'Are there any more people in the garden besides me?' Alice said, not choosing to notice the Rose's last remark.

'There's one other flower in the garden that can move about like you,' said the Rose. 'I wonder how you do it——' ('You're always wondering,' said the Tiger-lily), 'but she's more bushy than you are.'

'Is she like me?' Alice asked eagerly, for the thought crossed her mind, 'There's another little girl in the garden, some-where!'

'Well, she has the same awkward shape as you,' the Rose said: 'but she's redder—and her petals are shorter, I think.'

'They're done up close, like a dahlia,' said the Tiger-lily: 'not tumbled about, like yours.'

'But that's not *your* fault,' the Rose added kindly. 'You're beginning to fade, you know—and then one ca'n't help one's petals getting a little untidy.'

Alice didn't like this idea at all: so, to change the subject, she asked 'Does she ever come out here?'

'I daresay you'll see her soon,' said the Rose. 'She's one of the kind that has nine spikes,[1] you know.'

'Where does she wear them?' Alice asked with some curiosity.

'Why, all round her head, of course,' the Rose replied. 'I was wondering *you* hadn't got some too. I thought it was the regular rule.'

'She's coming!' cried the Larkspur. 'I hear her footstep, thump, thump, along the gravel-walk!'

Alice looked round eagerly and found that it was the Red Queen. 'She's grown a good deal!' was her first remark. She had indeed: when Alice first found her in the ashes, she had been only three inches high—and here she was, half a head taller than Alice herself!

'It's the fresh air that does it,'[2] said the Rose: 'wonderfully fine air it is, out here.'

'I think I'll go and meet her,' said Alice, for, though the flowers were interesting enough, she felt that it would be far grander to have a talk with a real Queen.

'You ca'n't possibly do that,' said the Rose: '*I* should advise you to walk the other way.'[3]

This sounded nonsense to Alice, so she said nothing, but set off at once towards the Red Queen. To her surprise she lost sight of her in a moment, and found herself walking in at the front-door again.

A little provoked, she drew back, and, after looking everywhere for the Queen (whom she spied out at last, a long way off), she thought she would try the plan, this time, of walking in the opposite direction.

It succeeded beautifully. She had not been walking a minute

before she found herself face to face with the Red Queen, and full in sight of the hill she had been so long aiming at.

'Where do you come from?' said the Red Queen. 'And where are you going? Look up, speak nicely, and don't twiddle your fingers all the time.'

Alice attended to all these directions, and explained, as well as she could, that she had lost her way.

'I don't know what you mean by *your* way,' said the Queen: 'all the ways about here belong to *me*—but why did you come out here at all?' she added in a kinder tone. 'Curtsey while you're thinking what to say. It saves time.'

Alice wondered a little at this, but she was too much in awe of the Queen to disbelieve it. 'I'll try it when I go home,' she thought to herself, 'the next time I'm a little late for dinner.'

'It's time for you to answer now,' the Queen said, looking at her watch: 'open your mouth a *little* wider when you speak, and always say "your Majesty."'

'I only wanted to see what the garden was like, your Majesty——'

'That's right,' said the Queen, patting her on the head, which Alice didn't like at all: 'though, when you say "garden" —*I*'*ve* seen gardens, compared with which this would be a wilderness.'

Alice didn't dare to argue the point, but went on: '—and I thought I'd try and find my way to the top of that hill——'

'When you say "hill,"' the Queen interrupted, '*I* could show you hills, in comparison with which you'd call that a valley.'

'No, I shouldn't,' said Alice, surprised into contradicting her at last: 'a hill *ca'n't* be a valley, you know. That would be nonsense——'

The Red Queen shook her head. 'You may call it "nonsense" if you like,' she said, 'but *I*'*ve* heard nonsense, compared with which that would be as sensible as a dictionary!'

Alice curtseyed again, as she was afraid from the Queen's tone that she was a *little* offended: and they walked on in silence till they got to the top of the little hill.[1]

For some minutes Alice stood without speaking, looking out in all directions over the country—and a most curious country it was. There were a number of tiny little brooks running straight across it from side to side, and the ground between was divided up into squares by a

number of little green hedges, that reached from brook to brook.

'I declare it's marked out just like a large chess-board!' Alice said at last. 'There ought to be some men moving about somewhere—and so there are!' she added in a tone of delight, and her heart began to beat quick with excitement as she went on. 'It's a great huge game of chess that's being played—all over the world—if this *is* the world at all, you know. Oh, what fun it is! How I *wish* I was one of them! I wouldn't mind being a Pawn, if only I might join—though of course I should *like* to be a Queen, best.'

She glanced rather shyly at the real Queen as she said this, but her companion only smiled pleasantly, and said 'That's easily managed. You can be the White Queen's Pawn, if you like, as Lily's too young to play; and you're in the Second Square to begin with: when you get to the Eighth Square you'll be a Queen——' Just at this moment, somehow or other, they began to run.

Alice never could quite make out, in thinking it over after-wards, how it was that they began: all she remembers is, that they were running hand in hand, and the Queen went so fast that it was all she could do to keep up with her: and still the Queen kept crying 'Faster! Faster!', but Alice felt she *could not* go faster, though she had no breath left to say so.

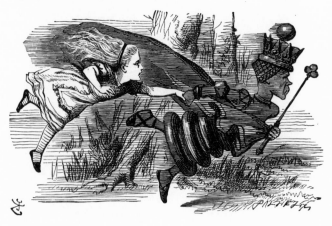

The most curious part of the thing was, that the trees and the other things round them never changed their places at all: however fast they went, they never seemed to pass anything. 'I wonder if all the things move along with us?' thought poor puzzled Alice. And the Queen seemed to guess her thoughts, for she cried 'Faster! Don't try to talk!'

Not that Alice had any idea of doing *that*. She felt as if she would never be able to talk again, she was getting so much out of breath: and still the Queen cried 'Faster! Faster!', and dragged her along. 'Are we nearly there?' Alice managed to pant out at last.

'Nearly there!' the Queen repeated. 'Why, we passed it ten minutes ago! Faster!' And they ran on for a time in silence, with the wind whistling in Alice's ears, and almost blowing her hair off her head, she fancied.

'Now! Now!' cried the Queen. 'Faster! Faster!' And they went so fast that at last they seemed to skim through the air, hardly touching the ground with their feet, till suddenly, just as Alice was getting quite exhausted, they stopped, and she found herself sitting on the ground, breathless and giddy.

The Queen propped her up against a tree, and said kindly, 'You may rest a little, now.'

Alice looked round her in great surprise. 'Why, I do believe we've been under this tree the whole time! Everything's just as it was!'

'Of course it is,' said the Queen. 'What would you have it?'

'Well, in *our* country,' said Alice, still panting a little, 'you'd generally get to somewhere else—if you ran very fast for a long time as we've been doing.'

'A slow sort of country!' said the Queen. 'Now, *here*, you see, it takes all the running *you* can do, to keep in the same place. If you want to get somewhere else, you must run at least twice as fast as that!'

'I'd rather not try, please!' said Alice. 'I'm quite content to stay here—only I *am* so hot and thirsty!'

'I know what *you'd* like!' the Queen said good-naturedly, taking a little box out of her pocket. 'Have a biscuit?'

Alice thought it would not be civil to say 'No,' though it wasn't at all what she wanted. So she took it, and ate it as well as she could: and it was *very* dry: and she thought she had never been so nearly choked in all her life.

'While you're refreshing yourself,' said the Queen, 'I'll just take the measurements.' And she took a ribbon out of her pocket, marked in inches, and began measuring the ground, and sticking little pegs in here and there.

'At the end of two yards,' she said, putting in a peg to mark the distance, 'I shall give you your directions—have another biscuit?'

'No, thank you,' said Alice: 'one's *quite* enough!'

'Thirst quenched, I hope?' said the Queen.

Alice did not know what to say to this, but luckily the Queen did not wait for an answer, but went on. 'At the end of *three* yards I shall repeat them—for fear of your forgetting them. At the end of *four*, I shall say good-bye. And at the end of *five*, I shall go!'

She had got all the pegs put in by this time, and Alice looked on with great interest as she returned to the tree, and then began slowly walking down the row.

At the two-yard peg she faced round, and said 'A pawn goes two squares in its first move, you know. So you'll go *very* quickly through the Third Square—by railway, I should think—and you'll find yourself in the Fourth Square in no time. Well, *that* square belongs to Tweedledum and Tweedledee—the Fifth is mostly water—the Sixth belongs to Humpty Dumpty—But you make no remark?'

'I—I didn't know I had to make one—just then,' Alice faltered out.

'You *should* have said,' the Queen went on in a tone of grave reproof, ' "It's extremely kind of you to tell me all this"—however, we'll suppose it said—the Seventh Square is all forest—however, one of the Knights will show you the way—and in the Eighth Square we shall be Queens together, and it's all feasting and fun!' Alice got up and curtseyed, and sat down again.

At the next peg the Queen turned again, and this time she said 'Speak in French when you ca'n't think of the English for a thing—turn out your toes as you walk—and remember who you are!' She did not wait for Alice to curtsey, this time, but walked on quickly to the next peg, where she turned for a moment to say 'Good-bye,' and then hurried on to the last.

How it happened, Alice never knew, but exactly as she came to the last peg, she was gone. Whether she vanished into the air, or whether she ran quickly into the wood ('and she *can* run very fast!' thought Alice), there was no way of guessing, but she was gone, and Alice began to remember that she was a Pawn, and that it would soon be time for her to move.

CHAPTER III

LOOKING-GLASS INSECTS

OF course the first thing to do was to make a grand survey of the country she was going to travel through. 'It's something very like learning geography,' thought Alice, as she stood on tiptoe in hopes of being able to see a little further. 'Principal rivers—there *are* none. Principal mountains—I'm on the only one, but I don't think it's got any name. Principal towns —why, what *are* those creatures, making honey down there? They ca'n't be bees—nobody ever saw bees a mile off, you know——' and for some time she stood silent, watching one of them that was bustling about among the flowers, poking its proboscis into them, 'just as if it was a regular bee,' thought Alice.

However, this was anything but a regular bee: in fact, it was an elephant[1]—as Alice soon found out, though the idea quite took her breath away at first. 'And what enormous flowers they must be!' was her next idea. 'Something like cottages with the roofs taken off, and stalks put to them—and what quantities of honey they must make! I think I'll go down and—no, I wo'n't go *just* yet,' she went on, checking herself just as she was beginning to run down the hill, and trying to find some excuse for turning shy so suddenly. 'It'll never do to go down among them without a good long branch to brush them away—and what fun it'll be when they ask me how I liked my walk. I shall say "Oh, I liked it well enough——" (here came the favourite little toss of the head), "only it *was* so dusty and hot, and the elephants *did* tease so!"

'I think I'll go down the other way,' she said after a pause; 'and perhaps I may visit the elephants later on. Besides, I *do* so want to get into the Third Square!'

So, with this excuse, she ran down the hill, and jumped over the first of the six little brooks.[1]

*   *   *   *   *

*   *   *   *

*   *   *   *   *

'Tickets, please!' said the Guard, putting his head in at the window. In a moment everybody was holding out a ticket: they were about the same size as the people, and quite seemed to fill the carriage.

'Now then! Show your ticket, child!' the Guard went on, looking angrily at Alice. And a great many voices all said together ('like the chorus of a song,' thought Alice) 'Don't keep him waiting, child! Why, his time is worth a thousand pounds a minute!'

'I'm afraid I haven't got one,' Alice said in a frightened tone: 'there wasn't a ticket-office where I came from.' And again the chorus of voices went on. 'There wasn't room for one where she came from. The land there is worth a thousand pounds[2] an inch!'

'Don't make excuses,' said the Guard: 'you should have bought one from the engine-driver.' And once more the chorus of voices went on with 'The man that drives the engine. Why, the smoke alone is worth a thousand pounds a puff!'

Alice thought to herself 'Then there's no use in speaking.' The voices didn't join in, *this* time, as she hadn't spoken, but, to her great surprise, they all *thought* in chorus (I hope you understand what *thinking in chorus* means—for I must confess that *I* don't), 'Better say nothing at all. Language is worth a thousand pounds a word!'

'I shall dream about a thousand pounds to-night, I know I shall!' thought Alice.

All this time the Guard was looking at her, first through a telescope, then through a microscope, and then through an

opera-glass. At last he said 'You're traveling the wrong way,' and shut up the window, and went away.

'So young a child,' said the gentleman sitting opposite to her, (he was dressed in white paper,) 'ought to know which way she's going, even if she doesn't know her own name!'

A Goat, that was sitting next to the gentleman in white, shut his eyes and said in a loud voice, 'She ought to know her way to the ticket-office, even if she doesn't know her alphabet!'

There was a Beetle sitting next the Goat (it was a very queer carriage-full of passengers altogether), and, as the rule seemed to be that they should all speak in turn, *he* went on with 'She'll have to go back from here as luggage!'

Alice couldn't see who was sitting beyond the Beetle, but a hoarse voice spoke next. 'Change engines——' it said, and there it choked and was obliged to leave off.

'It sounds like a horse,' Alice thought to herself. And an extremely small voice, close to her ear, said 'You might make a joke on that—something about "horse" and "hoarse," you know.'

Then a very gentle voice in the distance said, 'She must be labeled "Lass, with care,"[1] you know——'

And after that other voices went on ('What a number of people there are in the carriage!' thought Alice), saying 'She must go by post, as she's got a head on her——' 'She must be sent as a message by the telegraph——' 'She must draw the train herself the rest of the way——,' and so on.

But the gentleman dressed in white paper leaned forwards and whispered in her ear, 'Never mind what they all say, my dear, but take a return-ticket every time the train stops.'

'Indeed I sha'n't!' Alice said rather impatiently. 'I don't belong to this railway journey at all—I was in a wood just now—and I wish I could get back there!'

'You might make a joke on *that*,' said the little voice close to her ear: 'something about "you *would* if you could, you know".'

'Don't tease so,' said Alice, looking about in vain to see where the voice came from. 'If you're so anxious to have a joke made, why don't you make one yourself?'

The little voice sighed deeply. It was *very* unhappy, evidently, and Alice would have said something pitying to comfort it, 'if it would only sigh like other people!' she thought. But this was such a wonderfully small sigh, that she wouldn't have heard it at all, if it hadn't come *quite* close to her ear. The consequence of this was that it tickled her ear very much, and quite took off her thoughts from the unhappiness of the poor little creature.

'I know you are a friend,' the little voice went on: 'a dear friend, and an old friend. And you wo'n't hurt me, though I *am* an insect.'

'What kind of insect?' Alice inquired, a little anxiously. What she really wanted to know was, whether it could sting or not, but she thought this wouldn't be quite a civil question to ask.

'What, then you don't——' the little voice began, when it was drowned by a shrill scream from the engine, and everybody jumped up in alarm, Alice among the rest.

The Horse, who had put his head out of the window, quietly drew it in and said 'It's only a brook we have to jump over.' Everybody seemed satisfied with this, though Alice felt a little nervous at the idea of trains jumping at all. 'However, it'll take us into the Fourth Square, that's some comfort!' she said to herself. In another moment she felt the carriage rise straight up into the air, and in her fright she caught at the thing nearest to her hand, which happened to be the Goat's beard.[1]

         *   *   *   *   *

             *   *   *   *

      *   *   *   *   *

But the beard seemed to melt away as she touched it, and she found herself sitting quietly under a tree—while the Gnat (for that was the insect she had been talking to) was balancing itself on a twig just over her head, and fanning her with its wings.

It certainly was a *very* large Gnat: 'about the size of a chicken,' Alice thought. Still, she couldn't feel nervous with it, after they had been talking together so long.

'—then you don't like *all* insects?' the Gnat went on, as quietly as if nothing had happened.

'I like them when they can talk,' Alice said. 'None of them ever talk, where *I* come from.'

'What sort of insects do you rejoice in, where *you* come from?' the Gnat inquired.

'I don't *rejoice* in insects at all,' Alice explained, 'because I'm rather afraid of them—at least the large kinds. But I can tell you the names of some of them.'

'Of course they answer to their names?' the Gnat remarked carelessly.

'I never knew them do it.'

'What's the use of their having names,' the Gnat said, 'if they wo'n't answer to them?'

'No use to *them*,' said Alice; 'but it's useful to the people that name them, I suppose. If not, why do things have names at all?'

'I ca'n't say,' the Gnat replied. 'Further on, in the wood down there, they've got no names—however, go on with your list of insects: you're wasting time.'

'Well, there's the Horse-fly,' Alice began, counting off the names on her fingers.

'All right,' said the Gnat. 'Half way up that bush, you'll see

a Rocking-horse-fly, if you look. It's made entirely of wood, and gets about by swinging itself from branch to branch.'

'What does it live on?' Alice asked, with great curiosity.

'Sap and sawdust,' said the Gnat. 'Go on with the list.'

Alice looked at the Rocking-horse-fly with great interest, and made up her mind that it must have been just repainted, it looked so bright and sticky; and then she went on.

'And there's the Dragon-fly.'

'Look on the branch above your head,' said the Gnat, 'and there you'll find a Snap-dragon-fly. Its body is made of plum-pudding, its wings of holly-leaves, and its head is a raisin burning in brandy.'[1]

'And what does it live on?' Alice asked, as before.

'Frumenty[1] and mince-pie,' the Gnat replied; 'and it makes its nest in a Christmas-box.'

'And then there's the Butterfly,' Alice went on, after she had taken a good look at the insect with its head on fire, and had thought to herself, 'I wonder if that's the reason insects are so fond of flying into candles—because they want to turn into Snap-dragon-flies!'

'Crawling at your feet,' said the Gnat (Alice drew her feet back in some alarm), 'you may observe a Bread-and-butter-fly. Its wings are thin slices of bread-and-butter, its body is a crust, and its head is a lump of sugar.'

'And what does *it* live on?'

'Weak tea with cream in it.'

A new difficulty came into Alice's head. 'Supposing it couldn't find any?' she suggested.

'Then it would die, of course.'

'But that must happen very often,' Alice remarked thoughtfully.

'It always happens,' said the Gnat.

After this, Alice was silent for a minute or two, pondering. The Gnat amused itself meanwhile by humming round and round her head: at last it settled again and remarked 'I suppose you don't want to lose your name?'

'No, indeed,' Alice said, a little anxiously.

'And yet I don't know,' the Gnat went on in a careless tone: 'only think how convenient it would be if you could manage to go home without it! For instance, if the governess wanted to call you to your lessons, she would call out "Come here——," and there she would have to leave off, because there wouldn't be any name for her to call, and of course you wouldn't have to go, you know.'

'That would never do, I'm sure,' said Alice: 'the governess would never think of excusing me lessons for that. If she couldn't remember my name, she'd call me "Miss," as the servants do.'

'Well, if she said "Miss," and didn't say anything more,' the Gnat remarked, 'of course you'd miss your lessons. That's a joke. I wish *you* had made it.'

'Why do you wish *I* had made it?' Alice asked. 'It's a very bad one.'

But the Gnat only sighed deeply, while two large tears came rolling down its cheeks.

'You shouldn't make jokes,' Alice said, 'if it makes you so unhappy.'

Then came another of those melancholy little sighs, and this time the poor Gnat really seemed to have sighed itself away, for, when Alice looked up, there was nothing whatever to be seen on the twig, and, as she was getting quite chilly with sitting still so long, she got up and walked on.

She very soon came to an open field, with a wood on the other side of it: it looked much darker than the last wood, and Alice felt a *little* timid about going into it. However, on second thoughts, she made up her mind to go on: 'for I certainly won't go *back*,' she thought to herself, and this was the only way to the Eighth Square.

'This must be the wood,' she said thoughtfully to herself, 'where things have no names. I wonder what'll become of *my* name when I go in? I shouldn't like to lose it at all——because they'd have to give me another, and it would be almost certain to be an ugly one. But then the fun would be, trying to find the

creature that had got my old name! That's just like the
advertisements, you know, when people lose dogs——
"*answers to the name of 'Dash': had on a brass collar*"——just
fancy calling everything you met "Alice," till one of them
answered! Only they wouldn't answer at all, if they were
wise.'

She was rambling on in this way when she reached the
wood: it looked very cool and shady. 'Well, at any rate it's
a great comfort,' she said as she stepped under the trees, 'after
being so hot, to get into the—into the—into *what?*' she went
on, rather surprised at not being able to think of the word.
'I mean to get under the—under the—under *this*, you know!'
putting her hand on the trunk of the tree. 'What *does* it call
itself, I wonder? I do believe it's got no name—why, to be
sure it hasn't!'

She stood silent for a minute, thinking: then she suddenly
began again. 'Then it really *has* happened, after all! And now,
who am I? I *will* remember, if I can! I'm determined to do it!'
But being determined didn't help her much, and all she could
say, after a great deal of puzzling, was 'L, I *know* it begins
with L!'[1]

Just then a Fawn came wandering by: it looked at Alice
with its large gentle eyes, but didn't seem at all frightened.
'Here then! Here then!' Alice said, as she held out her hand
and tried to stroke it; but it only started back a little, and then
stood looking at her again.

'What do you call yourself?' the Fawn said at last. Such
a soft sweet voice it had!

'I wish I knew!' thought poor Alice. She answered, rather
sadly, 'Nothing, just now.'

'Think again,' it said: 'that wo'n't do.'

Alice thought, but nothing came of it. 'Please, would you
tell me what *you* call yourself?' she said timidly. 'I think that
might help a little.'

'I'll tell you, if you'll come a little further on,' the Fawn
said. 'I ca'n't remember *here*.'

So they walked on together through the wood, Alice with

her arms clasped lovingly round the soft neck of the Fawn, till they came out into another open field, and here the Fawn gave a sudden bound into the air, and shook itself free from Alice's arm. 'I'm a Fawn!' it cried out in a voice of delight. 'And, dear me! you're a human child!' A sudden look of alarm came into its beautiful brown eyes, and in another moment it had darted away at full speed.

Alice stood looking after it, almost ready to cry with vexation at having lost her dear little fellow-traveler so suddenly. 'However, I know my name now,' she said: 'that's *some* comfort. Alice—Alice—I wo'n't forget it again. And now, which of these finger-posts ought I to follow, I wonder?'

It was not a very difficult question to answer, as there was only one road through the wood, and the two finger-posts both pointed along it. 'I'll settle it,' Alice said to herself, 'when the road divides and they point different ways.'

But this did not seem likely to happen. She went on and on, a long way, but, wherever the road divided, there were sure to be two finger-posts pointing the same way, one marked 'TO TWEEDLEDUM'S HOUSE,' and the other 'TO THE HOUSE OF TWEEDLEDEE.'

'I do believe,' said Alice at last, 'that they live in the *same* house! I wonder I never thought of that before—But I ca'n't stay there long. I'll just call and say "How d'ye do?" and ask them the way out of the wood. If I could only get to the Eighth Square before it gets dark!' So she wandered on, talking to herself as she went, till, on turning a sharp corner, she came upon two fat little men, so suddenly that she could not help starting back, but in another moment she recovered herself, feeling sure that they must be[1]

CHAPTER IV

TWEEDLEDUM AND TWEEDLEDEE

THEY were standing under a tree, each with an arm round the other's neck, and Alice knew which was which in a moment, because one of them had 'DUM' embroidered on his collar, and the other 'DEE.' 'I suppose they've each got 'TWEEDLE' round at the back of the collar,' she said to herself.

They stood so still that she quite forgot they were alive, and she was just going round to see if the word 'TWEEDLE' was written at the back of each collar, when she was startled by a voice coming from the one marked 'DUM.'

'If you think we're wax-works,' he said, 'you ought to pay, you know. Wax-works weren't made to be looked at for nothing. Nohow!'

'Contrariwise,' added the one marked 'DEE,' 'if you think we're alive, you ought to speak.'

N

'I'm sure I'm very sorry,' was all Alice could say; for the words of the old song[1] kept ringing through her head like the ticking of a clock, and she could hardly help saying them out loud:—

> *'Tweedledum and Tweedledee*
> *Agreed to have a battle;*
> *For Tweedledum said Tweedledee*
> *Had spoiled his nice new rattle.*
>
> *Just then flew down a monstrous crow,*
> *As black as a tar-barrel;*
> *Which frightened both the heroes so,*
> *They quite forgot their quarrel.'*

'I know what you're thinking about,' said Tweedledum; 'but it isn't so, nohow.'

'Contrariwise,' continued Tweedledee, 'if it was so, it might be; and if it were so, it would be; but as it isn't, it ain't. That's logic.'

'I was thinking,' Alice said very politely, 'which is the best way out of this wood: it's getting so dark. Would you tell me, please?'

But the fat little men only looked at each other and grinned.

They looked so exactly like a couple of great schoolboys, that Alice couldn't help pointing her finger at Tweedledum, and saying 'First Boy!'

'Nohow!' Tweedledum cried out briskly, and shut his mouth up again with a snap.

'Next Boy!' said Alice, passing on to Tweedledee, though she felt quite certain he would only shout out 'Contrariwise!' and so he did.

'You've begun wrong!' cried Tweedledum. 'The first thing in a visit is to say "How d'ye do?" and shake hands!' And here the two brothers gave each other a hug, and then they held out the two hands that were free, to shake hands with her.

Alice did not like shaking hands with either of them first, for fear of hurting the other one's feelings; so, as the best way out of the difficulty, she took hold of both hands at once: the next moment they were dancing round in a ring. This seemed quite natural (she remembered afterwards), and she was not even surprised to hear music playing: it seemed to come from the tree under which they were dancing, and it was done (as well as she could make it out) by the branches rubbing one across the other, like fiddles and fiddle-sticks.

'But it certainly *was* funny,' (Alice said afterwards, when she was telling her sister the history of all this,) 'to find myself singing "*Here we go round the mulberry bush.*"[1] I don't know when I began it, but somehow I felt as if I'd been singing it a long long time!'

The other two dancers were fat, and very soon out of breath. 'Four times round is enough for one dance,' Tweedledum panted out, and they left off dancing as suddenly as they had begun: the music stopped at the same moment.

Then they let go of Alice's hands, and stood looking at her for a minute: there was a rather awkward pause, as Alice didn't know how to begin a conversation with people she had just been dancing with. 'It would never do to say "How d'ye do?" *now*,' she said to herself: 'we seem to have got beyond that, somehow!'

'I hope you're not much tired?' she said at last.

'Nohow. And thank you *very* much for asking,' said Tweedledum.

'So *much* obliged!' added Tweedledee. 'You like poetry?'

'Ye-es, pretty well—*some* poetry,' Alice said doubtfully. 'Would you tell me which road leads out of the wood?'

'What shall I repeat to her?' said Tweedledee, looking round at Tweedledum with great solemn eyes, and not noticing Alice's question.

'"*The Walrus and the Carpenter*"[2] is the longest,' Tweedledum replied, giving his brother an affectionate hug.

Tweedledee began instantly:

> '*The sun was shining*——'

Here Alice ventured to interrupt him. 'If it's *very* long,' she said, as politely as she could, 'would you please tell me first which road——'

Tweedledee smiled gently, and began again:

> '*The sun was shining on the sea,*
>   *Shining with all his might:*
> *He did his very best to make*
>   *The billows smooth and bright—*
> *And this was odd, because it was*
>   *The middle of the night.*
>
> *The moon was shining sulkily,*[1]
>   *Because she thought the sun*
> *Had got no business to be there*
>   *After the day was done—*
> *"It's very rude of him," she said,*
>   *"To come and spoil the fun!"*
>
> *The sea was wet as wet could be,*
>   *The sands were dry as dry.*
> *You could not see a cloud, because*
>   *No cloud was in the sky:*
> *No birds were flying overhead—*
>   *There were no birds to fly.*
>
> *The Walrus and the Carpenter*
>   *Were walking close at hand:*
> *They wept like anything to see*
>   *Such quantities of sand:*
> *"If this were only cleared away,"*
>   *They said, "it* would *be grand!"*
>
> *"If seven maids with seven mops*
>   *Swept it for half a year,*
> *Do you suppose," the Walrus said.*
>   *"That they could get it clear?"*

"*I doubt it,*" *said the* Carpenter,
    And shed a bitter tear.

"*O Oysters, come and walk with us!*"
    The Walrus did beseech.
"*A pleasant walk, a pleasant talk,*
    Along the briny beach:
We cannot do with more than four,
    To give a hand to each."

The eldest Oyster looked at him,
    But never a word he said:
The eldest Oyster winked his eye,
    And shook his heavy head—
Meaning to say he did not choose
    To leave the oyster-bed.

But four young Oysters hurried up,
    All eager for the treat:
Their coats were brushed, their faces washed,
    Their shoes were clean and neat—
And this was odd, because, you know,
    They hadn't any feet.

Four other Oysters followed them,
  And yet another four;
And thick and fast they came at last,
  And more, and more, and more—
All hopping through the frothy waves,
  And scrambling to the shore.

The Walrus and the Carpenter
  Walked on a mile or so,
And then they rested on a rock
  Conveniently low:
And all the little Oysters stood
  And waited in a row.

"The time has come," the Walrus said,
  "To talk of many things:
Of shoes—and ships—and sealing-wax—
  Of cabbages—and kings—
And why the sea is boiling hot—
  And whether pigs have wings"[1]

"But wait a bit," the Oysters cried,
  "Before we have our chat;
For some of us are out of breath,
  And all of us are fat!"
"No hurry!" said the Carpenter.
  They thanked him much for that.

"A loaf of bread," the Walrus said,
  "Is what we chiefly need:
Pepper and vinegar besides
  Are very good indeed—
Now, if you're ready, Oysters dear,
  We can begin to feed."

"But not on us!" the Oysters cried,
  Turning a little blue.
"After such kindness, that would be
  A dismal thing to do!"
"The night is fine," the Walrus said.
  "Do you admire the view?

"It was so kind of you to come!
  And you are very nice!"
The Carpenter said nothing but
  "Cut us another slice.
I wish you were not quite so deaf—
  I've had to ask you twice!"

"It seems a shame," the Walrus said,
  "To play them such a trick.
After we've brought them out so far,
  And made them trot so quick!"
The Carpenter said nothing but
  "The butter's spread too thick!"

"*I weep for you,*" *the Walrus said :*
  "*I deeply sympathize.*"
With sobs and tears he sorted out
  Those of the largest size,
Holding his pocket-handkerchief
  Before his streaming eyes.

"*O Oysters,*" *said the Carpenter,*
  "*You've had a pleasant run!*
Shall we be trotting home again?"
  But answer came there none—
And this was scarcely odd, because
  They'd eaten every one.'

'I like the Walrus best,' said Alice: 'because he was a *little*
sorry for the poor oysters.'

'He ate more than the Carpenter, though,' said Tweedledee.
'You see he held his handkerchief in front, so that the Carpenter couldn't count how many he took: contrariwise.'

'That was mean!' Alice said indignantly. 'Then I like the
Carpenter best—if he didn't eat so many as the Walrus.'

'But he ate as many as he could get,' said Tweedledum.

This was a puzzler. After a pause, Alice began, 'Well! They were *both* very unpleasant characters——' Here she checked herself in some alarm, at hearing something that sounded to her like the puffing of a large steam-engine in the wood near them, though she feared it was more likely to be a wild beast. 'Are there any lions or tigers about here?' she asked timidly.

'It's only the Red King snoring,' said Tweedledee.

'Come and look at him!' the brothers cried, and they each took one of Alice's hands, and led her up to where the King was sleeping.

'Isn't he a *lovely* sight?' said Tweedledum.

Alice couldn't say honestly that he was. He had a tall red night-cap on, with a tassel, and he was lying crumpled up into a sort of untidy heap, and snoring loud——'fit to snore his head off!' as Tweedledum remarked.

'I'm afraid he'll catch cold with lying on the damp grass,' said Alice, who was a very thoughtful little girl.

'He's dreaming now,' said Tweedledee: 'and what do you think he's dreaming about?'

Alice said 'Nobody can guess that.'

'Why, about *you!*' Tweedledee exclaimed, clapping his hands triumphantly. 'And if he left off dreaming about you, where do you suppose you'd be?'

'Where I am now, of course,' said Alice.

'Not you!' Tweedledee retorted contemptuously. 'You'd be nowhere. Why, you're only a sort of thing in his dream!'

'If that there King was to wake,' added Tweedledum, 'you'd go out—bang!—just like a candle!'

'I shouldn't!' Alice exclaimed indignantly. 'Besides, if *I'm* only a sort of thing in his dream, what are *you*, I should like to know?'

'Ditto,' said Tweedledum.

'Ditto, ditto!' cried Tweedledee.

He shouted this so loud that Alice couldn't help saying 'Hush! You'll be waking him, I'm afraid, if you make so much noise.'

'Well, it's no use *your* talking about waking him,' said Tweedledum, 'when you're only one of the things in his dream. You know very well you're not real.'

'I *am* real!' said Alice, and began to cry.

'You wo'n't make yourself a bit realler by crying,' Tweedledee remarked: 'there's nothing to cry about.'

'If I wasn't real,' Alice said—half-laughing through her tears, it all seemed so ridiculous—'I shouldn't be able to cry.'

'I hope you don't suppose those are *real* tears?' Tweedledum interrupted in a tone of great contempt.

'I know they're talking nonsense,' Alice thought to herself: 'and it's foolish to cry about it.' So she brushed away her tears, and went on, as cheerfully as she could, 'At any rate I'd better be getting out of the wood, for really it's coming on very dark. Do you think it's going to rain?'

Tweedledum spread a large umbrella over himself and his brother, and looked up into it. 'No, I don't think it is,' he said: 'at least—not under *here*. Nohow.'

'But it may rain *outside?*'

'It may—if it chooses,' said Tweedledee: 'we've no objection. Contrariwise.'

'Selfish things!' thought Alice, and she was just going to say 'Good-night' and leave them, when Tweedledum sprang out from under the umbrella, and seized her by the wrist.

'Do you see *that?*' he said, in a voice choking with passion, and his eyes grew large and yellow all in a moment, as he pointed with a trembling finger at a small white thing lying under the tree.

'It's only a rattle,' Alice said, after a careful examination of the little white thing. 'Not a rattle-*snake*, you know,' she added hastily, thinking that he was frightened: 'only an old rattle— quite old and broken.'

'I knew it was!' cried Tweedledum, beginning to stamp about wildly and tear his hair. 'It's spoilt, of course!' Here he

looked at Tweedledee, who immediately sat down on the ground, and tried to hide himself under the umbrella.

Alice laid her hand upon his arm, and said, in a soothing tone, 'You needn't be so angry about an old rattle.'

'But it *isn't* old!' Tweedledum cried, in a greater fury than ever. 'It's *new*, I tell you—I bought it yesterday—my nice NEW RATTLE!' and his voice rose to a perfect scream.

All this time Tweedledee was trying his best to fold up the umbrella, with himself in it: which was such an extraordinary thing to do, that it quite took off Alice's attention from the angry brother. But he couldn't quite succeed, and it ended in his rolling over, bundled up in the umbrella, with only his head out: and there he lay, opening and shutting his mouth and his large eyes——'looking more like a fish than anything else,' Alice thought.

'Of course you agree to have a battle?' Tweedledum said in a calmer tone.

'I suppose so,' the other sulkily replied, as he crawled out of the umbrella: 'only *she* must help us to dress up, you know.'

So the two brothers went off hand-in-hand into the wood, and returned in a minute with their arms full of things—such as bolsters, blankets, hearth-rugs, table-cloths, dish-covers and coal-scuttles. 'I hope you're a good hand at pinning and tying strings?' Tweedledum remarked. 'Every one of these things has got to go on, somehow or other.'

Alice said afterwards she had never seen such a fuss made about anything in all her life—the way those two bustled about—and the quantity of things they put on—and the trouble they gave her in tying strings and fastening buttons ——'Really they'll be more like bundles of old clothes than anything else, by the time they're ready!' she said to herself, as she arranged a bolster round the neck of Tweedledee, 'to keep his head from being cut off,' as he said.

'You know,' he added very gravely, 'it's one of the most serious things that can possibly happen to one in a battle— to get one's head cut off.'

Alice laughed loud: but she managed to turn it into a cough, for fear of hurting his feelings.

'Do I look very pale?' said Tweedledum, coming up to have his helmet tied on. (He *called* it a helmet, though it certainly looked much more like a saucepan.)

'Well—yes—a *little*,' Alice replied gently.

'I'm very brave, generally,' he went on in a low voice: 'only to-day I happen to have a headache.'

'And *I've* got a toothache!' said Tweedledee, who had over-heard the remark. 'I'm far worse than you!'

'Then you'd better not fight to-day,' said Alice, thinking it a good opportunity to make peace.

'We *must* have a bit of a fight, but I don't care about going on long,' said Tweedledum. 'What's the time now?'

Tweedledee looked at his watch, and said 'Half-past four.'

'Let's fight till six, and then have dinner,' said Tweedledum.

'Very well,' the other said, rather sadly: 'and *she* can watch us—only you'd better not come *very* close,' he added: 'I generally hit every thing I can see—when I get really excited.'

'And *I* hit every thing within reach,' cried Tweedledum, 'whether I can see it or not!'

Alice laughed. 'You must hit the *trees* pretty often, I should think,' she said.

Tweedledum looked round him with a satisfied smile. 'I don't suppose,' he said, 'there'll be a tree left standing, for ever so far round, by the time we've finished!'

'And all about a rattle!' said Alice, still hoping to make them a *little* ashamed of fighting for such a trifle.

'I shouldn't have minded it so much,' said Tweedledum, 'if it hadn't been a new one.'

'I wish the monstrous crow would come!' thought Alice.

'There's only one sword, you know,' Tweedledum said to his brother: 'but *you* can have the umbrella—it's quite as

sharp. Only we must begin quick. It's getting as dark as
it can.'

'And darker,' said Tweedledee.

It was getting dark so suddenly that Alice thought there
must be a thunderstorm coming on. 'What a thick black cloud
that is!' she said. 'And how fast it comes! Why, I do believe it's
got wings!'

'It's the crow!' Tweedledum cried out in a shrill voice of
alarm; and the two brothers took to their heels and were out
of sight in a moment.

Alice ran a little way into the wood, and stopped under
a large tree. 'It can never get at me *here*,' she thought: 'it's far
too large to squeeze itself in among the trees. But I wish it
wouldn't flap its wings so—it makes quite a hurricane in the
wood—here's somebody's shawl being blown away!'

CHAPTER V

SHE caught the shawl as she spoke, and looked about for the owner: in another moment the White Queen[1] came running wildly through the wood, with both arms stretched out wide, as if she were flying, and Alice very civilly went to meet her with the shawl.

'I'm very glad I happened to be in the way,' Alice said, as she helped her to put on her shawl again.

The White Queen only looked at her in a helpless frightened sort of way, and kept repeating something in a whisper to herself that sounded like 'Bread-and-butter, bread-and-butter,' and Alice felt that if there was to be any conversation at all, she must manage it herself. So she began rather timidly: 'Am I addressing the White Queen?'

'Well, yes, if you call that a-dressing,' the Queen said. 'It isn't *my* notion of the thing, at all.'

Alice thought it would never do to have an argument at the very beginning of their conversation, so she smiled and said 'If your Majesty will only tell me the right way to begin, I'll do it as well as I can.'

'But I don't want it done at all!' groaned the poor Queen. 'I've been a-dressing myself for the last two hours.'

It would have been all the better, as it seemed to Alice, if she had got some one else to dress her, she was so dreadfully untidy. 'Every single thing's crooked,' Alice thought to herself, 'and she's all over pins!——May I put your shawl straight for you?' she added aloud.

'I don't know what's the matter with it!' the Queen said, in a melancholy voice. 'It's out of temper, I think. I've pinned it here, and I've pinned it there, but there's no pleasing it!'

'It *ca'n't* go straight, you know, if you pin it all on one side,' Alice said, as she gently put it right for her; 'and, dear me, what a state your hair is in!'

'The brush has got entangled in it!' the Queen said with a sigh. 'And I lost the comb yesterday.'

Alice carefully released the brush, and did her best to get the hair into order. 'Come, you look rather better now!' she said, after altering most of the pins. 'But really you should have a lady's-maid!'

'I'm sure I'll take *you* with pleasure!' the Queen said. 'Twopence a week, and jam every other day.'

Alice couldn't help laughing, as she said 'I don't want you to hire *me*—and I don't care for jam.'

'It's very good jam,' said the Queen.

'Well, I don't want any *to-day*, at any rate.'

'You couldn't have it if you *did* want it,' the Queen said. 'The rule is, jam to-morrow and jam yesterday—but never jam *to-day*.'

'It *must* come sometimes to "jam to-day,"' Alice objected.

'No, it ca'n't,' said the Queen. 'It's jam every *other* day: to-day isn't any *other* day, you know.'

'I don't understand you,' said Alice. 'It's dreadfully confusing!'

'That's the effect of living backwards,' the Queen said kindly: 'it always makes one a little giddy at first——'

'Living backwards!' Alice repeated in great astonishment. 'I never heard of such a thing!'

'—but there's one great advantage in it, that one's memory works both ways.'

'I'm sure *mine* only works one way,' Alice remarked. 'I ca'n't remember things before they happen.'

'It's a poor sort of memory that only works backwards,' the Queen remarked.

'What sort of things do *you* remember best?' Alice ventured to ask.

'Oh, things that happened the week after next,' the Queen replied in a careless tone. 'For instance, now,' she went on, sticking a large piece of plaster on her finger as she spoke, 'there's the King's Messenger. He's in prison now, being punished: and the trial doesn't even begin till next Wednesday: and of course the crime comes last of all.'

'Suppose he never commits the crime?' said Alice.

'That would be all the better, wouldn't it?' the Queen said, as she bound the plaster round her finger with a bit of ribbon.

Alice felt there was no denying *that*. 'Of course it

o

would be all the better,' she said: 'but it wouldn't be all the better his being punished.'

'You're wrong *there*, at any rate,' said the Queen. 'Were *you* ever punished?'

'Only for faults,' said Alice.

'And you were all the better for it, I know!' the Queen said triumphantly.

'Yes, but then I *had* done the things I was punished for,' said Alice: 'that makes all the difference.'

'But if you *hadn't* done them,' the Queen said, 'that would have been better still; better, and better, and better!' Her voice went higher with each 'better,' till it got quite to a squeak at last.

Alice was just beginning to say 'There's a mistake some-where——,' when the Queen began screaming, so loud that she had to leave the sentence unfinished. 'Oh, oh, oh!' shouted the Queen, shaking her hand about as if she wanted to shake it off. 'My finger's bleeding! Oh, oh, oh, oh!'

Her screams were so exactly like the whistle of a steam-engine, that Alice had to hold both her hands over her ears.

'What *is* the matter?' she said, as soon as there was a chance of making herself heard. 'Have you pricked your finger?'

'I haven't pricked it *yet*,' the Queen said, 'but I soon shall—oh, oh, oh!'

'When do you expect to do it?' Alice asked, feeling very much inclined to laugh.

'When I fasten my shawl again,' the poor Queen groaned out: 'the brooch will come undone directly. Oh, oh!' As she said the words the brooch flew open, and the Queen clutched wildly at it, and tried to clasp it again.

'Take care!' cried Alice. 'You're holding it all crooked!' And she caught at the brooch; but it was too late: the pin had slipped, and the Queen had pricked her finger.

'That accounts for the bleeding, you see,' she said to Alice with a smile. 'Now you understand the way things happen here.'

'But why don't you scream *now?*' Alice asked, holding her hands ready to put over her ears again.

'Why, I've done all the screaming already,' said the Queen. 'What would be the good of having it all over again?'

By this time it was getting light. 'The crow must have flown away, I think,' said Alice: 'I'm so glad it's gone. I thought it was the night coming on.'

'I wish *I* could manage to be glad!' the Queen said. 'Only I never can remember the rule. You must be very happy, living in this wood, and being glad whenever you like!'

'Only it is so *very* lonely here!' Alice said in a melancholy voice; and, at the thought of her loneliness, two large tears came rolling down her cheeks.

'Oh, don't go on like that!' cried the poor Queen, wringing her hands in despair. 'Consider what a great girl you are. Consider what a long way you've come to-day. Consider what o'clock it is. Consider anything, only don't cry!'

Alice could not help laughing at this, even in the midst of her tears. 'Can *you* keep from crying by considering things?' she asked.

'That's the way it's done,' the Queen said with great decision: 'nobody can do two things at once, you know. Let's consider your age to begin with——how old are you?'

'I'm seven and a half, exactly.'

'You needn't say "exactually,"' the Queen remarked. 'I can believe it without that. Now I'll give *you* something to believe. I'm just one hundred and one, five months and a day.'

'I ca'n't believe *that!*' said Alice.

'Ca'n't you?' the Queen said in a pitying tone. 'Try again: draw a long breath, and shut your eyes.'

Alice laughed. 'There's no use trying,' she said: 'one *ca'n't* believe impossible things.'

'I daresay you haven't had much practice,' said the Queen. 'When I was your age, I always did it for half-an-hour a day. Why, sometimes I've believed as many as six impossible things before breakfast. There goes the shawl again!'

The brooch had come undone as she spoke, and a sudden

gust of wind blew the Queen's shawl across a little brook. The Queen spread out her arms again, and went flying after it, and this time she succeeded in catching it for herself. 'I've got it!' she cried in a triumphant tone. 'Now you shall see me pin it on again, all by myself!'

'Then I hope your finger is better now?' Alice said very politely, as she crossed the little brook after the Queen.

```
     *         *         *         *         *         *
          *         *         *         *         *
     *         *         *         *         *         *
```

'Oh, much better!' cried the Queen, her voice rising into a squeak as she went on. 'Much be-etter! Be-etter! Be-e-e-etter! Be-e-ehh!' The last word ended in a long bleat, so like a sheep that Alice quite started.

She looked at the Queen, who seemed to have suddenly wrapped herself up in wool. Alice rubbed her eyes, and looked again. She couldn't make out what had happened at all. Was she in a shop?[1] And was that really—was it really a *sheep* that was sitting on the other side of the counter? Rub as she would, she could make nothing more of it: she was in a little dark shop, leaning with her elbows on the counter, and opposite to her was an old Sheep, sitting in an arm-chair, knitting, and every now and then leaving off to look at her through a great pair of spectacles.

'What is it you want to buy?' the Sheep said at last, looking up for a moment from her knitting.

'I don't *quite* know yet,' Alice said very gently. 'I should like to look all round me first, if I might.'

'You may look in front of you, and on both sides, if you like,' said the Sheep; 'but you ca'n't look *all* round you—unless you've got eyes at the back of your head.'

But these, as it happened, Alice had *not* got: so she contented herself with turning round, looking at the shelves as she came to them.

The shop seemed to be full of all manner of curious things —but the oddest part of it all was that, whenever she looked

hard at any shelf, to make out exactly what it had on it, that particular shelf was always quite empty, though the others round it were crowded as full as they could hold.

'Things flow about so here!' she said at last in a plaintive tone, after she had spent a minute or so in vainly pursuing a large bright thing, that looked sometimes like a doll and sometimes like a work-box, and was always in the shelf next above the one she was looking at. 'And this one is the most provoking of all—but I'll tell you what——' she added, as a sudden thought struck her. 'I'll follow it up to the very top shelf of all. It'll puzzle it to go through the ceiling, I expect!'

But even this plan failed: the "thing" went through the ceiling as quietly as possible, as if it were quite used to it.

'Are you a child or a teetotum?'[1] the Sheep said, as she took up another pair of needles. 'You'll make me giddy soon, if you go on turning round like that.' She was now working with fourteen pairs at once, and Alice couldn't help looking at her in great astonishment.

'How *can* she knit with so many?' the puzzled child thought to herself. 'She gets more and more like a porcupine every minute!'

'Can you row?' the Sheep asked, handing her a pair of knitting-needles as she spoke.

'Yes, a little—but not on land—and not with needles——' Alice was beginning to say, when suddenly the needles turned into oars in her hands, and she found they were in a little boat, gliding along between banks: so there was nothing for it but to do her best.

'Feather!'[1] cried the Sheep, as she took up another pair of needles.

This didn't sound like a remark that needed any answer: so Alice said nothing, but pulled away. There was something very queer about the water, she thought, as every now and then the oars got fast in it, and would hardly come out again.

'Feather! Feather!' the Sheep cried again, taking more needles. 'You'll be catching a crab[2] directly.'

'A dear little crab!' thought Alice. 'I should like that.'

'Didn't you hear me say "Feather"?' the Sheep cried angrily, taking up quite a bunch of needles.

'Indeed I did,' said Alice: 'you've said it very often—and very loud. Please where *are* the crabs?'

'In the water, of course!' said the Sheep, sticking some of the needles into her hair, as her hands were full. 'Feather, I say!'

'*Why* do you say "Feather" so often?' Alice asked at last, rather vexed. 'I'm not a bird!'

'You are,' said the Sheep: 'you're a little goose.'

This offended Alice a little, so there was no more conversation for a minute or two, while the boat glided gently on, sometimes among beds of weeds (which made the oars stick fast in the water, worse than ever), and sometimes under trees, but always with the same tall river-banks frowning over their heads.

'Oh, please! There are some scented rushes!' Alice cried in a sudden transport of delight. 'There really are—and *such* beauties!'

'You needn't say "please" to *me* about 'em,' the Sheep said, without looking up from her knitting: 'I didn't put 'em there, and I'm not going to take 'em away.'

'No, but I meant—please, may we wait and pick some?' Alice pleaded. 'If you don't mind stopping the boat for a minute.'

'How am *I* to stop it?' said the Sheep. 'If you leave off rowing, it'll stop of itself.'

So the boat was left to drift down the stream as it would, till it glided gently in among the waving rushes. And then the little sleeves were carefully rolled up, and the little arms were plunged in elbow-deep, to get hold of the rushes a good long way down before breaking them off—and for a while Alice forgot all about the Sheep and the knitting, as she bent over the side of the boat, with just the ends of her tangled hair dipping into the water—while with bright eager eyes she caught at one bunch after another of the darling scented rushes.

'I only hope the boat won't tipple over!' she said to herself. 'Oh, *what* a lovely one! Only I couldn't quite reach it.' And it certainly *did* seem a little provoking ('almost as if it happened on purpose,' she thought) that, though she managed to pick plenty of beautiful rushes as the boat glided by, there was always a more lovely one that she couldn't reach.

'The prettiest are always further!' she said at last, with a sigh at the obstinacy of the rushes in growing so far off, as, with flushed cheeks and dripping hair and hands, she scrambled back into her place, and began to arrange her new-found treasures.

What mattered it to her just then that the rushes had begun to fade, and to lose all their scent and beauty, from the very moment that she picked them? Even real scented rushes, you know, last only a very little while—and these, being dream-rushes, melted away almost like snow, as they lay in heaps at her feet—but Alice hardly noticed this, there were so many other curious things to think about.

They hadn't gone much farther before the blade of one of the oars got fast in the water and *wouldn't* come out again (so Alice explained it afterwards), and the consequence was that the handle of it caught her under the chin, and, in spite of a series of little shrieks of 'Oh, oh, oh!' from poor Alice, it swept her straight off the seat, and down among the heap of rushes.

However, she wasn't a bit hurt, and was soon up again: the Sheep went on with her knitting all the while, just as if nothing had happened. 'That was a nice crab you caught!' she remarked, as Alice got back into her place, very much relieved to find herself still in the boat.

'Was it? I didn't see it,' said Alice, peeping cautiously over the side of the boat into the dark water. 'I wish it hadn't let go—I should so like a little crab to take home with me!' But the Sheep only laughed scornfully, and went on with her knitting.

'Are there many crabs here?' said Alice.

'Crabs, and all sorts of things,' said the Sheep: 'plenty of choice, only make up your mind. Now, what *do* you want to buy?'

'To buy!' Alice echoed in a tone that was half astonished and half frightened—for the oars, and the boat, and the river, had vanished all in a moment, and she was back again in the little dark shop.

'I should like to buy an egg,[1] please,' she said timidly. 'How do you sell them?'

'Fivepence farthing for one—twopence for two,' the Sheep replied.

'Then two are cheaper than one?' Alice said in a surprised tone, taking out her purse.

'Only you *must* eat them both, if you buy two,' said the Sheep.

'Then I'll have *one*, please,' said Alice, as she put the money down on the counter. For she thought to herself, 'They mightn't be at all nice, you know.'

The Sheep took the money, and put it away in a box: then she said 'I never put things into people's hands—that would never do—you must get it for yourself.' And so saying, she went off to the other end of the shop, and set the egg upright on a shelf.

'I wonder *why* it wouldn't do?' thought Alice, as she groped her way among the tables and chairs, for the shop was very dark towards the end. 'The egg seems to get further away the

more I walk towards it. Let me see, is this a chair? Why, it's
got branches, I declare! How very odd to find trees growing
here! And actually here's a little brook! Well, this is the very
queerest shop I ever saw!'

    *   *   *   *   *   *

      *   *   *   *   *

    *   *   *   *   *   *

So she went on, wondering more and more at every step,
as everything turned into a tree the moment she came up to
it, and she quite expected the egg to do the same.

CHAPTER VI

HUMPTY DUMPTY

HOWEVER, the egg only got larger and larger, and more and more human: when she had come within a few yards of it, she saw that it had eyes and a nose and mouth; and, when she had come close to it, she saw clearly that it was HUMPTY DUMPTY himself. 'It ca'n't be anybody else!' she said to herself. 'I'm as certain of it, as if his name were written all over his face!'

It might have been written a hundred times, easily, on that enormous face. Humpty Dumpty was sitting, with his legs crossed like a Turk, on the top of a high wall—such a narrow one that Alice quite wondered how he could keep his balance— and, as his eyes were steadily fixed in the opposite direction, and he didn't take the least notice of her, she thought he must be a stuffed figure, after all.

'And how exactly like an egg he is!' she said aloud, standing with her hands ready to catch him, for she was every moment expecting him to fall.

'It's *very* provoking,' Humpty Dumpty said after a long silence, looking away from Alice as he spoke, 'to be called an egg—*very!*'

'I said you *looked* like an egg, Sir,' Alice gently explained. 'And some eggs are very pretty, you know,' she added, hoping to turn her remark into a sort of compliment.

'Some people,' said Humpty Dumpty, looking away from her as usual, 'have no more sense than a baby!'

Alice didn't know what to say to this: it wasn't at all like conversation, she thought, as he never said anything to *her*; in fact, his last remark was evidently addressed to a tree—so she stood and softly repeated to herself:—

'*Humpty Dumpty sat on a wall:*[1]
Humpty Dumpty had a great fall.
All the King's horses and all the King's men
Couldn't put Humpty Dumpty in his place again.'

'That last line is much too long for the poetry,' she added, almost out loud, forgetting that Humpty Dumpty would hear her.

'Don't stand chattering to yourself like that,' Humpty Dumpty said, looking at her for the first time, 'but tell me your name and your business.'

'My *name* is Alice, but——'

'It's a stupid name enough!' Humpty Dumpty interrupted impatiently. 'What does it mean?'

'*Must* a name mean something?' Alice asked doubtfully.

'Of course it must,' Humpty Dumpty said with a short laugh: '*my* name means the shape I am—and a good handsome shape it is, too. With a name like yours, you might be any shape, almost.'[2]

'Why do you sit out here all alone?' said Alice, not wishing to begin an argument.

'Why, because there's nobody with me!' cried Humpty Dumpty. 'Did you think I didn't know the answer to *that*? Ask another.'

'Don't you think you'd be safer down on the ground?' Alice went on, not with any idea of making another riddle, but simply in her good-natured anxiety for the queer creature. 'That wall is so *very* narrow!'

'What tremendously easy riddles you ask!' Humpty Dumpty growled out. 'Of course I don't think so! Why, if ever I *did* fall off—which there's no chance of—but *if* I did——' Here he pursed up his lips, and looked so solemn and grand that Alice could hardly help laughing. '*If* I *did* fall,' he went on, '*the King has promised me*—ah, you may turn pale, if you like! You didn't think I was going to say that, did you? *The King has promised me—with his very own mouth*—to—to——'

'To send all his horses and all his men,' Alice interrupted, rather unwisely.

'Now I declare that's too bad!' Humpty Dumpty cried, breaking into a sudden passion. 'You've been listening at doors—and behind trees—and down chimneys—or you couldn't have known it!'

'I haven't, indeed!' Alice said very gently. 'It's in a book.'

'Ah, well! They may write such things in a *book*,' Humpty Dumpty said in a calmer tone. 'That's what you call a History of England, that is. Now, take a good look at me! I'm one that has spoken to a King, *I* am: mayhap you'll never see such

another: and, to show you I'm not proud, you may shake hands with me!' And he grinned almost from ear to ear, as he leant forwards (and as nearly as possible fell off the wall in doing so) and offered Alice his hand. She watched him a little anxiously as she took it. 'If he smiled much more the ends of his mouth might meet behind,' she thought: 'and then I don't know *what* would happen to his head! I'm afraid it would come off!'

'Yes, all his horses and all his men,' Humpty Dumpty went on. 'They'd pick me up again in a minute, *they* would! However, this conversation is going on a little too fast: let's go back to the last remark but one.'

'I'm afraid I ca'n't quite remember it,' Alice said, very politely.

'In that case we start afresh,' said Humpty Dumpty, 'and it's my turn to choose a subject——' ('He talks about it just as if it was a game!' thought Alice.) 'So here's a question for you. How old did you say you were?'

Alice made a short calculation, and said 'Seven years and six months.'

'Wrong!' Humpty Dumpty exclaimed triumphantly. 'You never said a word like it!'

'I thought you meant "How old *are* you?"' Alice explained.

'If I'd meant that, I'd have said it,' said Humpty Dumpty.

Alice didn't want to begin another argument, so she said nothing.

'Seven years and six months!' Humpty Dumpty repeated thoughtfully. 'An uncomfortable sort of age. Now if you'd asked *my* advice, I'd have said "Leave off at seven"——but it's too late now.'

'I never ask advice about growing,' Alice said indignantly.

'Too proud?' the other enquired.

Alice felt even more indignant at this suggestion. 'I mean,' she said, 'that one ca'n't help growing older.'

'*One* ca'n't, perhaps,' said Humpty Dumpty; 'but *two* can. With proper assistance, you might have left off at seven.'

'What a beautiful belt you've got on!' Alice suddenly remarked. (They had had quite enough of the subject of age, she thought: and, if they really were to take turns in choosing subjects, it was *her* turn now.) 'At least,' she corrected herself

on second thoughts, 'a beautiful cravat, I should have said—
no, a belt, I mean—I beg your pardon!' she added in dismay,
for Humpty Dumpty looked thoroughly offended, and she
began to wish she hadn't chosen that subject. 'If only I knew,'
she thought to herself, 'which was neck and which was
waist!'

Evidently Humpty Dumpty was very angry, though he said
nothing for a minute or two. When he *did* speak again, it was
in a deep growl.

'It is a—*most—provoking*—thing,' he said at last, 'when
a person doesn't know a cravat from a belt!'

'I know it's very ignorant of me,' Alice said, in so humble
a tone that Humpty Dumpty relented.

'It's a cravat, child, and a beautiful one, as you say. It's
a present from the White King and Queen. There now!'

'Is it really?' said Alice, quite pleased to find that she *had*
chosen a good subject, after all.

'They gave it me,' Humpty Dumpty continued thoughtfully, as he crossed one knee over the other and clasped
his hands round it, 'they gave it me—for an un-birthday
present.'

'I beg your pardon?' Alice said with a puzzled air.

'I'm not offended,' said Humpty Dumpty.

'I mean, what *is* an un-birthday present?'

'A present given when it isn't your birthday, of course.'

Alice considered a little. 'I like birthday presents best,' she
said at last.

'You don't know what you're talking about!' cried Humpty
Dumpty. 'How many days are there in a year?'

'Three hundred and sixty-five,' said Alice.

'And how many birthdays have you?'

'One.'

'And if you take one from three hundred and sixty-five,
what remains?'

'Three hundred and sixty-four, of course.'

Humpty Dumpty looked doubtful. 'I'd rather see that done
on paper,' he said.

Alice couldn't help smiling as she took out her memorandum-book, and worked the sum for him:

$$365$$
$$1$$
$$\overline{364}$$

Humpty Dumpty took the book, and looked at it carefully. 'That seems to be done right——' he began.

'You're holding it upside down!' Alice interrupted.

'To be sure I was!' Humpty Dumpty said gaily, as she turned it round for him. 'I thought it looked a little queer. As I was saying, that *seems* to be done right—though I haven't time to look it over thoroughly just now—and that shows that there are three hundred and sixty-four days when you might get un-birthday presents——'

'Certainly,' said Alice.

'And only *one* for birthday presents, you know. There's glory for you!'

'I don't know what you mean by "glory,"' Alice said.

Humpty Dumpty smiled contemptuously. 'Of course you don't—till I tell you. I meant "there's a nice knock-down argument for you!"'

'But "glory" doesn't mean "a nice knock-down argument,"' Alice objected.

'When *I* use a word,'[1] Humpty Dumpty said, in rather a scornful tone, 'it means just what I choose it to mean—neither more nor less.'

'The question is,' said Alice, 'whether you *can* make words mean so many different things.'

'The question is,' said Humpty Dumpty, 'which is to be master——that's all.'

Alice was too much puzzled to say anything; so after a minute Humpty Dumpty began again. 'They've a temper, some of them—particularly verbs: they're the proudest—adjectives you can do anything with, but not verbs—however,

I can manage the whole lot of them! Impenetrability!¹ That's what *I* say!'

'Would you tell me, please,' said Alice, 'what that means?'

'Now you talk like a reasonable child,' said Humpty Dumpty, looking very much pleased. 'I meant by "impenetrability" that we've had enough of that subject, and it would be just as well if you'd mention what you mean to do next, as I suppose you don't mean to stop here all the rest of your life.'

'That's a great deal to make one word mean,' Alice said in a thoughtful tone.

'When I make a word do a lot of work like that,' said Humpty Dumpty, 'I always pay it extra.'

'Oh!' said Alice. She was too much puzzled to make any other remark.

'Ah, you should see 'em come round me of a Saturday night,' Humpty Dumpty went on, wagging his head gravely from side to side, 'for to get their wages, you know.'

(Alice didn't venture to ask what he paid them with; and so you see I ca'n't tell *you*.)

'You seem very clever at explaining words, Sir,' said Alice. 'Would you kindly tell me the meaning of the poem² called "Jabberwocky"?'

'Let's hear it,' said Humpty Dumpty. 'I can explain all the poems that ever were invented—and a good many that haven't been invented just yet.'

This sounded very hopeful, so Alice repeated the first verse:—

> '*'Twas brillig, and the slithy toves*
>   *Did gyre and gimble in the wabe:*
> *All mimsy were the borogoves,*
>   *And the mome raths outgrabe.*'

'That's enough to begin with,' Humpty Dumpty interrupted: 'there are plenty of hard words there. "*Brillig*" means four o'clock in the afternoon—the time when you begin *broiling* things for dinner.'

P

'That'll do very well,' said Alice: 'and "*slithy*"?'

'Well, "*slithy*" means "lithe and slimy." "Lithe" is the same as "active." You see it's like a portmanteau—there are two meanings packed up into one word.'

'I see it now,' Alice remarked thoughtfully: 'and what are "*toves*"?'

'Well, "*toves*" are something like badgers—they're something like lizards—and they're something like corkscrews.'

'They must be very curious-looking creatures.'

'They are that,' said Humpty Dumpty: 'also they make their nests under sun-dials—also they live on cheese.'

'And what's to "*gyre*" and to "*gimble*"?'

'To "*gyre*" is to go round and round like a gyroscope. To "*gimble*" is to make holes like a gimblet.'

'And "*the wabe*" is the grass-plot round a sun-dial, I suppose?' said Alice, surprised at her own ingenuity.

'Of course it is. It's called "*wabe*," you know, because it goes a long way before it, and a long way behind it——'

'And a long way beyond it on each side,' Alice added.

'Exactly so. Well then, "*mimsy*" is "flimsy and miserable" (there's another portmanteau for you). And a "*borogove*" is a thin shabby-looking bird with its feathers sticking out all round—something like a live mop.'

'And then "*mome raths*"?' said Alice. 'I'm afraid I'm giving you a great deal of trouble.'

'Well, a "*rath*" is a sort of green pig: but "*mome*" I'm not certain about. I think it's short for "from home"—meaning that they'd lost their way, you know.'

'And what does "*outgrabe*" mean?'

'Well, "*outgribing*" is something between bellowing and whistling, with a kind of sneeze in the middle: however, you'll hear it done, maybe—down in the wood yonder—and, when you've once heard it, you'll be *quite* content. Who's been repeating all that hard stuff to you?'

'I read it in a book,' said Alice. 'But I *had* some poetry repeated to me much easier than that, by—Tweedledee, I think it was.'

'As to poetry, you know,' said Humpty Dumpty, stretching out one of his great hands, '*I* can repeat poetry as well as other folk, if it comes to that——'

'Oh, it needn't come to that!' Alice hastily said, hoping to keep him from beginning.

'The piece I'm going to repeat,' he went on without noticing her remark, 'was written entirely for your amusement.'

Alice felt that in that case she really *ought* to listen to it; so she sat down, and said 'Thank you' rather sadly.

'*In winter, when the fields are white,*[1]
I sing this song for your delight——

only I don't sing it,' he added, as an explanation.

'I see you don't,' said Alice.

'If you can *see* whether I'm singing or not, you've sharper eyes than most,' Humpty Dumpty remarked severely. Alice was silent.

'*In spring, when woods are getting green,*
I'll try and tell you what I mean:'

'Thank you very much,' said Alice.

'*In summer, when the days are long,*
Perhaps you'll understand the song:

In autumn, when the leaves are brown,
Take pen and ink, and write it down.'

'I will, if I can remember it so long,' said Alice.

'You needn't go on making remarks like that,' Humpty Dumpty said: 'they're not sensible, and they put me out.'

'*I sent a message to the fish:*
I told them "This is what I wish."

The little fishes of the sea,
They sent an answer back to me.

The little fishes' answer was
"We cannot do it, Sir, because——"'

'I'm afraid I don't quite understand,' said Alice.

'It gets easier further on,' Humpty Dumpty replied.

'*I sent to them again to say*
"It will be better to obey."

The fishes answered, with a grin,
"Why, what a temper you are in!"'

I told them once, I told them twice:
They would not listen to advice.

I took a kettle large and new,
Fit for the deed I had to do.

My heart went hop, my heart went thump:
I filled the kettle at the pump.

Then some one came to me and said
"The little fishes are in bed."

I said to him, I said it plain,
"Then you must wake them up again."

I said it very loud and clear:
I went and shouted in his ear.'

Humpty Dumpty raised his voice almost to a scream as he repeated this verse, and Alice thought, with a shudder, 'I wouldn't have been the messenger for *anything!*'

> '*But he was very stiff and proud:*
> *He said "You needn't shout so loud!"*
>
> *And he was very proud and stiff:*
> *He said "I'd go and wake them, if——"*
>
> *I took a corkscrew from the shelf:*
> *I went to wake them up myself.*
>
> *And when I found the door was locked,*
> *I pulled and pushed and kicked and knocked.*
>
> *And when I found the door was shut,*
> *I tried to turn the handle, but——'*

There was a long pause.

'Is that all?' Alice timidly asked.

'That's all,' said Humpty Dumpty. 'Good-bye.'

This was rather sudden, Alice thought: but, after such a *very* strong hint that she ought to be going, she felt that it would hardly be civil to stay. So she got up, and held out her hand. 'Good-bye, till we meet again!' she said as cheerfully as she could.

'I shouldn't know you again if we *did* meet,' Humpty Dumpty replied in a discontented tone, giving her one of his fingers to shake: 'you're so exactly like other people.'

'The face is what one goes by, generally,' Alice remarked in a thoughtful tone.

'That's just what I complain of,' said Humpty Dumpty. 'Your face is the same as everybody has—the two eyes, so——' (marking their places in the air with his thumb) 'nose in the middle, mouth under. It's always the same. Now if you had the two eyes on the same side of the nose, for instance—or the mouth at the top—that would be *some* help.'

'It wouldn't look nice,' Alice objected. But Humpty Dumpty only shut his eyes, and said 'Wait till you've tried.'

Alice waited a minute to see if he would speak again, but, as he never opened his eyes or took any further notice of her, she said 'Good-bye!' once more, and, getting no answer to this, she quietly walked away: but she couldn't help saying to herself, as she went, 'Of all the unsatisfactory——' (she repeated this aloud, as it was a great comfort to have such a long word to say) 'of all the unsatisfactory people I *ever* met——' She never finished the sentence, for at this moment a heavy crash shook the forest from end to end.

CHAPTER VII

THE LION AND THE UNICORN

THE next moment soldiers came running through the wood, at first in twos and threes, then ten or twenty together, and at last in such crowds that they seemed to fill the whole forest. Alice got behind a tree, for fear of being run over, and watched them go by.

She thought that in all her life she had never seen soldiers so uncertain on their feet: they were always tripping over something or other, and whenever one went down, several more always fell over him, so that the ground was soon covered with little heaps of men.

Then came the horses. Having four feet, these managed rather better than the foot-soldiers; but even *they* stumbled now and then; and it seemed to be a regular rule that, whenever a horse stumbled, the rider fell off instantly. The confusion got worse every moment, and Alice was very glad to get out of the wood into an open place, where she found the White King seated on the ground, busily writing in his memorandum-book.

'I've sent them all!' the King cried in a tone of delight, on seeing Alice. 'Did you happen to meet any soldiers, my dear, as you came through the wood?'

'Yes, I did,' said Alice: 'several thousand, I should think.'

'Four thousand two hundred and seven, that's the exact number,' the King said, referring to his book. 'I couldn't send all the horses, you know, because two of them are wanted in the game. And I haven't sent the two Messengers, either. They're both gone to the town. Just look along the road, and tell me if you can see either of them.'

'I see nobody on the road,' said Alice.

'I only wish *I* had such eyes,' the King remarked in a fret-ful tone. 'To be able to see Nobody! And at that distance too! Why, it's as much as *I* can do to see real people, by this light!'

All this was lost on Alice, who was still looking intently along the road, shading her eyes with one hand. 'I see some-body now!' she exclaimed at last. 'But he's coming very slowly —and what curious attitudes he goes into!' (For the Messenger kept skipping up and down, and wriggling like an eel, as he came along, with his great hands spread out like fans on each side.)

'Not at all,' said the King. 'He's an Anglo-Saxon Messenger —and those are Anglo-Saxon attitudes.[1] He only does them when he's happy. His name is Haigha.'[2] (He pronounced it so as to rhyme with "mayor.")

'I love my love with an H[3],' Alice couldn't help beginning, 'because he is Happy. I hate him with an H, because he is Hideous. I fed him with—with—with Ham-sandwiches and Hay. His name is Haigha, and he lives——'

'He lives on the Hill,' the King remarked simply, without the least idea that he was joining in the game, while Alice was still hesitating for the name of a town beginning with H. 'The other Messenger's called Hatta. I must have *two*, you know— to come and go. One to come, and one to go.'

'I beg your pardon?' said Alice.

'It isn't respectable to beg,' said the King.

'I only meant that I didn't understand,' said Alice. 'Why one to come and one to go?'

'Don't I tell you?' the King repeated impatiently. 'I must have *two*—to fetch and carry. One to fetch, and one to carry.'

At this moment the Messenger arrived: he was far too much out of breath to say a word, and could only wave his hands about, and make the most fearful faces at the poor King.

'This young lady loves you with an H,' the King said, introducing Alice in the hope of turning off the Messenger's attention from himself—but it was of no use—the Anglo-Saxon attitudes only got more extraordinary every moment, while the great eyes rolled wildly from side to side.

'You alarm me!' said the King. 'I feel faint——Give me a ham sandwich!'

On which the Messenger, to Alice's great amusement, opened a bag that hung round his neck, and handed a sand-wich to the King, who devoured it greedily.

'Another sandwich!' said the King.

'There's nothing but hay left now,' the Messenger said, peeping into the bag.

'Hay, then,' the King murmured in a faint whisper.

Alice was glad to see that it revived him a good deal. 'There's nothing like eating hay when you're faint,' he remarked to her, as he munched away.

'I should think throwing cold water over you would be better,' Alice suggested: '—or some sal-volatile.'[1]

'I didn't say there was nothing *better*,' the King replied. 'I said there was nothing *like* it.' Which Alice did not venture to deny.

'Who did you pass on the road?' the King went on, holding out his hand to the Messenger for some more hay.

'Nobody,'[2] said the Messenger.

'Quite right,' said the King: 'this young lady saw him too. So of course Nobody walks slower than you.'

'I do my best,' the Messenger said in a sullen tone. 'I'm sure nobody walks much faster than I do!'

'He ca'n't do that,' said the King, 'or else he'd have been here first. However, now you've got your breath, you may tell us what's happened in the town.'

'I'll whisper it,' said the Messenger, putting his hands to his mouth in the shape of a trumpet and stooping so as to get close to the King's ear. Alice was sorry for this, as she wanted to hear the news too. However, instead of whispering, he simply shouted, at the top of his voice, 'They're at it again!'

'Do you call *that* a whisper?' cried the poor King, jumping up and shaking himself. 'If you do such a thing again, I'll have you buttered! It went through and through my head like an earthquake!'

'It would have to be a very tiny earthquake!' thought Alice. 'Who are at it again?' she ventured to ask.

'Why, the Lion and the Unicorn, of course,' said the King.

'Fighting for the crown?'

'Yes, to be sure,' said the King: 'and the best of the joke is, that it's *my* crown all the while! Let's run and see them.' And they trotted off, Alice repeating to herself, as she ran, the words of the old song:—

'*The Lion and the Unicorn were fighting for the crown:*[1]
The Lion beat the Unicorn all round the town.
Some gave them white bread, some gave them brown:
Some gave them plum-cake and drummed them out of town.'

'Does——the one——that wins——get the crown?' she asked, as well as she could, for the run was putting her quite out of breath.

'Dear me, no!' said the King. 'What an idea!'

'Would you—be good enough——' Alice panted out, after running a little further, 'to stop a minute—just to get—one's breath again?'

'I'm *good* enough,' the King said, 'only I'm not *strong* enough. You see, a minute goes by so fearfully quick. You might as well try to stop a Bandersnatch!'

Alice had no more breath for talking; so they trotted on in silence, till they came into sight of a great crowd, in the middle of which the Lion and Unicorn were fighting. They were in such a cloud of dust, that at first Alice could not make out

which was which; but she soon managed to distinguish the
Unicorn by his horn.

They placed themselves close to where Hatta, the other
Messenger, was standing watching the fight, with a cup of
tea in one hand and a piece of bread-and-butter in the
other.

'He's only just out of prison, and he hadn't finished his
tea when he was sent in,' Haigha whispered to Alice: 'and
they only give them oyster-shells in there—so you see
he's very hungry and thirsty. How are you, dear child?'
he went on, putting his arm affectionately round Hatta's
neck.

Hatta looked round and nodded, and went on with his
bread-and-butter.

'Were you happy in prison, dear child?' said Haigha.

Hatta looked round once more, and this time a tear or two
trickled down his cheek; but not a word would he say.

'Speak, ca'n't you!' Haigha cried impatiently. But Hatta
only munched away, and drank some more tea.

'Speak, wo'n't you!' cried the King. 'How are they getting on with the fight?'

Hatta made a desperate effort, and swallowed a large piece of bread-and-butter. 'They're getting on very well,' he said in a choking voice: 'each of them has been down about eighty-seven times.'

'Then I suppose they'll soon bring the white bread and the brown?' Alice ventured to remark.

'It's waiting for 'em now,' said Hatta; 'this is a bit of it as I'm eating.'

There was a pause in the fight just then, and the Lion and the Unicorn sat down, panting, while the King called out 'Ten minutes allowed for refreshments!' Haigha and Hatta set to work at once, carrying round trays of white and brown bread. Alice took a piece to taste, but it was *very* dry.

'I don't think they'll fight any more today,' the King said to Hatta: 'go and order the drums to begin.' And Hatta went bounding away like a grasshopper.

For a minute or two Alice stood silent, watching him. Suddenly she brightened up. 'Look, look!' she cried, point-ing eagerly. 'There's the White Queen running across the country! She came flying out of the wood over yonder—— How fast those Queens *can* run!'[1]

'There's some enemy after her, no doubt,' the King said, without even looking round. 'That wood's full of them.'

'But aren't you going to run and help her?' Alice asked, very much surprised at his taking it so quietly.

'No use, no use!' said the King. 'She runs so fearfully quick. You might as well try to catch a Bandersnatch! But I'll make a memorandum about her, if you like——She's a dear good creature,' he repeated softly to himself, as he opened his memorandum-book. 'Do you spell "creature" with a double "e"?'

At this moment the Unicorn sauntered by them, with his

hands in his pockets. 'I had the best of it this time?' he said
to the King, just glancing at him as he passed.

'A little—a little,' the King replied, rather nervously.
'You shouldn't have run him through with your horn, you
know.'

'It didn't hurt him,' the Unicorn said carelessly, and he was
going on, when his eye happened to fall upon Alice: he turned
round instantly, and stood for some time looking at her with
an air of the deepest disgust.

'What—is—this?' he said at last.

'This is a child!' Haigha replied eagerly, coming in front of
Alice to introduce her, and spreading out both his hands
towards her in an Anglo-Saxon attitude. 'We only found it
to-day. It's as large as life, and twice as natural!'

'I always thought they were fabulous monsters!' said the
Unicorn. 'Is it alive?'

'It can talk,' said Haigha solemnly.

The Unicorn looked dreamily at Alice, and said 'Talk,
child.'

Alice could not help her lips curling up into a smile as she
began: 'Do you know, I always thought Unicorns were
fabulous monsters, too? I never saw one alive before!'

'Well, now that we *have* seen each other,' said the Unicorn, 'if you'll believe in me, I'll believe in you. Is that a
bargain?'

'Yes, if you like,' said Alice.

'Come, fetch out the plum-cake, old man!' the Unicorn
went on, turning from her to the King. 'None of your brown
bread for me!'

'Certainly—certainly!' the King muttered, and beckoned
to Haigha. 'Open the bag!' he whispered. 'Quick! Not that
one—that's full of hay!'

Haigha took a large cake out of the bag, and gave it to Alice
to hold, while he got out a dish and carving-knife. How they
all came out of it Alice couldn't guess. It was just like a
conjuring-trick,[1] she thought.

The Lion had joined them while this was going on: he

looked very tired and sleepy, and his eyes were half shut. 'What's this!' he said, blinking lazily at Alice, and speaking in a deep hollow tone that sounded like the tolling of a great bell.

'Ah, what *is* it, now?' the Unicorn cried eagerly. 'You'll never guess! *I* couldn't.'

The Lion looked at Alice wearily. 'Are you animal—or vegetable—or mineral?' he said, yawning at every other word.

'It's a fabulous monster!' the Unicorn cried out, before Alice could reply.

'Then hand round the plum-cake, Monster,' the Lion said, lying down and putting his chin on his paws. 'And sit down, both of you,' (to the King and the Unicorn): 'fair play with the cake, you know!'

The King was evidently very uncomfortable at having to sit down between the two great creatures; but there was no other place for him.

'What a fight we might have for the crown, *now!*' the Unicorn said, looking slyly up at the crown, which the poor King was nearly shaking off his head, he trembled so much.

'I should win easy,' said the Lion.

'I'm not so sure of that,' said the Unicorn.

'Why, I beat you all round the town, you chicken!' the Lion replied angrily, half getting up as he spoke.

Here the King interrupted, to prevent the quarrel going on: he was very nervous, and his voice quite quivered. 'All round the town?' he said. 'That's a good long way. Did you go by the old bridge, or the market-place? You get the best view by the old bridge.'

'I'm sure I don't know,' the Lion growled out as he lay down again. 'There was too much dust to see anything. What a time the Monster is, cutting up that cake!'

Alice had seated herself on the bank of a little brook, with the great dish on her knees, and was sawing away diligently with the knife. 'It's very provoking!' she said, in reply to the Lion (she was getting quite used to being called 'the Monster'). 'I've cut several slices already, but they always join on again!'

'You don't know how to manage Looking-glass cakes,' the Unicorn remarked. 'Hand it round first, and cut it afterwards.'

This sounded nonsense, but Alice very obediently got up, and carried the dish round, and the cake divided itself into three pieces as she did so. '*Now* cut it up,' said the Lion, as she returned to her place with the empty dish.

'I say, this isn't fair!' cried the Unicorn, as Alice sat with the knife in her hand, very much puzzled how to begin. 'The Monster has given the Lion twice as much[1] as me!'

'She's kept none for herself, anyhow,' said the Lion. 'Do you like plum-cake, Monster?'

But before Alice could answer him, the drums began.

Where the noise came from, she couldn't make out: the air seemed full of it, and it rang through and through her head till she felt quite deafened. She started to her feet and sprang across the little brook in her terror,

    *   *   *   *   *   *

       *   *   *   *   *

    *   *   *   *   *   *

Q

and had just time to see the Lion and the Unicorn rise to their feet, with angry looks at being interrupted in their feast, before she dropped to her knees, and put her hands over her ears, vainly trying to shut out the dreadful uproar.

'If *that* doesn't "drum them out of town,"' she thought to herself, 'nothing ever will!'

CHAPTER VIII

AFTER a while the noise seemed gradually to die away, till all was dead silence, and Alice lifted up her head in some alarm. There was no one to be seen, and her first thought was that she must have been dreaming about the Lion and the Unicorn and those queer Anglo-Saxon Messengers. However, there was the great dish still lying at her feet, on which she had tried to cut the plum-cake, 'So I wasn't dreaming, after all,' she said to herself, 'unless—unless we're all part of the same dream. Only I do hope it's *my* dream, and not the Red King's! I don't like belonging to another person's dream,' she went on in a rather complaining tone: 'I've a great mind to go and wake him, and see what happens!'

At this moment her thoughts were interrupted by a loud shouting of 'Ahoy! Ahoy! Check!' and a Knight, dressed in crimson armour, came galloping down upon her, brandishing a great club. Just as he reached her, the horse stopped suddenly: 'You're my prisoner!' the Knight cried, as he tumbled off his horse.

Startled as she was, Alice was more frightened for him than for herself at the moment, and watched him with some anxiety as he mounted again. As soon as he was comfortably in the saddle, he began once more 'You're my——' but here another voice broke in 'Ahoy! Ahoy! Check!' and Alice looked round in some surprise for the new enemy.

This time it was a White Knight. He drew up at Alice's side, and tumbled off his horse just as the Red Knight had done: then he got on again, and the two Knights sat and looked at each other for some time without speaking. Alice looked from one to the other in some bewilderment.

'She's *my* prisoner, you know!' the Red Knight said at last.

'Yes, but then *I* came and rescued her!' the White Knight replied.

'Well, we must fight for her, then,' said the Red Knight, as he took up his helmet (which hung from the saddle, and was something the shape of a horse's head) and put it on.

'You will observe the Rules of Battle, of course?' the White Knight remarked, putting on his helmet too.

'I always do,' said the Red Knight, and they began banging away at each other with such fury that Alice got behind a tree to be out of the way of the blows.

'I wonder, now, what the Rules of Battle are,' she said to herself, as she watched the fight, timidly peeping out from her hiding-place. 'One Rule seems to be, that if one Knight hits the other, he knocks him off his horse; and, if he misses, he tumbles off himself—and another Rule seems to be that they hold their clubs with their arms, as if they were Punch and

Judy——What a noise they make when they tumble! Just like a whole set of fire-irons falling into the fender! And how quiet the horses are! They let them get on and off them just as if they were tables!'

Another Rule of Battle, that Alice had not noticed, seemed to be that they always fell on their heads; and the battle ended with their both falling off in this way, side by side. When they got up again, they shook hands, and then the Red Knight mounted and galloped off.

'It was a glorious victory,[1] wasn't it?' said the White Knight, as he came up panting.

'I don't know,' Alice said doubtfully. 'I don't want to be anybody's prisoner. I want to be a Queen.'

'So you will, when you've crossed the next brook,' said the White Knight. 'I'll see you safe to the end of the wood—and then I must go back, you know. That's the end of my move.'

'Thank you very much,' said Alice. 'May I help you off with your helmet?' It was evidently more than he could manage by himself: however she managed to shake him out of it at last.

'Now one can breathe more easily,' said the Knight, putting back his shaggy hair with both hands, and turning his gentle face and large mild eyes to Alice. She thought she had never seen such a strange-looking soldier in all her life.

He was dressed in tin armour, which seemed to fit him very badly, and he had a queer-shaped little deal box fastened across his shoulders, upside-down, and with the lid hanging open. Alice looked at it with great curiosity.

'I see you're admiring my little box,' the Knight said in a friendly tone. 'It's my own invention—to keep clothes and sandwiches in. You see I carry it upside-down, so that the rain ca'n't get in.'

'But the things can get *out*,' Alice gently remarked. 'Do you know the lid's open?'

'I didn't know it,' the Knight said, a shade of vexation passing over his face. 'Then all the things must have fallen out! And the box is no use without them.' He unfastened it as he spoke, and was just going to throw it into the bushes, when a sudden thought seemed to strike him, and he hung it carefully on a tree. 'Can you guess why I did that?' he said to Alice.

Alice shook her head.

'In hopes some bees may make a nest in it—then I should get the honey.'

'But you've got a bee-hive—or something like one—fastened to the saddle,' said Alice.

'Yes, it's a very good bee-hive,' the Knight said in a discontented tone, 'one of the best kind. But not a single bee has come near it yet. And the other thing is a mouse-trap. I suppose the mice keep the bees out—or the bees keep the mice out, I don't know which.'

'I was wondering what the mouse-trap was for,' said Alice. 'It isn't very likely there would be any mice on the horse's back.'[1]

'Not very likely, perhaps,' said the Knight; 'but, if they *do* come, I don't choose to have them running all about.'

'You see,' he went on after a pause, 'it's as well to be provided for *everything*. That's the reason the horse has all those anklets round his feet.'

'But what are they for?' Alice asked in a tone of great curiosity.

'To guard against the bites of sharks,' the Knight replied. 'It's an invention of my own. And now help me on. I'll go with you to the end of the wood——What's that dish for?'

'It's meant for plum-cake,' said Alice.

'We'd better take it with us,' the Knight said. 'It'll come in handy if we find any plum-cake. Help me to get it into this bag.'

This took a long time to manage, though Alice held the bag open very carefully, because the Knight was so *very* awkward in putting in the dish: the first two or three times that he tried he fell in himself instead. 'It's rather a tight fit, you see,' he said, as they got it in at last; 'there are so many candlesticks in the bag.' And he hung it to the saddle, which was already loaded with bunches of carrots, and fire-irons, and many other things.

'I hope you've got your hair well fastened on?' he continued, as they set off.

'Only in the usual way,' Alice said, smiling.

'That's hardly enough,' he said, anxiously. 'You see the wind is so *very* strong here. It's as strong as soup.'

'Have you invented a plan for keeping the hair from being blown of?' Alice enquired.

'Not yet,' said the Knight. 'But I've got a plan for keeping it from *falling* off.'

'I should like to hear it, very much.'

'First you take an upright stick,' said the Knight. 'Then you make your hair creep up it, like a fruit-tree. Now the reason hair falls off is because it hangs *down*—things never fall *upwards*, you know. It's a plan of my own invention. You may try it if you like.'

It didn't sound a comfortable plan, Alice thought, and for a few minutes she walked on in silence, puzzling over the idea, and every now and then stopping to help the poor Knight, who certainly was *not* a good rider.

Whenever the horse stopped (which it did very often), he

fell off in front; and, whenever it went on again (which it generally did rather suddenly), he fell off behind. Otherwise he kept on pretty well, except that he had a habit of now and then falling off sideways; and, as he generally did this on the side on which Alice was walking, she soon found that it was the best plan not to walk *quite* close to the horse.

'I'm afraid you've not had much practice in riding,' she ventured to say, as she was helping him up from his fifth tumble.

The Knight looked very much surprised, and a little offended at the remark. 'What makes you say that?' he asked, as he scrambled back into the saddle, keeping hold of Alice's hair with one hand, to save himself from falling over on the other side.

'Because people don't fall off quite so often, when they've had much practice.'

'I've had plenty of practice,' the Knight said very gravely: 'plenty of practice!'

Alice could think of nothing better to say than 'Indeed?' but she said it as heartily as she could. They went on a little way in silence after this, the Knight with his eyes shut, muttering to himself, and Alice watching anxiously for the next tumble.

'The great art of riding,'[1] the Knight suddenly began in a loud voice, waving his right arm as he spoke, 'is to keep——' Here the sentence ended as suddenly as it had begun, as the Knight fell heavily on the top of his head exactly in the path where Alice was walking. She was quite frightened this time, and said in an anxious tone, as she picked him up, 'I hope no bones are broken?'

'None to speak of,' the Knight said, as if he didn't mind breaking two or three of them. 'The great art of riding, as I was saying, is—to keep your balance properly. Like this, you know——'

He let go the bridle, and stretched out both his arms to show Alice what he meant, and this time he fell flat on his back, right under the horse's feet.

'Plenty of practice!' he went on repeating, all the time that Alice was getting him on his feet again. 'Plenty of practice!'

'It's too ridiculous!' cried Alice, losing all her patience this time. 'You ought to have a wooden horse on wheels, that you ought!'

'Does that kind go smoothly?' the Knight asked in a tone of great interest, clasping his arms round the horse's neck as he spoke, just in time to save himself from tumbling off again.

'Much more smoothly than a live horse,' Alice said, with a little scream of laughter, in spite of all she could do to prevent it.

'I'll get one,' the Knight said thoughtfully to himself. 'One or two—several.'

There was a short silence after this, and then the Knight went on again. 'I'm a great hand at inventing things. Now, I daresay you noticed, the last time you picked me up, that I was looking rather thoughtful?'

'You *were* a little grave,' said Alice.

'Well, just then I was inventing a new way of getting over a gate—would you like to hear it?'

'Very much indeed,' Alice said politely.

'I'll tell you how I came to think of it,' said the Knight. 'You see, I said to myself "The only difficulty is with the feet: the *head* is high enough already." Now, first I put my head on the top of the gate—then the head's high enough—then I stand on my head—then the feet are high enough, you see— then I'm over, you see.'

'Yes, I suppose you'd be over when that was done,' Alice said thoughtfully: 'but don't you think it would be rather hard?'

'I haven't tried it yet,' the Knight said, gravely; 'so I ca'n't tell for certain—but I'm afraid it *would* be a little hard.'

He looked so vexed at the idea, that Alice changed the subject hastily. 'What a curious helmet you've got!' she said cheerfully. 'Is that your invention too?'

The Knight looked down proudly at his helmet, which hung from the saddle. 'Yes,' he said; 'but I've invented a better one than that—like a sugar-loaf. When I used to wear it, if I fell off the horse, it always touched the ground directly. So I had a *very* little way to fall, you see—But there *was* the danger of falling *into* it, to be sure. That happened to me once —and the worst of it was, before I could get out again, the other White Knight came and put it on. He thought it was his own helmet.'

The Knight looked so solemn about it that Alice did not dare to laugh. 'I'm afraid you must have hurt him,' she said in a trembling voice, 'being on the top of his head.'

'I had to kick him, of course,' the Knight said, very seriously. 'And then he took the helmet off again—but it took hours and hours to get me out. I was as fast as—as lightning, you know.'

'But that's a different kind of fastness,' Alice objected.

The Knight shook his head. 'It was all kinds of fastness with me, I can assure you!' he said. He raised his hands in some excitement as he said this, and instantly rolled out of the saddle, and fell headlong into a deep ditch.

Alice ran to the side of the ditch to look for him. She was rather startled by the fall, as for some time he had kept on very well, and she was afraid that he really *was* hurt this time. However, though she could see nothing but the soles of his feet, she was much relieved to hear that he was talking on in his usual tone. 'All kinds of fastness,' he repeated: 'but it was careless of him to put another man's helmet on—with the man in it, too.'

'How *can* you go on talking so quietly, head downwards?' Alice asked, as she dragged him out by the feet, and laid him in a heap on the bank.

The Knight looked surprised at the question. 'What does it matter where my body happens to be?' he said. 'My mind goes on working all the same. In fact, the more head-downwards I am, the more I keep inventing new things.'

'Now the cleverest thing of the sort that I ever did,' he went

on after a pause, 'was inventing a new pudding during the meat-course.'

'In time to have it cooked for the next course?' said Alice. 'Well, that *was* quick work, certainly!'

'Well, not the *next* course,' the Knight said in a slow thoughtful tone: 'no, certainly not the next *course*.'

'Then it would have to be the next day. I suppose you wouldn't have two pudding-courses in one dinner?'

'Well, not the *next* day,' the Knight repeated as before: 'not the next *day*. In fact,' he went on, holding his head down, and his voice getting lower and lower, 'I don't believe that pudding ever *was* cooked! In fact, I don't believe that pudding ever *will* be cooked! And yet it was a very clever pudding to invent.'

'What did you mean it to be made of?' Alice asked, hoping to cheer him up, for the poor Knight seemed quite low-spirited about it.

'It began with blotting-paper,' the Knight answered with a groan.

'That wouldn't be very nice, I'm afraid——'

'Not very nice *alone*,' he interrupted, quite eagerly: 'but you've no idea what a difference it makes, mixing it with other things—such as gunpowder and sealing-wax. And here I must leave you.' They had just come to the end of the wood.

Alice could only look puzzled: she was thinking of the pudding.

'You are sad,' the Knight said in an anxious tone: 'let me sing you a song to comfort you.'

'Is it very long?' Alice asked, for she had heard a good deal of poetry that day.

'It's long,' said the Knight, 'but it's very, *very* beautiful. Everybody that hears me sing it—either it brings the *tears* into their eyes, or else——'

'Or else what?' said Alice, for the Knight had made a sudden pause.

'Or else it doesn't, you know. The name of the song[1] is called "*Haddocks' Eyes*."'

'Oh, that's the name of the song, is it?' Alice said, trying to feel interested.

'No, you don't understand,' the Knight said, looking a little vexed. 'That's what the name is *called*. The name really *is* "*The Aged Aged Man*."'

'Then I ought to have said "That's what the *song* is called"?' Alice corrected herself.

'No, you oughtn't: that's quite another thing! The *song* is called "*Ways And Means*": but that's only what it's *called*, you know!'

'Well, what *is* the song, then?' said Alice, who was by this time completely bewildered.

'I was coming to that,' the Knight said. 'The song really *is* "*A-sitting On A Gate*": and the tune's my own invention.'

So saying, he stopped his horse and let the reins fall on its neck: then, slowly beating time with one hand, and with a faint smile lighting up his gentle foolish face, as if he enjoyed the music of his song, he began.

Of all the strange things that Alice saw in her journey Through The Looking-Glass, this was the one that she always remembered most clearly. Years afterwards she could bring the whole scene back again, as if it had been only yesterday—the mild blue eyes and kindly smile of the Knight —the setting sun gleaming through his hair, and shining on his armour in a blaze of light that quite dazzled her—the horse quietly moving about, with the reins hanging loose on his neck, cropping the grass at her feet—and the black shadows of the forest behind—all this she took in like a picture, as, with one hand shading her eyes, she leant against a tree, watching the strange pair, and listening, in a half-dream, to the melancholy music of the song.

'But the tune *isn't* his own invention,' she said to herself: 'it's "*I give thee all, I can no more.*"'[1] She stood and listened very attentively, but no tears came into her eyes.

'I'll tell thee everything I can:[2]
    There's little to relate.
I saw an aged aged man,
    A-sitting on a gate.
"Who are you, aged man?" I said.
    "And how is it you live?"
And his answer trickled through my head,
    Like water through a sieve.

He said "I look for butterflies
    That sleep among the wheat:
I make them into mutton-pies,
    And sell them in the street.
I sell them unto men," he said,
    "Who sail on stormy seas;
And that's the way I get my bread—
    A trifle, if you please."

But I was thinking of a plan
    To dye one's whiskers green,
And always use so large a fan
    That they could not be seen.

So, having no reply to give
   To what the old man said,
I cried "Come, tell me how you live!"
   And thumped him on the head.

His accents mild took up the tale:
   He said "I go my ways,
And when I find a mountain-rill,
   I set it in a blaze;
And thence they make a stuff they call
   Rowland's Macassar-Oil[1] —
Yet twopence-halfpenny is all
   They give me for my toil."

But I was thinking of a way
   To feed oneself on batter,
And so go on from day to day
   Getting a little fatter.
I shook him well from side to side,
   Until his face was blue:
"Come, tell me how you live," I cried,
   "And what it is you do!"

He said "I hunt for haddocks' eyes
  Among the heather bright,
And work them into waistcoat-buttons
  In the silent night.
And these I do not sell for gold
  Or coin of silvery shine,
But for a copper halfpenny,
  And that will purchase nine.

"I sometimes dig for buttered rolls,
  Or set limed twigs[1] *for crabs:*
I sometimes search the grassy knolls
  For wheels of Hansom-cabs.
And that's the way" (he gave a wink)
  "By which I get my wealth—
And very gladly will I drink
  Your Honour's noble health."

I heard him then, for I had just
  Completed my design
To keep the Menai bridge[2] *from rust*
  By boiling it in wine.
I thanked him much for telling me
  The way he got his wealth,
But chiefly for his wish that he
  Might drink my noble health.

And now, if e'er by chance I put
  My fingers into glue,
Or madly squeeze a right-hand foot
  Into a left-hand shoe,
Or if I drop upon my toe
  A very heavy weight,
I weep, for it reminds me so
Of that old man I used to know—
Whose look was mild, whose speech was slow,
Whose hair was whiter than the snow,

Whose face was very like a crow,
With eyes, like cinders, all aglow,
Who seemed distracted with his woe,
Who rocked his body to and fro,
And muttered mumblingly and low,
As if his mouth were full of dough,
Who snorted like a buffalo——
That summer evening long ago,
   A-sitting on a gate.'

As the Knight sang the last words of the ballad, he gathered up the reins, and turned his horse's head along the road by which they had come. 'You've only a few yards to go,' he said, 'down the hill and over that little brook, and then you'll be a Queen——But you'll stay and see me off first?' he added as Alice turned with an eager look in the direction to which he pointed. 'I sha'n't be long. You'll wait and wave your handkerchief when I get to that turn in the road![I] I think it'll encourage me, you see.'

'Of course I'll wait,' said Alice: 'and thank you very much for coming so far—and for the song—I liked it very much.'

'I hope so,' the Knight said doubtfully: 'but you didn't cry so much as I thought you would.'

So they shook hands, and then the Knight rode slowly away into the forest. 'It wo'n't take long to see him *off*, I expect,' Alice said to herself, as she stood watching him. 'There he goes! Right on his head as usual! However, he gets on again pretty easily—that comes of having so many things hung round the horse——' So she went on talking to herself, as she watched the horse walking leisurely along the road, and the Knight tumbling off, first on one side and then on the other. After the fourth or fifth tumble he reached the turn, and then she waved her handkerchief to him, and waited till he was out of sight.

'I hope it encouraged him,' she said, as she turned to run down the hill: 'and now for the last brook, and to be a Queen! How grand it sounds!' A very few steps brought her to the

:dge of the brook. 'The Eighth Square at last!'[1] she cried as
:he bounded across,

      *   *   *   *   *   *
          *   *   *   *   *
   *   *   *   *   *   *

and threw herself down to rest on a lawn as soft as moss, with
little flower-beds dotted about it here and there. 'Oh, how glad
I am to get here! And what *is* this on my head?' she exclaimed
in a tone of dismay, as she put her hands up to something very
heavy, that fitted tight all round her head.

'But how *can* it have got there without my knowing it?' she
said to herself, as she lifted it off, and set it on her lap to make
out what it could possibly be.

It was a golden crown.

CHAPTER IX

QUEEN ALICE

'WELL, this *is* grand!' said Alice. 'I never expected I should be a Queen so soon—and I'll tell you what it is, your Majesty,' she went on, in a severe tone (she was always rather fond of scolding herself), 'it'll never do for you to be lolling about on the grass like that! Queens have to be dignified, you know!'

So she got up and walked about—rather stiffly just at first, as she was afraid that the crown might come off: but she comforted herself with the thought that there was nobody to see her, 'and if I really am a Queen,' she said as she sat down again, 'I shall be able to manage it quite well in time.'

Everything was happening so oddly that she didn't feel a bit surprised at finding the Red Queen and the White Queen sitting close to her, one on each side: she would have liked very much to ask them how they came there, but she feared it would not be quite civil. However, there would be no harm, she thought, in asking if the game was over. 'Please, would you tell me——' she began, looking timidly at the Red Queen.

'Speak when you're spoken to!' the Queen sharply interrupted her.

'But if everybody obeyed that rule,' said Alice, who was always ready for a little argument, 'and if you only spoke when you were spoken to, and the other person always waited for *you* to begin, you see nobody would ever say anything, so that——'

'Ridiculous!' cried the Queen. 'Why, don't you see, child——' here she broke off with a frown, and, after thinking for a minute, suddenly changed the subject of the conversation. 'What do you mean by "If you really are a Queen"? What right have you to call yourself so? You ca'n't be a

Queen, you know, till you've passed the proper examination. And the sooner we begin it, the better.'

'I only said "if"!' poor Alice pleaded in a piteous tone.

The two Queens looked at each other, and the Red Queen remarked, with a little shudder, 'She *says* she only said "if"——'

'But she said a great deal more than that!' the White Queen moaned, wringing her hands. 'Oh, ever so much more than that!'

'So you did, you know,' the Red Queen said to Alice. 'Always speak the truth—think before you speak—and write it down afterwards.'

'I'm sure I didn't mean——' Alice was beginning, but the Red Queen interrupted her impatiently.

'That's just what I complain of! You *should* have meant! What do you suppose is the use of a child without any meaning? Even a joke should have some meaning—and a child's more important than a joke, I hope. You couldn't deny that, even if you tried with both hands.'

'I don't deny things with my *hands*,' Alice objected.

'Nobody said you did,' said the Red Queen. 'I said you couldn't if you tried.'

'She's in that state of mind,' said the White Queen, 'that she wants to deny *something*—only she doesn't know what to deny!'

'A nasty, vicious temper,' the Red Queen remarked; and then there was an uncomfortable silence for a minute or two.

The Red Queen broke the silence by saying, to the White Queen, 'I invite you to Alice's dinner-party this afternoon.'

The White Queen smiled feebly, and said 'And I invite *you*.'

'I didn't know I was to have a party at all,' said Alice; 'but, if there *is* to be one, I think *I* ought to invite the guests.'

'We gave you the opportunity of doing it,' the Red Queen remarked: 'but I daresay you've not had many lessons in manners yet?'

'Manners are not taught in lessons,' said Alice. 'Lessons teach you to do sums, and things of that sort.'

'Can you do Addition?' the White Queen asked. 'What's one and one and one and one and one and one and one and one and one and one?'

'I don't know,' said Alice. 'I lost count.'

'She ca'n't do Addition,' the Red Queen interrupted. 'Can you do Subtraction? Take nine from eight.'

'Nine from eight I ca'n't, you know,' Alice replied very readily: 'but——'

'She ca'n't do Substraction,' said the White Queen. 'Can you do Division? Divide a loaf by a knife—what's the answer to *that?*'

'I suppose——' Alice was beginning, but the Red Queen answered for her. 'Bread-and-butter, of course. Try another Subtraction sum. Take a bone from a dog: what remains?'

Alice considered. 'The bone wouldn't remain, of course, if I took it—and the dog wouldn't remain: it would come to bite me—and I'm sure *I* shouldn't remain!'

'Then you think nothing would remain?' said the Red Queen.

'I think that's the answer.'

'Wrong, as usual,' said the Red Queen: 'the dog's temper would remain.'

'But I don't see how——'

'Why, look here!' the Red Queen cried. 'The dog would lose its temper, wouldn't it?'

'Perhaps it would,' Alice replied cautiously.

'Then if the dog went away, its temper would remain!' the Queen exclaimed triumphantly.

Alice said, as gravely as she could, 'They might go different ways.' But she couldn't help thinking to herself 'What dreadful nonsense we *are* talking!'

'She ca'n't do sums a *bit!*' the Queens said together, with great emphasis.

'Can *you* do sums?' Alice said, turning suddenly on the White Queen, for she didn't like being found fault with so much.

The Queen gasped and shut her eyes. 'I can do Addition,' she said, 'if you give me time—but I ca'n't do Substraction under *any* circumstances!'

'Of course you know your A B C?' said the Red Queen.

'To be sure I do,' said Alice.

'So do I,' the White Queen whispered: 'we'll often say it over together, dear. And I'll tell you a secret—I can read words of one letter! Isn't *that* grand? However, don't be discouraged. You'll come to it in time.'

Here the Red Queen began again. 'Can you answer useful questions?' she said. 'How is bread made?'

'I know *that!*' Alice cried eagerly. 'You take some flour——'

'Where do you pick the flower?' the White Queen asked. 'In a garden or in the hedges?'

'Well, it isn't *picked* at all,' Alice explained: 'it's *ground*——'

'How many acres of ground?' said the White Queen. 'You mustn't leave out so many things.'

'Fan her head!' the Red Queen anxiously interrupted. 'She'll be feverish after so much thinking.' So they set to work and fanned her with bunches of leaves, till she had to beg them to leave off, it blew her hair about so.

'She's all right again now,' said the Red Queen. 'Do you know Languages? What's the French for fiddle-de-dee?'[1]

'Fiddle-de-dee's not English,' Alice replied gravely.

'Who ever said it was?' said the Red Queen.

Alice thought she saw a way out of the difficulty, this time. 'If you'll tell me what language "fiddle-de-dee" is, I'll tell you the French for it!' she exclaimed triumphantly.

But the Red Queen drew herself up rather stiffly, and said 'Queens never make bargains.'

'I wish Queens never asked questions,' Alice thought to herself.

'Don't let us quarrel,' the White Queen said in an anxious tone. 'What is the cause of lightning?'

'The cause of lightning,' Alice said very decidedly, for she felt quite certain about this, 'is the thunder—no, no!' she hastily corrected herself. 'I meant the other way.'

'It's too late to correct it,' said the Red Queen: 'when you've once said a thing, that fixes it, and you must take the consequences.'

'Which reminds me——' the White Queen said, looking down and nervously clasping and unclasping her hands, 'we had *such* a thunderstorm last Tuesday—I mean one of the last set of Tuesdays, you know.'

Alice was puzzled. 'In *our* country,' she remarked, 'there's only one day at a time.'

The Red Queen said 'That's a poor thin way of doing things. Now *here*, we mostly have days and nights two or three at a time, and sometimes in the winter we take as many as five nights together—for warmth, you know.'

'Are five nights warmer than one night, then?' Alice ventured to ask.

'Five times as warm, of course.'

'But they should be five times as *cold*, by the same rule——'

'Just so!' cried the Red Queen. 'Five times as warm, *and*

five times as cold—just as I'm five times as rich as you are,
and five times as clever!'

Alice sighed and gave it up. 'It's exactly like a riddle with no
answer!' she thought.

'Humpty Dumpty saw it too,' the White Queen went on in
a low voice, more as if she were talking to herself. 'He came
to the door with a corkscrew in his hand——'

'What did he want?' said the Red Queen.

'He said he *would* come in,' the White Queen went on,
'because he was looking for a hippopotamus. Now, as it
happened, there wasn't such a thing in the house, that morning.'

'Is there generally?' Alice asked in an astonished tone.

'Well, only on Thursdays,' said the Queen.

'I know what he came for,' said Alice: 'he wanted to punish
the fish, because——'

Here the White Queen began again. 'It was *such* a thunderstorm, you ca'n't think!' ('She *never* could, you know,' said
the Red Queen.) 'And part of the roof came off, and ever so
much thunder got in—and it went rolling round the room
in great lumps—and knocking over the tables and things
—till I was so frightened, I couldn't remember my own
name!'

Alice thought to herself 'I never should *try* to remember my
name in the middle of an accident! Where would be the use of
it?' but she did not say this aloud, for fear of hurting the poor
Queen's feelings.

'Your Majesty must excuse her,' the Red Queen said to
Alice, taking one of the White Queen's hands in her own, and
gently stroking it: 'she means well, but she ca'n't help saying
foolish things, as a general rule.'

The White Queen looked timidly at Alice, who felt she
ought to say something kind, but really couldn't think of anything at the moment.

'She never was really well brought up,' the Red Queen went
on: 'but it's amazing how good-tempered she is! Pat her on
the head, and see how pleased she'll be!' But this was more
than Alice had courage to do.

'A little kindness—and putting her hair in papers[1]—would do wonders with her——'

The White Queen gave a deep sigh, and laid her head on Alice's shoulder. 'I *am* so sleepy!' she moaned.

'She's tired, poor thing!' said the Red Queen. 'Smooth her hair—lend her your nightcap—and sing her a soothing lullaby.'

'I haven't got a nightcap with me,' said Alice, as she tried to obey the first direction: 'and I don't know any soothing lullabies.'

'I must do it myself, then,' said the Red Queen, and she began:—

> *'Hush-a-by lady,[2] in Alice's lap!*
> *Till the feast's ready, we've time for a nap.*
> *When the feast's over, we'll go to the ball—*
> *Red Queen, and White Queen, and Alice, and all!*

'And now you know the words,' she added, as she put her head down on Alice's other shoulder, 'just sing it through to *me*. I'm getting sleepy, too.' In another moment both Queens were fast asleep, and snoring loud.

'What *am* I to do?' exclaimed Alice, looking about in great perplexity, as first one round head, and then the other, rolled down from her shoulder, and lay like a heavy lump in her lap. 'I don't think it *ever* happened before, that any one had to take care of two Queens asleep at once! No, not in all the History of England—it couldn't, you know, because there never was more than one Queen at a time. Do wake up, you heavy things!' she went on in an impatient tone; but there was no answer but a gentle snoring.

The snoring got more distinct every minute, and sounded more like a tune: at last she could even make out words, and she listened so eagerly that, when the two great heads suddenly vanished from her lap, she hardly missed them.

She was standing before an arched doorway, over which were the words 'QUEEN ALICE' in large letters, and on each side of the arch there was a bell-handle; one was marked 'Visitors' Bell,' and the other 'Servants' Bell.'

'I'll wait till the song's over,' thought Alice, 'and then I'll ring the—the—*which* bell must I ring?' she went on, very much puzzled by the names. 'I'm not a visitor, and I'm not a servant. There *ought* to be one marked "Queen," you know——'

Just then the door opened a little way, and a creature with a long beak put its head out for a moment and said 'No admittance till the week after next!' and shut the door again with a bang.

Alice knocked and rang in vain for a long time; but at last a very old Frog, who was sitting under a tree, got up and hobbled slowly towards her: he was dressed in bright yellow, and had enormous boots on.

'What is it, now?' the Frog said in a deep hoarse whisper.

Alice turned round, ready to find fault with anybody. 'Where's the servant whose business it is to answer the door?' she began angrily.

'Which door?' said the Frog.

Alice almost stamped with irritation at the slow drawl in which he spoke. '*This* door, of course!'

The Frog looked at the door with his large dull eyes for
a minute: then he went nearer and rubbed it with his thumb,
as if he were trying whether the paint would come off: then
he looked at Alice.

'To answer the door?' he said. 'What's it been asking of?'
He was so hoarse that Alice could scarcely hear him.

'I don't know what you mean,' she said.

'I speaks English, doesn't I?' the Frog went on. 'Or are you
deaf? What did it ask you?'

'Nothing!' Alice said impatiently. 'I've been knocking
at it!'

'Shouldn't do that—shouldn't do that——' the Frog
muttered. 'Wexes it, you know.' Then he went up and gave
the door a kick with one of his great feet. 'You let *it* alone,'

he panted out, as he hobbled back to his tree, 'and it'll let
you alone, you know.'

At this moment the door was flung open, and a shrill voice
was heard singing:—.

'*To the Looking-Glass world it was Alice that said*[1]
"*I've a sceptre in hand I've a crown on my head.*
Let the Looking-Glass creatures, whatever they be
Come and dine with the Red Queen, the White Queen,
  and me!"'

And hundreds of voices joined in the chorus:—

'*Then fill up the glasses as quick as you can,*
  And sprinkle the table with buttons and bran:
  Put cats in the coffee, and mice in the tea—
  And welcome Queen Alice with thirty-times-three!'

Then followed a confused noise of cheering, and Alice
thought to herself 'Thirty times three makes ninety. I wonder
if any one's counting?' In a minute there was silence again,
and the same shrill voice sang another verse:—

'"*O Looking-Glass creatures,*' quoth Alice, "*draw near!*
  '*Tis an honour to see me, a favour to hear:*
  '*Tis a privilege high to have dinner and tea*
  Along with the Red Queen, the White Queen, and me!"'

Then came the chorus again:—

'*Then fill up the glasses with treacle and ink,*
  Or anything else that is pleasant to drink:
  Mix sand with the cider, and wool with the wine—
  And welcome Queen Alice with ninety-times-nine!'

'Ninety times nine!' Alice repeated in despair. 'Oh, that'll
never be done! I'd better go in at once——' and in she went,
and there was a dead silence the moment she appeared.

Alice glanced nervously along the table, as she walked up
the large hall, and noticed that there were about fifty guests,
of all kinds: some were animals, some birds, and there were
even a few flowers among them. 'I'm glad they've come without waiting to be asked,' she thought: 'I should never have
known who were the right people to invite!'

There were three chairs at the head of the table: the Red
and White Queens had already taken two of them, but the
middle one was empty. Alice sat down in it, rather uncomfortable at the silence, and longing for some one to
speak.

At last the Red Queen began. 'You've missed the soup and
fish,' she said. 'Put on the joint!' And the waiters set a leg of
mutton before Alice, who looked at it rather anxiously, as she
had never had to carve a joint before.

'You look a little shy:
let me introduce you to
that leg of mutton,' said
the Red Queen. 'Alice
——Mutton: Mutton——
Alice.' The leg of mutton
got up in the dish and
made a little bow to Alice;
and Alice returned the
bow, not knowing whether
to be frightened or amused.

'May I give you a slice?'
she said, taking up the
knife and fork, and looking
from one Queen to the
other.

'Certainly not,' the Red
Queen said, very deci-
dedly: 'it isn't etiquette to
cut any one you've been introduced to. Remove the joint!' And
the waiters carried it off, and brought a large plum-pudding in
its place.

'I wo'n't be introduced to the pudding, please,' Alice said
rather hastily, 'or we shall get no dinner at all. May I give
you some?'

But the Red Queen looked sulky, and growled 'Pudding
——Alice: Alice——Pudding. Remove the pudding!', and
the waiters took it away so quickly that Alice couldn't return
its bow.

However, she didn't see why the Red Queen should be the
only one to give orders; so, as an experiment, she called out
'Waiter! Bring back the pudding!', and there it was again in
a moment, like a conjuring-trick. It was so large that she
couldn't help feeling a *little* shy with it, as she had been with
the mutton: however, she conquered her shyness by a great
effort, and cut a slice and handed it to the Red Queen.

'What impertinence!' said the Pudding.[1] 'I wonder how
you'd like it, if I were to cut a slice out of *you*, you creature!'

It spoke in a thick, suety sort of voice, and Alice hadn't
a word to say in reply: she could only sit and look at it and
gasp.

'Make a remark,' said the Red Queen: 'it's ridiculous to
leave all the conversation to the pudding!'

'Do you know, I've had such a quantity of poetry repeated
to me to-day,' Alice began, a little frightened at finding
that, the moment she opened her lips, there was dead silence,
and all eyes were fixed upon her; 'and it's a very curious
thing, I think—every poem was about fishes in some way.
Do you know why they're so fond of fishes, all about
here?'

She spoke to the Red Queen, whose answer was a little wide
of the mark. 'As to fishes,' she said, very slowly and solemnly,
putting her mouth close to Alice's ear, 'her White Majesty
knows a lovely riddle—all in poetry—all about fishes. Shall
she repeat it?'

'Her Red Majesty's very kind to mention it,' the White
Queen murmured into Alice's other ear, in a voice like the
cooing of a pigeon. 'It would be *such* a treat! May I?'

'Please do,' Alice said very politely.

The White Queen laughed with delight, and stroked Alice's cheek. Then she began:

> '"*First, the fish must be caught.*"[1]
> *That is easy: a baby, I think, could have caught it.*
> "*Next, the fish must be bought.*"
> *That is easy: a penny, I think, would have bought it.*
>
> "*Now cook me the fish!*"
> *That is easy, and will not take more than a minute.*
> "*Let it lie in a dish!*"
> *That is easy, because it already is in it.*
>
> "*Bring it here! Let me sup!*"
> *It is easy to set such a dish on the table.*
> "*Take the dish-cover up!*"
> *Ah,* that *is so hard that I fear I'm unable!*
>
> *For it holds it like glue—*
> *Holds the lid to the dish, while it lies in the middle:*
> *Which is easiest to do,*
> *Un-dish-cover the fish, or dishcover the riddle?*'

'Take a minute to think about it, and then guess,' said the Red Queen. 'Meanwhile, we'll drink your health—Queen Alice's health!' she screamed at the top of her voice, and all the guests began drinking it directly, and very queerly they managed it: some of them put their glasses upon their heads like extinguishers,[2] and drank all that trickled down their faces—others upset the decanters, and drank the wine as it ran off the edges of the table—and three of them (who looked like kangaroos) scrambled into the dish of roast mutton, and began eagerly lapping up the gravy, 'just like pigs in a trough!' thought Alice.

'You ought to return thanks in a neat speech,' the Red Queen said, frowning at Alice as she spoke.

'We must support you, you know,' the White Queen

whispered, as Alice got up to do it, very obediently, but a little frightened.

'Thank you very much,' she whispered in reply, 'but I can do quite well without.'

'That wouldn't be at all the thing,' the Red Queen said very decidedly: so Alice tried to submit to it with a good grace.

('And they *did* push so!' she said afterwards, when she was telling her sister the history of the feast. 'You would have thought they wanted to squeeze me flat!')

In fact it was rather difficult for her to keep in her place while she made her speech: the two Queens pushed her so, one on each side, that they nearly lifted her up into the air. 'I rise to return thanks——' Alice began: and she really *did* rise as she spoke, several inches; but she got hold of the edge of the table, and managed to pull herself down again.

'Take care of yourself!' screamed the White Queen, seizing Alice's hair with both her hands. 'Something's going to happen!'

And then (as Alice afterwards described it) all sorts of things happened in a moment. The candles all grew up to the ceiling, looking something like a bed of rushes with fireworks at the top. As to the bottles, they each took a pair of plates, which they hastily fitted on as wings, and so, with forks for legs, went fluttering about in all directions: 'and very like birds they look,' Alice thought to herself, as well as she could in the dreadful confusion that was beginning.

At this moment she heard a hoarse laugh at her side, and turned to see what was the matter with the White Queen; but, instead of the Queen, there was the leg of mutton sitting in the chair. 'Here I am!' cried a voice from the soup-tureen,[1] and Alice turned again, just in time to see the Queen's broad good-natured face grinning at her for a moment over the edge of the tureen, before she disappeared into the soup.

There was not a moment to be lost. Already several of the guests were lying down in the dishes, and the soup-ladle was walking up the table towards Alice's chair, and beckoning to her impatiently to get out of its way.

'I ca'n't stand this any longer!' she cried, as she jumped up and seized the tablecloth with both hands: one good pull, and plates, dishes, guests, and candles came crashing down together in a heap on the floor.

'And as for *you*,' she went on, turning fiercely upon the Red Queen, whom she considered as the cause of all the

mischief—but the Queen was no longer at her side—she had suddenly dwindled down to the size of a little doll, and was now on the table, merrily running round and round after her own shawl, which was trailing behind her.

At any other time, Alice would have felt surprised at this, but she was far too much excited to be surprised at anything *now*. 'As for *you*,' she repeated, catching hold of the little creature in the very act of jumping over a bottle which had just lighted upon the table, 'I'll shake you into a kitten,[1] that I will!'

CHAPTER X

SHAKING

SHE took her off the table as she spoke, and shook her backwards and forwards with all her might.

The Red Queen made no resistance whatever: only her face grew very small, and her eyes got large and green: and still, as Alice went on shaking her, she kept on growing shorter—and fatter—and softer—and rounder—and——

CHAPTER XI

WAKING

——and it really *was* a kitten, after all.

CHAPTER XII

'YOUR Red Majesty shouldn't purr so loud,' Alice said, rubbing her eyes, and addressing the kitten, respectfully, yet with some severity. 'You woke me out of oh! such a nice dream! And you've been along with me, Kitty—all through the Looking-Glass world. Did you know it, dear?'

It is a very inconvenient habit of kittens (Alice had once made the remark) that, whatever you say to them, they *always* purr. 'If they would only purr for "yes," and mew for "no," or any rule of that sort,' she had said, 'so that one could keep up a conversation! But how *can* you talk with a person if they *always* say the same thing?'

On this occasion the kitten only purred: and it was impossible to guess whether it meant "yes" or "no."

So Alice hunted among the chessmen on the table till she had found the Red Queen: then she went down on her knees on the hearth-rug, and put the kitten and the Queen to look at each other. 'Now, Kitty!' she cried, clapping her hands triumphantly. 'Confess that was what you turned into!'

('But it wouldn't look at it,' she said, when she was explaining the thing afterwards to her sister: 'it turned away its head, and pretended not to see it: but it looked a *little* ashamed of itself, so I think it *must* have been the Red Queen.')

'Sit up a little more stiffly, dear!' Alice cried with a merry laugh. 'And curtsey while you're thinking what to—what to purr. It saves time, remember!' And she caught it up and gave it one little kiss, 'just in honour of its having been a Red Queen.'

'Snowdrop, my pet!' she went on, looking over her shoulder at the White Kitten, which was still patiently undergoing its

toilet, 'when *will* Dinah have finished with your White Majesty, I wonder? That must be the reason you were so untidy in my dream.——Dinah! Do you know that you're scrubbing a White Queen? Really, it's most disrespectful of you!

'And what did *Dinah* turn to, I wonder?' she prattled on, as she settled comfortably down, with one elbow on the rug, and her chin in her hand, to watch the kittens. 'Tell me, Dinah, did you turn to Humpty Dumpty? I *think* you did— however, you'd better not mention it to your friends just yet, for I'm not sure.

'By the way, Kitty, if only you'd been really with me in my dream, there was one thing you *would* have enjoyed——I had such a quantity of poetry said to me, all about fishes! To-morrow morning you shall have a real treat. All the time you're eating your breakfast, I'll repeat "The Walrus and the Carpenter" to you; and then you can make believe it's oysters, dear!

'Now, Kitty, let's consider who it was that dreamed it all
This is a serious question, my dear, and you should *not* go on
licking your paw like that—as if Dinah hadn't washed you
this morning! You see, Kitty, it *must* have been either me or
the Red King. He was part of my dream, of course—but then
I was part of his dream, too! *Was* it the Red King, Kitty?
You were his wife, my dear, so you ought to know——
Oh, Kitty, *do* help to settle it! I'm sure your paw can wait!'
But the provoking kitten only began on the other paw, and
pretended it hadn't heard the question.

Which do *you* think it was?

A BOAT, beneath a sunny sky[1]
Lingering onward dreamily
In an evening of July—

Children three that nestle near,
Eager eye and willing ear,
Pleased a simple tale to hear—

Long has paled that sunny sky:
Echoes fade and memories die:
Autumn frosts have slain July.

Still she haunts me, phantomwise,
Alice moving under skies
Never seen by waking eyes.

Children yet, the tale to hear,
Eager eye and willing ear,
Lovingly shall nestle near.

In a Wonderland they lie,
Dreaming as the days go by,
Dreaming as the summers die:

Ever drifting down the stream—
Lingering in the golden gleam—
Life, what is it but a dream?

THE END

CHRISTMAS-GREETINGS[1]

[FROM A FAIRY TO A CHILD]

LADY dear, if Fairies may
    For a moment lay aside
Cunning tricks and elfish play,
    'Tis at happy Christmas-tide.

We have heard the children say—
    Gentle children, whom we love—
Long ago, on Christmas Day,
    Came a message from above.

Still, as Christmas-tide comes round,
    They remember it again—
Echo still the joyful sound
    'Peace on earth, good-will to men!'

Yet the hearts must childlike be
    Where such heavenly guests abide;
Unto children, in their glee,
    All the year is Christmas-tide!

Thus, forgetting tricks and play
    For a moment, Lady dear,
We would wish you, if we may,
    Merry Christmas, glad New Year!

Christmas, 1867.

TO ALL CHILD-READERS OF
'ALICE'S ADVENTURES IN WONDERLAND'[1]

DEAR CHILDREN,

At Christmas-time a few grave words are not quite out of place, I hope, even at the end of a book of nonsense—and I want to take this oportunity of thanking the thousands of children who have read 'Alice's Adventures in Wonderland,' for the kindly interest they have taken in my little dream-child.

The thought of the many English firesides where happy faces have smiled her a welcome, and of the many English children to whom she has brought an hour of (I trust) innocent amusement, is one of the brightest and pleasantest thoughts of my life. I have a host of young friends already, whose names and faces I know—but I cannot help feeling as if, through 'Alice's Adventures' I had made friends with many many other dear children, whose faces I shall never see.

To all my little friends, known and unknown, I wish with all my heart, 'A Merry Christmas and a Happy New Year.' May God bless you, dear children, and make each Christmas-tide, as it comes round to you, more bright and beautiful than the last—bright with the presence of that unseen Friend, who once on earth blessed little children—and beautiful with memories of a loving life, which has sought and found that truest kind of happiness, the only kind that is really worth the having, the happiness of making others happy too!

Your affectionate Friend,

LEWIS CARROLL

Christmas, 1871

AN EASTER GREETING
TO EVERY CHILD WHO LOVES
'*ALICE*'[1]

Dear Child,

Please to fancy, if you can, that you are reading a real letter, from a real friend whom you have seen, and whose voice you can seem to yourself to hear wishing you, as I do now with all my heart, a happy Easter.

Do you know that delicious dreamy feeling when one first wakes on a summer morning, with the twitter of birds in the air, and the fresh breeze coming in at the open window——when, lying lazily with eyes half shut, one sees as in a dream green boughs waving, or waters rippling in a golden light? It is a pleasure very near to sadness, bringing tears to one's eyes like a beautiful picture or poem. And is not that a Mother's gentle hand that undraws your curtains, and a Mother's sweet voice that summons you to rise? To rise and forget, in the bright sunlight, the ugly dreams that frightened you so when all was dark——to rise and enjoy another happy day, first kneeling to thank that unseen Friend, who sends you the beautiful sun?

Are these strange words from a writer of such tales as 'Alice'? And is this a strange letter to find in a book of nonsense? It may be so. Some perhaps may blame me for thus mixing together things grave and gay; others may smile and think it odd that any one should speak of solemn things at all, except in church and on a Sunday: but I think—nay, I am sure—that some children will read this gently and lovingly, and in the spirit in which I have written it.

For I do not believe God means us thus to divide life into two halves——to wear a grave face on Sunday, and to think it out-of-place to even so much as mention Him on a week-day. Do you think He cares to see only kneeling figures, and to hear only tones of prayer——and that He does not also love to see the lambs leaping in the sunlight, and to hear the merry voices of the children, as they roll among the hay? Surely their innocent laughter is as sweet in His ears as the grandest anthem that ever rolled up from the 'dim religious light' of some solemn cathedral?

And if I have written anything to add to those stores of innocent and healthy amusement that are laid up in books for the children I love so well, it is surely something I may hope to look back upon without shame and sorrow (as how much of life must then be recalled!) when my turn comes to walk through the valley of shadows.

This Easter sun will rise on you, dear child, feeling your 'life in every limb,' and eager to rush out into the fresh morning air ——and many an Easter-day will come and go, before it finds you feeble and gray-headed, creeping wearily out to bask once more in the sunlight——but it is good, even now, to think sometimes of that great morning when the 'Sun of Righteousness shall arise with healing in his wings.'

Surely your gladness need not be the less for the thought that you will one day see a brighter dawn than this——when lovelier sights will meet your eyes than any waving trees or rippling waters—— when angel-hands shall undraw your curtains, and sweeter tones than ever loving Mother breathed shall wake you to a new and glorious day——and when all the sadness, and the sin, that darkened life on this little earth, shall be forgotten like the dreams of a night that is past!

Your affectionate friend,

LEWIS CARROLL

Easter, 1876

TEXTUAL NOTES

66, *97*, the editions of 1866 and 1897. A few variants appear in other editions: *65* is the 1865 edition printed at Oxford but withdrawn before publication. Other editions under dates: where two appeared in one year a superior figure is employed for the second—e.g. *67*, *67²*. The various editions and impressions are differentiated on the title-pages by the appropriate number of thousands, as follows:

1867: Fifth Thousand   *1867²*: Tenth Thousand
1870: Twenty-first Thousand *1870²*: Twenty-fifth Thousand
1886: Seventy-ninth Thousand
1897: Eighty-sixth Thousand

In *Through the Looking-Glass* the only alterations from the first (*1872*) edition are the corrections of three misprints, made in the first reprint, until the revised edition of *1897* (*97* in the following notes) which is the Sixty-first Thousand.

Page	Line	
16	19	*et passim* sh'a'nt] shan't 66
17	28	*et passim* Wo'n't] won't 66
18	2	*was*] was 66
18	11	*et passim* ca'n't] can't 66
19	5	doesn't 67² 97: don't 66
22	15	its tail] his tail 66
24	10	I'm] I am 66
26	21	stood] sat 66
26	24	*all*] all 66
33	20	*you*] you 66
41	29	and the] and as (*deleted*) the 66
47	11	*them*] them 66
47	23	but] and 66
52	9	for 67² 97: of 66
53	5	*air*] air 66
53	8	*not*] not 66
55	7	the Duchess said 67 97: said the Duchess 66
56	24	made 66 97: been 65
56	35	felt that it 67 97: felt it 66
57	5	go 67 97: walk 66
57	12	go 67 97: walk 66
62	32	upon] on to 66: on 67

Page	Line	
70	31	AND THE QUEEN] AND QUEEN 66
72	5	backs] back 67
72	6	the pack] their pack 70
81	14	otherwise than] otherwise that 66
81	26	people] they 66
93	27-30	*When . . . sound*] *added in* 86 97
93	35	down 86 97: down again 66
94	12	repeated 86 97: repeated impatiently 66
94	17-23	*How . . . by—*' 86 97: 66 *has only* How the owl and the oyster were sharing a pie—'
94	31	another] a 66
95	2	voice 86 97: voice sometimes 66
98	24	said] *added* 66
100	2	hadn't begun 67 97: hadn't but just begun 66
100	7	*begins*] begins 66
106	2	prove that I] prove I 66
106	8-10	'That . . . Alice.] 66 *has*: 'That *proves* his guilt,' said the Queen. 'It proves nothing of the sort!' said Alice.
106	15	said very gravely] said gravely 66
106	17-18	There . . . verses:—] These were the verses the White Rabbit read:—66
107	30-2	'*If she should . . . indeed!*] *added in* 97
108	7	*fits*] fits 66
109	5	*you*] you 66
110	3	upon 67 97: on 66
110	18	about little Alice herself:] of little Alice herself, and 66
127	16	*that*] that 72
134	14	*wabe* 72 (*second impression*), 97: wade 72
141	1-2	'They're done . . . like yours.'] 72 *has*: 'Her petals are done up close, almost like a dahlia' the Tiger-lily interrupted: 'not tumbled about anyhow, like yours.'
141	9	kind that has nine spikes, you know] thorny kind 72
141	10	them] the thorns 72
148	26	*was*] was 72
148	26	*did*] did 72
148	29	*do*] do 72
149	23	*this*] this 72
152	12	*all*] all 72
156	36	*here*] here 72
159	8	going] looking 72
169	15	*isn't*] isn't 72
169	16	*new*] new 72

Page	*Line*	
171	21	*you*] you *72*
174	10	*you*] you *72*
174	18	jam *to-day*] jam to-day *72*
177	1	*now*] now *72*
185	14	stuffed figure, after all] stuffed figure after all *72*: stuffed figure *80*
202	34	into sight] in sight *72*
225	34	*is*] is *72*
226	13	*that*] that *72*

EXPLANATORY NOTES

ABBREVIATIONS

A.A.   *The Annotated Alice.* Edited by Martin Gardner. *New York*, 1960.

A.A.U.   *Alice's Adventures Underground.* By Lewis Carroll, 1886. [Facsimile of story written for Alice Liddell 1862-3.]

Hamlyn   *The Works of Lewis Carroll.* Edited and Introduced by Roger Lancelyn Green. Paul Hamlyn Ltd., 1965.

Collingwood S. Dodgson Collingwood, *The Life and Letters of Lewis Carroll*, 1898.

M-M   *Misch-Masch* (family magazine and scrapbook prepared by Dodgson 1853-62). First published in its entirety 1932.

J.O.H.   *Popular Rhymes and Nursery Tales of England*, collected by James Orchard Halliwell [later Halliwell-Phillips], 1849 etc. Edn. of *c.* 1860.

O.E.D.   *Oxford English Dictionary.*

Page 3. *Prima*: Lorina Charlotte Liddell (11 May 1849-29 October 1930); *Secunda*: Alice Pleasance Liddell (4 May 1852-15 November 1934); *Tertia*: Edith Mary Liddell (23 January 1854-26 June 1876).

Page 5. (1) *on the Stage*: *Alice in Wonderland. A Dream Play for Children, in two Acts . . . By H. Savile Clarke. Music by Walter Slaughter. 1886.* Opened at the Prince of Wales Theatre, London, on 23 December 1886.
    (2) *Oyster*: See *infra*, notes to pp. 73-4, for original version of this song.

Page 6. *the Nursery 'Alice'*: *The Nursery Alice . . . With Text adapted to Nursery Readers by Lewis Carroll, 1889.*

Page 10. *Orange Marmalade*: M. A. Liddell wrote (*Observer*, 9 February 1958): 'According to the story in my family, the original recipe for Cooper's Oxford Marmalade was given to Mrs. Cooper by my grandmother, the wife of Dean Liddell. . . . If, as suggested, the recipe must have come from Scotland, presumably my grandmother obtained the recipe from the Dean's mother, who was a Miss Lyon, a member of the family that subsequently became the Bowes-Lyons.'

Page 11. (1) *Dinah*: the tabby cat which the Liddell children owned at the

time, and Alice's especial pet; named from the popular music-hall song
'Villikins and his Dinah'.

(2) *Do cats eat bats?*: probably suggested by the children's classic *Th
Gold Thread* (1861) by Norman MacLeod, p. 40:

> And I waken up the bat,
> Who flies off with a scream,
> For he thinks that I'm the cat
> Pouncing on him in his dream.

Page 12. *a tiny golden key*: may have been suggested by his friend George
MacDonald's poem 'The Golden Key', published in *Victoria Regis*, 1861.
MacDonald's famous allegorical fairy story of the same name was not
published until 1867 (*Dealings with the Fairies*), but his tales circulated in
manuscript for years before publication, and Dodgson may well have
read it by 1862.

Page 13. (1) *how she longed . . . bright flowers*: dedicated Freudians seriously
identify this as referring to Dodgson sitting in the sub-librarian's room
off the great Library at Christ Church, looking out into the Deanery
garden, and lusting after Alice Liddell year after year as she grew from
fascinating child into lovely maiden. But Dodgson was sub-Librarian for
only a year and a half, ending in January 1857 when Alice was under five
years old. He had no *entrée* to that room thereafter.

(2) *several nice little stories*: such as the various volumes of *Cautionary
Tales* by Elizabeth Turner (d. 1846), frequently reprinted until the end
of the century. They were later parodied by Hilaire Belloc.

Page 18. *Ada . . . Mabel*: Dodgson doubtless made sure these could not
be identified. But in the original story written out for Alice Liddell they
appear as Gertrude and Florence—both names of cousins of the Liddell
children.

Page 19. (1) *I shall never get to twenty at that rate*: Martin Gardner, himself a mathematician, explains in *The Annotated Alice* (N.Y., 1960), p. 38,
that 'the multiplication table traditionally stops with the twelves, so if
you continue this nonsense progression . . . you end with 4 times 12 (the
highest she can go) is 19—just one short of twenty.'

(2) *How doth the little crocodile . . .*: a parody of the first two stanzas of
'Against Idleness and Mischief' by Isaac Watts (1674–1748), from his
Divine Songs Attempted in Easy Language for the Use of Children (1715)
—a poem which the Liddells, like most other children of their class at
that time, were expected to be able to 'stand up and recite':

> How doth the little busy Bee
> Improve each shining Hour,
> And gather Honey all the Day
> From ev'ry op'ning Flow'r!

How skilfully she builds her Cell!
How neat she spreads the Wax;
And labours hard to store it well
With the sweet Food she makes.

Page 20. (1) *Alice had been to the seaside once in her life*: if this has any definite reference to Alice Liddell, it refers to her visit to Llandudno in the summer of 1861. Dean Liddell purchased the old Gogarth Abbey site a little distance from the town, on the west side of the Great Orme's Head, this year, and the house 'Penmorfa' (nucleus of the present Gogarth Abbey Hotel) was built there for him. The Liddells first occupied 'Penmorfa' in 1865: in spite of a legend to the contrary, Dodgson never visited them there nor stayed with them. If he paid any visit to Llandudno while the Liddells were there, it must have been in 1861—but there is no evidence even for this.

(2) *bathing-machines*: changing rooms on wheels, resembling the old-style gipsy caravan. These were drawn by horses down to just below the high-tide line, and the bathers who had changed in them could enter the sea directly down steps at the back. Many were fitted with awnings over these steps both to offer further privacy and to prevent exposure to the sun: both fashion and medical theory were against sunburn for women until well after the end of the Victorian period.

Page 21. (1) *her brother*: Edward Henry Liddell (1847–1911), 'Harry'. Dodgson tutored him, not very successfully, for a while in 1856. Harry was a 'child-friend' until he went to boarding-school.

(2) *Latin Grammar*: probably that by Benjamin Hall Kennedy first published in 1843 and frequently revised: best known as *The Public School Latin Primer* (1866; anon.) and *The Public School Latin Grammar* (1871; anon.), both developed from the original anonymous volume.

(3) *The first sentence in her French lesson-book*: the first sentence from the first lesson in *La Bagatelle: Intended to introduce children of three or four years old to some knowledge of the French Language*, 1804. There were many reprints at least up to 1856 and 1861. (Hugh O'Brien in the *Irish Times*, 5 April 1963, and again in *Notes and Queries* (ccviii), December 1963, 461, finds other echoes from this book in the early chapters of *Alice* —but they are very tenuous.)

Page 23. (1) *I hate cats and dogs*: probably suggested by the rain on the picnic of 17 June. Someone would have said: 'It's raining cats and dogs.'

(2) *a Duck*: the Revd. Robinson Duckworth (1834–1911), Fellow of Trinity College, Oxford, and later Canon of Westminster. He was on both picnics (17 June and 4 July). Dodgson inscribed a copy of the facsimile of *Alice's Adventures Underground* (1886): 'The Duck from the Dodo.' *a Dodo*: Dodgson himself ('Do-do-Dodgson' when he stammered). *a Lory*: 'a parrot-like bird of the family Loriinae'—here representing

T

256 EXPLANATORY NOTES

Lorina Liddell. *an Eaglet*: a sound-equivalent for Edith Liddell. *several other curious creatures*: originally Dodgson's aunt, Lucy Lutwidge (1805–80) and his sisters Frances (1828–1903), and Elizabeth (1830–1916).

Page 24. the Mouse: although there is no indication that she was on the picnic, this character 'who seemed to be a person of some authority among them' must be based on the Liddells' governess, Miss Prickett, since the Mouse gives the history lesson from the actual book which Miss Prickett was using with the children.

Page 25. 'William the Conqueror. . . . the insolence of his Normans': accurate quotation from Havilland Chepmell's *A Short Course of History*, 1862, pp. 143–4.

Page 26. (1) *Caucus-race*: a Caucus is a committee called to decide general action of the group or party—but here it seems to be used simply as a Nonsense name, though Martin Gardner suggests (*A.A.*, p. 48) that 'committee members generally do a lot of running around in circles, getting nowhere, and with everybody wanting a political plum'. It was substituted as a method for getting dry after the Pool of Tears for the fire in the little cottage in *A.A.U.* by which the party actually dried themselves after the picnic on 17 June.

(2) *all must have prizes*: J. Barrett Davies has suggested (*T.L.S.*, 26 January 1965) that Dodgson had in mind *Aeneid* v. 305 et seq: 'Nemo ex hoc numero mihi non donatus abibit . . . Omnibus hic erit unos honos' —'None out of this number will I let go without a gift . . . one and all shall be honoured thus' [J. W. Mackail's translation].

Page 31. Mary Ann: almost as common an equivalent for 'servant-girl' in the nineteenth century as Abigail had been in the eighteenth.

Page 37. a crowd of little animals: these are particularized in *A.A.U.*— 'guinea-pigs, white-mice, squirrels, and "Bill", a little green lizard', so were probably suggested by the Liddell children's pets.

Page 42. Repeat 'You are old, Father William': a parody of another didactic poem which Victorian children were expected to learn and recite on demand. The original is 'The Old Man's Comforts' by Robert Southey, first published in *The Annual Anthology*, i (1799). The first two of eight stanzas run:

> You are old, Father William, the young man cried,
>   The few locks that are left you are grey,
> You are hale, Father William, a hearty old man,
>   Now tell me the reason, I pray.
>
> In the days of my youth, Father William replied,
>   I remember'd that youth would fly fast,
> And abused not my health and my vigour at first,
>   That I never might need them at last.

Page 43. *one shilling the box*: in *A.A.U.* it cost five shillings.

Page 49. *As she said this*: in *A.A.U.* this continues as after the same words on page 68 when she finds the door in the tree. All the intervening material was added from other stories when Dodgson was rewriting for publication.

Page 53. *It's a Cheshire-Cat*: between 1850 and 1852 there was a correspondence in *Notes and Queries* on the origin of the phrase 'to grin like a Cheshire Cat'. Various reasons were suggested: (1) because Cheshire was a County Palatine (ii. 377); (2) because Cheshire cheese was made in the shape of a cat (ii. 412); (3) because the sign-painters tried to paint snarling leopards (as on the Royal Arms) and only succeeded in producing grinning Cats (v. 402). It is worth noting that the Liddell coat of arms sported three leopards' heads. (The last of these explanations is the most likely, and in proof may be produced the carved head in the crypt under the tower at Brimstage, Wirral, which is obviously intended for a snarling lion or leopard, but is so like a grinning cat that the local inn (pulled down about 1910) was called 'The Red Cat' and bore a suitable sign.) Dodgson subscribed to *Notes and Queries* from its inception until his death: his well-marked set is now owned by Iona and Peter Opie.

Page 54. *Speak roughly to your little boy*: parody of 'Speak Gently' by David Bates. Published anonymously in *Sharpe's Magazine* (London), v. 256, February 1848 (perhaps reprinted from some American periodical) and included by Bates in his volume of verse *The Eolian* (Philadelphia, 1849), pp. 15–16. The relevant stanza (the third out of nine—there are only eight in *The Eolian*) runs:

> Speak gently to the little child!
>   Its love be sure to gain;
> Teach it in accents soft and mild—
>   It may not long remain.

Page 56. *it was neither more nor less than a pig*: C. W. Scott-Giles, O.B.E., Fitzalan Pursuivant of Arms Extraordinary, suggested (at first frivolously, in *Punch*, 15 August 1928, but later more seriously in *The Times* and finally in the *Sunday Times*, 25 July 1965) that Dodgson took several ideas from history (doubtless derived from what the Liddell children were learning at the time) as background for incidents and even characters. 'An answer to the question "Where was Alice's Duke?" ', he wrote, 'can be found if we consider the identity of the baby. A duke's son who turned into a pig—who can this be but Richard of Gloucester who came to the throne as Richard III, took the white boar as his badge, and was called "the hog" in political lampoons? When he was born, in October 1452, his father, Richard Duke of York, was living in retirement following an unsuccessful first attempt to oust Somerset from the royal counsels. In view of the antagonism between York and Queen Margaret, it is not

surprising that the Duke should have been omitted from the royal invitation to play croquet. Margaret's determination to maintain the Lancastrian
supremacy, and to exclude York from power, is reflected in *Alice* by the
Queen's insistence on red roses in the royal garden, and the gardeners'
painting with Lancastrian red the intruding white roses of York.'

Page 57. a Hatter . . . a March Hare . . . they're both mad: the phrases 'as
mad as a Hatter', 'as mad as a March hare' were both current by the
mid-Victorian period. There had been a correspondence in *Notes and
Queries* on the madness of hatters (was 'hatter' a corruption of 'adder',
or were hatters, in fact, prone to madness due to the mercury used in
curing felt). Hares caper and run round in circles in March, which is
their mating season. C. W. Scott-Giles suggests that Dodgson also had
in mind Mortimer, Earl of March from whom Richard Duke of York
claimed the throne in 1460 (see previous note).

Page 58. You're mad. . . . You must be . . . or you wouldn't have come here:
perhaps an echo of *Macbeth*, I. v. 33: 'The king comes here tonight.'
'Thou'rt mad to say it.'

Page 59. (1) a grin without a cat: the correspondence in *Notes and Queries*
faded out, leaving the grin unexplained.

(2) *the Hatter*: is said to have been suggested by Theophilus Carter,
at one time a servitor at Christ Church and later a furniture dealer with
a shop in the High at Oxford. He was the inventor of 'the Alarm Clock
Bed' (exhibited at the Great Exhibition in 1851) which tipped its occu-
pant out at the correct time—or, more frequently, the incorrect time when
it went wrong, or was tampered with by practical jokers. Carter was
known in Oxford as the Mad Hatter; he bore a singular resemblance to
Gladstone, and tried to heighten it by dressing like the Prime Minister
and standing at the door of his shop, wearing a top hat. Tenniel is supposed
to have come to Oxford on purpose to sketch him for the book (see letters
in *The Times*, 13, 19, 20 March 1931).

Dodgson's nephew, S. D. Collingwood, says (*Life and Letters of Lewis
Carroll*, 1898, p. 47) that the dining-hall was still divided into 'messes'
in 1851, and in Dodgson's mess was 'among others, one who still lives in
Alice in Wonderland as the "Hatter"'. Carter is not in *Alumni Oxonienses*,
but may simply have waited on the mess.

Page 60. Why is a raven like a writing-desk?: see Dodgson's Preface to
the 1897 edition (*supra*, p. 6) for a suggested answer. An answer current
among children before Dodgson published his, was 'because neither
can climb a tree'. An answer given in the American *Cyclopaedia of Puzzles*
(1914), p. 114, is 'because Poe wrote on both'. Many other solutions have
been proposed.

Page 62. (1) *What day of the month is it?*: the month was May (see p. 58) and the date, given by Alice, was the 4th. This was Alice Liddell's birthday, and suggests that Dodgson originally told the separate story of the Mad Tea-Party at her birthday party. The fact that the Battle of Tewkesbury took place on 4 May (1471), which Scott-Giles uses to strengthen his theory, seems to be only coincidence—but may have suggested the idea of a link with the Wars of the Roses.

As Alice was probably seven in *Wonderland* (she was seven and a half in *Through the Looking-Glass*; see p. 177) the birthday of Alice Liddell on which the story was told should have been 1859; but all events that can be dated are in 1862. Unfortunately Dodgson's *Diary* for both dates (1859 and 1862) are missing.

(2) *Two days wrong*: 'it would be possible to measure time by the phases of the moon, and this is the principle of the Mad Hatter's watch . . . on that day, 4 May 1862, there were exactly two days' difference between the two ways of reckoning the date. As the amount varies with every month and year, there can be no doubt that Dodgson consulted an almanac and based his calculations upon it' (Alexander L. Taylor, *The White Knight: a Study of C. L. Dodgson*, 1952, p. 57).

Page 63. *Twinkle, twinkle, little bat!*: parody of Jane Taylor's poem 'The Star' in *Rhymes for the Nursery* (1806) of which the first stanza runs:

> Twinkle, twinkle, little star!
> How I wonder what you are.
> Up above the world so high,
> Like a diamond in the sky.

The 'Bat' was substituted out of compliment to Professor Bartholomew Price, Dodgson's tutor and friend, whose nickname it was. (Oral information from the late Miss Price, his daughter.)

Page 64. (1) *murdering the time*: playing badly out of time.

(2) *it's always tea-time*: according to Alice Liddell, it was always tea-time when she and her sisters visited Dodgson in his rooms—they had tea at 8.30 after the wet picnic on 17 June. (See 'Alice's Recollection of Carrollian Days, told to her son, Caryl Hargreaves', *Cornhill Magazine*, July 1932.) But 6 p.m. was the children's usual tea-time—the time of the permanent Mad Tea-Party.

Page 65. *Elsie, Lacie, and Tillie*: these were the three Liddell girls—Elsie a 'sound' equivalent of 'L. C.'—Lorina's initials; Lacie an anagram of Alice; and Tillie short for Matilda which was Edith's nickname.

Page 66. *It was a treacle-well*: medicinal springs in Oxfordshire were known as 'treacle-wells'. There is one at Binsey, near Oxford.

Page 67. *put the Dormouse into the teapot*: Victorian children were accustomed to keep dormice as pets. A favourite artificial nest in which a tame dormouse might hibernate was an old tea-pot filled with moss or dried grass. Miss Marghanita Laski quotes Charlotte M. Yonge, *John Keble's Parish*, 1898, pp. 191–2: 'the smooth round dormouse (or sleep-mouse, as the children call it) is a favourite gift imprisoned in an old teapot' (*T.L.S.*, 6 May 1965).

Page 68. Just as she said this . . .: here Dodgson returns to the original *A.A.U.* (see *supra*, note to p. 49).

Page 69. painting them red: (see *supra*, note to p. 56).

Page 70. (1) *this grand procession*: the introduction of the pack of playing cards into the story was probably due to the game of *Court Circular* which Dodgson invented for the Liddell children and had printed in January 1860, and in a revised form in April 1862. Both are reprinted in *Hamlyn*, pp. 1009–12.

Page 72. Off with her head!: the best known line from *Richard III* throughout the nineteenth century was: 'Off with his head! So much for Buckingham!'—the first part of the line from Shakespeare (III. iv. 74), the second from Colley Cibber's eighteenth-century adaptation, which was still normally used, e.g. by Sir Henry Irving. Hugh O'Brien (*Irish Times*, 26 February 1965) suggests that Dodgson is continuing with history books, here trying to soften the executions in the reign of Queen Elizabeth, notably that of Mary Queen of Scots, as rather frighteningly described in Mrs. Markham's famous *History of England* (1823). But he can produce only the fact that in *A.A.U.* the Queen of Hearts is also 'Marchioness of Mock Turtles' which he says is a parody of the name 'Mrs. Markham'. The Liddells are very likely to have used 'Mrs. Markham' as well as Havilland Chepmell, and would certainly have found the reference to Richard III 'who was called the hog because his badge was a white boar' (edn. of 1866, p. 204)—but there seem to be no specific references.

Page 73. (1) *a curious croquet-ground*: croquet was a favourite game with the Liddell children, and Dodgson played it often with Alice and her sisters in the Deanery garden. He invented for them a new version of the game, *Croquet Castles*, which he had printed privately at Oxford on 4 May 1863 (see *The Lewis Carroll Picture Book*, 1899, p. 271). (*Croquet Castles* is reprinted in *Hamlyn*.)

(2) *live flamingoes*: they were ostriches in *A.A.U.* (Ostriches bury their heads in the sand—as a child often does the head of a croquet mallet in the turf.)

Page 74. about once a minute: the section from here to p. 82 line 16 did not appear in *A.A.U.*

Page 76. A cat may look at a king: sixteenth-century proverb (M. P. Tilley, *A Dictionary of the Proverbs in England*, 1950, no. C141). In *J.O.H.* (see *infra*, note to p. 160), pp. 271–2, citing MS. dated 1652.

Page 79. *camomile*: a bitter medicine given to children of the Victorian period as a cure for bilious attacks, etc. Cf. Beatrix Potter, *Peter Rabbit* (1902), p. 56: 'Peter was not very well during the evening. His mother put him to bed, and made some camomile tea; and she gave a dose of it to Peter! "One table-spoonful to be taken at bed-time".'

Page 80. (1) *Oh, 'tis love, 'tis love, that makes the world go round*: ultimately derived from the last line of Dante's *'l'amor che muove il sole e l'attre stelle'* (*Paradiso*, xxxiii. 145), but here from a song, 'The Dawn of Love', anon., Birmingham, *c.* 1820, later adapted in a popular version—of which this is the first line.

(2) . . . *everybody minding their own business*: perhaps an echo of 'everybody's business is nobody's business'—Walton, *Compleat Angler*, 1653, Part I, ch. 2.

(3) *Take care of the sense and the sounds will take care of themselves*: parody of 'Take care of the pence and the pounds will take care of themselves', a proverb, already common in the seventeenth century, cf. Ray, *Collection of English Proverbs*, 1678, p. 188: 'That *penny* is well spent that saves a groat', and 'Who will not keep a *penny* shall never have many'.

(4) *Birds of a feather flock together*: Ray (op. cit., p. 101) gives this exact proverb, with examples of many similar ones from Homer onwards.

Page 81. (1) *Be what you would seem to be*: perhaps an echo of *A Midsummer Night's Dream*, IV. i. 72, 'Be as thou wast wont to be'.

(2) *as pigs have to fly*: perhaps thinking of the nursery rhyme beginning: 'Dickory, Dickory dare! The pig flew up in the air!'

Page 82. *Mock Turtle Soup*: 'calf's head dressed with sauces and condiments so as to resemble a turtle', current by 1763, and hence a soup made (usually from calf's head) to resemble turtle soup (1783). The appearance of the Mock Turtle, with calf's head and feet but a turtle's shell, was suggested to Tenniel by Canon Duckworth (F. R. G. Duckworth in the *Sunday Times*, 11 May 1952.)

Page 83. *a Gryphon*: this classical monster (the crest of Trinity College of which Duckworth was a Fellow) may have got into the story by way of the collections of crests which the children were making. (On 1 August 1862 Dodgson records in his *Diary* that he went to the Deanery to arrange for another river trip 'and remained a short time, for me to write the names in the books for crests etc. which I have given to Alice and Edith, and to hear them play their trio and sing "Beautiful Star"'.) Besides gryphons, and the lion and unicorn in the Royal Coat of Arms, the books would have included the Liddell family coat, which sported three leopard heads, full-face and snarling—suggesting the Cheshire Cat.

Page 86. (1) *Reeling and Writhing*: these, and the other lessons, are all puns on the usual educational subjects—Reading, Writing, Addition, Subtraction, Multiplication, Division, History, Geography, Drawing,

Sketching, Painting in Oils, Latin, Greek—most of them adapted to the aquatic setting.

(2) *the Drawling-master*: some private joke must have been intended. The Liddell children were taught drawing by John Ruskin, who came once a week, at about this time.

Page 88. Quadrille: the most difficult of the fashionable dances of the time—as the Liddells, who had private dancing lessons, would have discovered. The Lobster-Quadrille is a parody of this—and may have been suggested by the parody of the Nigger Minstrel Song 'Sally Come Up' (words by T. Ramsey, music by E. W. Mackney) which was a favourite of the Liddells. (On 3 July 1862 Dodgson lunched at the Deanery, and recorded that 'the three sang "Sally Come Up" with great spirit'. Dodgson parodied this in *A.A.U.* as follows:

> Beneath the waters *of* the sea
> Are lobsters thick as thick can be—
> They love to dance with you and me,
>   My own, my gentle Salmon!
> Salmon come up! Salmon go down!
> Salmon come twist your tail around!
> Of all the fishes *of* the sea
>   There's none so good as Salmon!)

Page 90. 'Will you walk a little faster?': the song which Dodgson substituted for the 'Sally Come Up' parody is itself a parody, but of the well-known nursery poem ' "Will you walk into my parlour?" said the spider to the fly', by Mary Howitt, published in her *Sketches of Natural History*, 1834, p. 131.

Page 91. their tails in their mouths . . .: whitings were always fried with their tails through their eyes and covered in breadcrumbs. 'When I wrote that,' Dodgson told Miss M. E. Manners in 1889, 'I believed that whiting really did have their tails in their mouths, but I have since been told that fishmongers put the tail through the eye.' (*Collingwood*, p. 402.)

Page 93. 'Tis the voice of the Lobster . . .: parody of 'The Sluggard' by Isaac Watts (*Divine Songs for Children*, 1715; edn. of 1727, pp. 44–5). The first stanza runs:

> 'Tis the Voice of the *Sluggard*; I hear him complain
> *You have wak'd me too soon, I must slumber again.*
> As the Door on its Hinges, so he on his Bed,
> Turns his Sides and his Shoulders, and his heavy Head.

Until the 1886 edition of *Alice* only the first 4 lines of the first stanza appeared. The next 4 lines of this stanza, and the last 6 lines of the second stanza were added for Savile Clarke's play and then incorporated in the book. (See *supra*, p. 5.)

Page 94. (1) *I passed by his garden*: the third stanza of 'The Sluggard' begins:

> I past by his Garden, and saw the wild Bryar,
> The Thorn and the Thistle grow broader and higher . . .

Before the 1886 revision the two lines in *Alice* ran:

> I passed by his garden, and marked, with one eye,
> How the owl and the oyster were sharing a pie.

For William Boyd's *Songs from Alice's Adventures in Wonderland* (1870) Dodgson added two lines:

> While the duck and the Dodo, the lizard and cat
> Were swimming in milk round the brim of a hat.

John Mackay Shaw in his Catalogue of *The Parodies of Lewis Carroll and their Originals* (Florida State University Library, 1960) suggests that the eight-line second stanza (after the first line which follows Watts) parodies William Roscoe's *The Butterfly's Ball* (1806)—but, beyond the metre, there is no resemblance. If another original is needed, *The Peacock at Home* (1807; by Catherine Anne Dorset, *née* Turner) seems much nearer, e.g.:

> The Razor-Bill carv'd for the famishing group
> And the Spoon-Bill obligingly ladled the soup.

But Dodgson probably intended no more than to branch out from the original line by Watts into some extravagance of his own. He may have had Edward Lear's 'The Owl and the Pussy Cat' (1871) in mind—even if the spoon was not runcible.

(2) *Turtle Soup*: parody of 'Beautiful Star', words and music by J. M. Sayles (date of first edition unknown, but J. H. Byron parodied it in 1860 in his burlesque *Cinderella*) of which the first stanza runs:

> Beautiful star in heav'n so bright
> Softly falls thy silv'ry light,
> As thou movest from earth so far,
> Star of the evening, beautiful star,
>> Beau - ti-ful star,
>> Beau - ti-ful star,
> Star-r of the eve-ning,
>> Beautiful, beautiful star.

Dodgson records in his *Diary* hearing Alice and Edith sing 'Beautiful Star' on 1 August 1862.

Page 95. *Beautiful Soup! Who cares for fish*: this has no equivalent in 'Beautiful Star', but may have been suggested by Dodgson's own parody

U

of 'Maidens of Zia' in his early burlesque opera written for his marionette theatre, *La Guiga di Bragia*:

> You know, love, I never wish
> For any other dish,
> So don't get any fish—

This burlesque, written about 1850, had its first and apparently only publication in the *Queen*, clxx, no. 4430 (18 November 1931), 37-40 and 66.

Page 96. Alice had never been in a court of justice before: Dodgson records in his *Diary* that he visited the Assize Court on 13 July 1863 where he heard 'some very petty cases, but they were interesting to me, as I have seen so little of trials'. In *A.A.U.* the whole trial occupies only about a page— as compared with two full chapters in the version expanded for publication.

Page 98. (1) *The Queen of Hearts, she made some tarts*: half the first stanza of 'On a Pack of Cards', anonymous poem published in *The European Magazine*, April 1782. The poem was in four stanzas, one for each suit— but the first may have been a traditional rhyme, and is certainly quoted alone in most subsequent collections of Nursery Rhymes. Dodgson quotes the same slightly variant version as Charles Lamb who prefixed this one stanza to his *King and Queen of Hearts* (1805).

(2) *Fourteenth of March*: the reference to the Concert on this or the succeeding dates may have been a topical reference (so far unidentified) which the children would have understood. Or it may be simply intended to refer to the Ides of March—with the date uncertain owing to the March Hare's faulty watch.

Page 105. Rule Forty-two: no reason is forthcoming for this number, but it was a favourite with Dodgson: the age of the narrator in *Phantasmagoria* (1869); the number of another Rule in the Preface to *The Hunting of the Snark* (1876), and the number of boxes the Baker had left on the beach in the same poem.

Page 106. They told me you had been to her: these verses were improved from an earlier version (which had two extra stanzas) published in the *Comic Times*, 8 September 1855. The poem is called 'She's All My Fancy Painted Him'—which is also the first line of the first (cancelled) stanza— and this line alone is a parody of William Mee's ballad 'Alice Gray' (published about 1815) which begins:

> She's all my fancy painted her—
> Ye gods! She is divine;
> But her heart it is another's—
> It never can be mine . . .

Dodgson published a much closer parody of this ballad under the title 'Disillusionized' in *College Rhymes*, June 1862. (Collingwood reprinted it,

docked of one eight-line stanza, as 'My Fancy': the complete poem may
be found in *Hamlyn*, p. 826.) If Dodgson's first parody revised and re-
used in *Alice* had any other original, it has not so far been traced; but the
last stanza seems to bear a close resemblance to the stanza set before
ch. XXIII of Maturin's *Melmoth the Wanderer* (1820):

> If he to thee no answer give,
>   I'll give to thee a sign;
> A secret known to nought that live,
>   Save but to me and mine

('not identified—possibly by Maturin'; Douglas Grant's note in O.E.N.
edition, 1968, p. 555—his query in *Notes and Queries* had failed to produce
any response).

Dodgson had preceded his poem in the *Comic Times* with the note:
'This effecting fragment was found in MS. among the papers of the well-
known author of *Was it You or I?* a tragedy, and the two popular novels,
Sister and Son and *The Niece's Legacy, or the Grateful Grandfather*'. None
of these can be traced—but if the poem is a parody, then titles are probably parodies too.

Page 116. (1) *happy summer days*: the last words of *Alice's Adventures in
Wonderland*.

(2) *pleasance*: Alice Liddell's second name. Dodgson altered it in proof
from 'pleasures'.

Page 117. *Advertisement*: [60th thousand]: this was a loose sheet inserted
in copies of the first edition (1893) of *Sylvie and Bruno Concluded*, and
possibly of the 61st thousand of *Through the Looking-Glass* (1897).

Page 118. *the chess-problem*: 'the chess framework is full of absurdities
and impossibilities'—Falconer Madan, *Handbook*, 1931, pp. 48–9;
'Carroll's description of the chess problem, which underlies the book's
action, is accurate'—Martin Gardner, *A.A.*, 1960, pp. 170–2: both give
their reasons at some length.

For an even fuller study, describing why the game can be accepted as
correct, see I. Lloyd Davies, 'Looking-Glass Chess', in *The Anglo-Welsh
Review*, xix, 189–91 (no. 43), Autumn 1970.

On 28 August 1878 Dodgson wrote to Macmillans: 'I have made an
annoying discovery in the forty-second thousand of *Through the Looking-
Glass*—Both the Kings are omitted from the chess diagram.' They were
still there in the 10th thousand but had vanished by the 40th. Dodgson
demanded an errata slip—of which no copy has survived.

Use of editions with faulty chess diagram may partly account for
strictures on the game. The first paragraph of this 'Preface' had appeared
in the 'People's Edition' of *Through the Looking-Glass* since 1887.

Page 123. *the white kitten had nothing to do with it*: Kathleen Tillotson points out most convincingly that Dodgson in the opening paragraph was subconsciously recollecting the beginning of a parody of Dickens' *The Cricket on the Hearth* in 'Advice to an intending Serialist' by William Edmondstoune Aytoun (1813–65) published in *Blackwood's Magazine*, lx (November 1845), 590–605; 'Lewis Carroll and the Kitten on the Hearth', *English*, viii. 45 (1950), 136–8.

Laura M. Ragg's insistence (in *English*, viii. 46 (1951), 216–17) that the scene was derived from the interest Dodgson and her husband (Archdeacon) Lonsdale Ragg took in the Common Room cat and its two kittens is disproved by chronology: Ragg only came up to Christ Church as an undergraduate in 1885, and became a Student in 1891. Dodgson first refers to him in his *Diary* in 1893.

Page 125. (1) *Do you know what tomorrow is?*: presumably 5 November (Guy Fawkes Day) celebrated with a big bonfire in Peckwater Quad at Christ Church. This also fits in with Alice's age—'seven and a half exactly' (see p. 177, line 24), since Alice Liddell was born on 4 May. This again suggests 1859 for the supposed year, though identifiable events come from 1862–3.

(2) *Snowdrop*: said to be the name of a kitten belonging to one of Dodgson's child-friends, Mary the daughter of George MacDonald (author of *The Princess and the Goblin*, etc.) to whom he wrote some of his earliest and best nonsense letters. Named after the fairy-tale 'Snowdrop' in the dramatic version by Mrs. MacDonald acted by the children in 1866 and included in her *Chamber Dramas for Children* (1870).

Page 134. *Jabberwocky*: the first four lines were written by Dodgson in 1855 as a 'Stanza of Anglo-Saxon Poetry' and copied into the MS. family magazine *Misch-Masch*, with 'learned' footnotes on all the difficult words—not always retained in Humpty-Dumpty's explanation (cf. pp. 191–3). This has frequently been reproduced, e.g. on pp. 239–40 of *Hamlyn*.

Of the poem itself (apart from the early stanza used as a prologue and epilogue) Collingwood tells us (*Life*, 1898, p. 143) that 'Lewis Carroll composed this poem while staying with his cousins, the Misses Wilcox, at Whitburn, near Sutherland. To while away an evening the whole party sat down to a game of verse making, and "Jabberwocky" was his contribution.' The poem is not mentioned in Dodgson's *Diary*, but the visit to Whitburn must have been that paid in December 1867. (This part of the *Diary* is very scant, and mostly written up afterwards: all he says of the visit is on 31 December: 'On the 27th I went over to Whitburn, returning to Croft today.')

Among the Whitburn party may have been a mutual cousin, Menella Bute Smedley (1820–77), the poetess; and it seems certain that Dodgson

ısed a poem of hers as basis for the story of how the beamish boy slew
ʰe monster under the Tumtum tree. The poem was *The Shepherd of the
Giant Mountains*, adapted from the German of Fouqué, which had first
ıppeared in *Sharpe's London Magazine*—1, nos. 19 and 20, 298-300,
326-8 (7 and 21 March 1846)—which was edited by Menella's brother
Frank, whom Dodgson also knew well, and from which he had already
parodied 'Speak Softly' in *Wonderland* (see *supra*, note to p. 54).

The poem tells how a shepherd-boy killed a fearsome griffin which
was harrying the flocks, following it to the gigantic tree where it had its
nest, which he burns, and stabbing the griffin to the heart with 'his herds-
man's staff, iron-tipped and sharpened'; and how he thereby won the
hand of the Duke's daughter, whose father greeted him after his triumph
with: 'Come to my heart, my true and gallant son'. (How memorable this
poem was is shown by Kipling, who describes it and the illustration
accompanying it in his early story 'Baa, Baa, Black Sheep' based on his
own childhood.)

brillig: spelt 'bryllyg' in *M-M*, where the meaning given is '(derived
from the verb to *bryl* or *broil*), the time of broiling dinner, i.e. the close
of the afternoon'. Humpty-Dumpty (ch. VI) agrees: '*Brillig* means four
o'clock in the afternoon—the time when you begin *broiling* things for
dinner.'

Slithy: *M-M* and H-D agree—'lithe and slimy'—'You see', explains
H-D, 'it's like a portmanteau—there are two meanings packed up into
one word.'

toves did gyre and gimble: *M-M* and H-D agree.

wabe: *M-M* gives '(derived from the verb to *swab* or *soak*). The side of
a hill (from its being *soaked* by the rain).'

mimsy: *M-M* gives merely '(whence *mimserable* and *miserable*)' which
H-D improves on: '*mimsy* is "flimsy" and "miserable".'

borogoves: *M-M* gives 'An extinct kind of Parrot. They had no wings,
beaks turned up, and made their nests under sundials. Lived on veal.'
'The first "o" in "borogoves" is pronounced like the "o" in "borrow".
I have heard people try to give it the sound of "o" in "worry". Such is
Human Perversity.' Preface to *The Hunting of the Snark* (1876), p. x.

The borogove as depicted by Tenniel is said to have originated in a
peculiar stuffed bird sent from South America to the Revd. W. D. Parish,
Vicar of Selmeston, Sussex, Dodgson's friend from 1863 until his death
in 1904. The bird disintegrated considerably during its journey to England
but 'not to be disappointed, the late Vicar had its head and long legs
mounted on a stand. It was shown to Lewis Carroll who became in-
fatuated with it and a picture of this curious looking "make-up" was printed
in his book *Through the Looking-Glass*'. (Obituary of W. D. Parish in
Sussex Daily News, 24 September 1904.)

mome: *M-M* gives '(hence *Solemome*, *solemone* and *solemn*), grave'.

H-D's explanations of both 'wabe' and 'mome' are great improvements on *M-M*.

raths: *M-M* gives 'A species of land turtle. Head erect; mouth like a shark; forelegs curved out so that the animal walked on its knees; smooth green body: lived on swallows and oysters.' H-D gives 'a sort of green pig'. Possibly Dodgson did not know the dictionary meaning of 'enclosure' or 'hill-fort'.

outgrabe: *M-M* gives 'past tense of the verb to *outgribe*. (It is connected with the old verb to *grike* or *shrike*, from which are derived "shriek" and "creak"). Squeaked.' But H-D gives a much better meaning—without etymology.

Jabberwock: in 1887 Dodgson invented a meaning for this word for a Girls' Latin School at Boston, U.S.A., whose editor wrote to ask his permission to use it as the name for a magazine. He found that 'the Anglo-Saxon word "wocer" or "wocor" signifies "offspring" or "fruit". Taking "jabber" in its ordinary acceptation of "excited and voluble discussion", this would give the meaning of "the result of much excited discussion" ' (*Collingwood*, p. 274). But, like the answer to the Hatter's riddle, this was only an afterthought.

frumious: another 'portmanteau-word'. Dodgson says [Preface to *The Hunting of the Snark*] 'take the two words "fuming" and "furious". Make up your mind that you will say both words . . . if you have that rarest of gifts, a perfectly balanced mind, you will say "frumious".'

Bandersnatch: Dodgson may well have known (even before he became an enthusiastic reader of Kipling) that 'bandar' was Hindustani for a monkey. 'Bandarsnatch' would so well describe Kaa or Bagheera!

vorpal: on 18 December 1877 Dodgson wrote to his child-friend Maud Standen: 'I am afraid I cannot explain "vorpal blade" for you—nor yet "tulgey wood" . . .'.

manxome: it has been suggested (e.g. by Martin Gardner) that Dodgson intended some allusion to the Isle of Man. But this seems very tenuous— the Jabberwock certainly has a tail in Tenniel's illustration, and there is no suggestion of three legs.

Tumtum: O.E.D. gives three meanings—the sound of a stringed instrument, an Indian dog-cart, and an alternative for tummy. But none seems to have any direct connection.

uffish: in the letter to Maud Standen quoted above Dodgson says: 'I did once make an explanation for "uffish thought"—It seems a state of mind when the voice is gruffish, the manner roughish, and the temper huffish.'

whiffling: 'to move lightly' or 'to make a light whistling sound'—so O.E.D., with dates before *Through the Looking-Glass*. But by 1903 the boys in Ernest Thompson Seton's *Two Little Savages* know the word only from Jabberwocky.

burbled: in the letter to Maud Standen, Dodgson goes on: 'Then again, as to "burble": if you take the three verbs "<u>b</u>leat", "m<u>ur</u>mur" and "war<u>ble</u>", and select the bits I have underlined, it certainly *makes* "burble": though I am afraid I can't distinctly remember having made it in that way.'

snicker-snack: an obvious onomatopoeia, but Dodgson probably had 'snickersnee' in mind, the 'cut-and-thrust knife', as in Thackeray's ballad 'Little Billee': 'Jack pulled out his snickersnee.'

galumphing: now accepted into the language; *O.E.D.* refers it to Dodgson, but says 'perhaps a fusion of *gallop* and *triumphing*'.

beamish: not invented. A variant of 'beaming', *O.E.D.*, from 1530.

Callooh: a species of Arctic duck, so named from its call (*O.E.D.*). But Dodgson need not have known of it.

chortled: also now a part of the language and ascribed to Dodgson by *O.E.D.*, where it is said to be a blend of 'chuckle' and 'snort'.

'Burble', 'galumphing', 'frabjous', and 'chortle' were helped to their place in the dictionary by Kipling's frequent use of them in *Stalky & Co.* (1899), presumably in recollection of their use in his own schooldays (1878–22).

Dodgson used many of his invented words and names from 'Jabberwock' in *The Hunting of the Snark* (1876).

Page 137. The Garden of Live Flowers: this chapter and part of the next seem to be the only section of *Through the Looking-Glass* that can be traced back to an outing with the Liddells, as in the case of the wet picnic and the following one in *Wonderland*. Being invited to lunch 'at Hetton Lawn, Charlton Kings (old Mrs. Liddell's)', he records in his *Diary*: '[1863] *Ap: 4. (Sat)*. Reached Cheltenham by 11.30 a.m. I found Alice waiting with Miss Prickett [the governess] at the station, and walked with them to Charlton Kings, about one and a half miles. In the afternoon we went a large party in the carriage up to Birdlip, where Ina, Alice and Miss Prickett got out, and walked back with me over Leckhampton Hill. Except for the high wind, the day could hardly have been better for the view: the children were in the wildest spirits. I stayed dinner and for the evening—then to the Belle Vue Hotel.' Dodgson spent most of Monday 6th (which was rainy) at Hetton Lawn, and visited the Liddells again on Tuesday 7th: 'Went over for the last time to Charlton Kings, and walked into Cheltenham with Alice, Edith and Miss Prickett.'

This was, in fact, the visit which Alice remembered in old age—when Dodgson came to see them while they were on holiday, but stayed at an hotel. Only—it was at Charlton Kings and not at Llandudno.

Page 138. Tiger-lily: Dodgson had a Passion-flower, until he discovered the religious origin of the name. The idea of the talking-flowers is based on Tennyson's *Maud* (1855), Pt. I, Section XXII, esp. stanza x: 'There has fallen a splendid tear / From the passion-flower at the gate,' etc.

Page 139. *the Rose*: Rhoda Caroline Anne Liddell (1858-1947).

Page 140. *a Violet*: Violet Constance Liddell (1864-1927). She was still only a baby when Dodgson ceased visiting the Liddell children (summer 1864), hence the Tiger-lily's next remark: 'As if *you* ever saw anybody!' etc.

Page 141. (1) *one of the kind that has nine spikes*: this is a revision in the 1897 edition (see Textual Notes, 141, 1-2). It originally ran: 'She's one of the thorny kind'. This identifies the Red Queen with Miss Prickett the governess, whose nickname was 'Pricks'. In his article 'Alice on the Stage' (*The Theatre*, April 1887) Dodgson described the Red Queen as: 'formal and strict, yet not unkindly; pedantic to the tenth degree, the concentrated essence of all governesses!' (See *Hamlyn*, p. 237.)

(2) *It's the fresh air that does it*: the 'high wind' on Leckhampton Hill.

(3) *I should advise you to walk the other way*: if you walk *towards* the reflection of an object in a mirror, you are walking *away* from the object—and vice versa.

Page 143. *they got to the top of the little hill*: Leckhampton Hill. From it the plain of Gloucestershire does indeed seem to be spread out like a chessboard divided by hedges.

Page 148. *it was an elephant*: perhaps suggested by the 'Ballad of Bedlam' in *Punch's Almanack* for 1862:

> The elephant with the cheerful voice
> Sings blithely on the spray.

Page 149. (1) *the six little brooks*: the story of the railway journey may have originated on the actual journey Dodgson made with the Liddells on 16 April 1863 on their way back to Oxford from Charlton Kings. Dodgson met them at Gloucester—'The train from Cheltenham at 2.40 brought the three Liddells and Miss Prickett: we had a very merry journey to Oxford together.'

It is worth noting that the main line between Gloucester and Didcot passes over the Swill Brook, the Derry Brook, the River Key, the River Cole, the Childrey Brook, and the Letcombe Brook—the two 'Rivers' being so near their sources as to be in fact brooks also. (See *Notes and Queries* (ccxiv), June 1969, 217-18.)

(2) *a thousand pounds*: it has been suggested that this is in fact the line of a popular song, or contemporary advertisement—but no original has so far been discovered.

Page 150. *Lass, with care*: parody of 'Glass, with care'.

Page 152. *the Goat's beard*: Alice caught hold of 'the old lady's hair' in the original manuscript (no longer extant), but this was changed at Tenniel's suggestion. (See letter dated 1 June 1870 in *Collingwood*, pp. 147-9. In the same letter Tenniel advises Dodgson to omit 'the "wasp" chapter'; and Collingwood quotes him as saying that 'a *wasp in a wig* is altogether beyond the appliances of art.' These two references are all we know about the omitted chapter.)

Page 153. *a raisin burning in brandy*: Snapdragon was an old game, usually played at Christmas, when players tried to snatch raisins out of a dish of burning brandy and eat them while still alight. Cf. J. H. Ewing, *Snapdragon and Old Father Christmas*, 1888; Patrick R. Chalmers, 'Snapdragon', in his *A Peck o' Maut*, 1914, pp. 61-3.

Page 154. *Frumenty*: 'a dish made of hulled wheat boiled in milk and seasoned with cinnamon, sugar, etc.' (*O.E.D.*).

Page 156. *I know it begins with L*: Liddell.

Page 158. *feeling sure that they must be*: Martin Gardner (*A.A.*, p. 228) points out that, as there is no stop at the end of the sentence, Dodgson intended the title of the next Chapter to be read with it as a couplet:

Feeling sure that they must be
TWEEDLEDUM AND TWEEDLEDEE.

Page 160. *the old song*: this, like the other Nursery Rhymes, was probably quoted by Dodgson from memory. But he would have known J. O. Halliwell [later Halliwell-Phillips], *Popular Rhymes and Nursery Tales of England* (1849), probably in the revised edition of *c*. 1860, which was current (undated) for many years. See pp. 86-7 (no. ccccxviii) for 'Tweedledum and Tweedledee' (not quite accurately quoted by Dodgson), and Iona and Peter Opie, *The Oxford Dictionary of Nursery Rhymes*, 1951, p. 418, for origin of the verses.

Page 161. (1) *Here we go round the mulberry bush*: an old children's 'Game Rhyme' for a 'ring-dance'. *J.O.H.* (pp. 224-5) gives 'Here we go round the bramble-bush' as a variant to the 'mulberry bush'. Both variants are quoted by him as traditional.

(2) *The Walrus and the Carpenter*: the first of these characters was suggested by the stuffed walrus in the Sunderland Museum which Dodgson had known since childhood. The Carpenter is said to derive from one Asdell, whom Dodgson may have met when visiting Tennyson in the Isle of Wight in 1859 (see correspondence in *T.L.S.*, 14 September-19 October 1951). But Dodgson attached no importance to the trade or appearance of his character, offering Tenniel a Baronet or a Butterfly if easier to draw (letter to Harry Furniss, quoted in 'New Lewis Carroll Letters to Harry Furniss', *Pearson's Magazine*, December 1930, p. 635. Date of letter not given, but *c*. 1886).

The poem is, to a certain extent, a parody of Thomas Hood's 'The Dream of Eugene Aram' (first published in *The Gem* in 1829), but of the metre and style rather than anything else. The first stanza of Hood's poem runs:

> 'Twas in the prime of summer time,
>   An evening calm and cool,
>   And four and twenty happy boys
>   Came bounding out of school:
> There were some that ran and some that leapt
>   Like troutlets in a pool.

Page 162. *The moon was shining sulkily*: Rear-Admiral Noel Wright suggested (*T.L.S.*, 14 September 1951) that Dodgson had in mind a passage from J. R. Bellot's *Journal d'un voyage aux mers polaires* (1854), p. 94, describing the midnight sun: 'Le soleil, indépendamment des effets de la réfraction, devrait se coucher, mais il promène pendant plus d'une heure sur l'horizon un immense globe de feu resplendissant entre des nuages de poupre et d'or. La lune, qui est pleine depuis hier, se lève, et fait un piteux contraste par la simplicité de son disque d'un rouge pâle; elle semble bien à plaindre.' But Dodgson does say 'no cloud was in the sky'; and it is not certain whether he knew enough French to read Bellot's *Journal*—though he was learning it in 1867 'in the hope of visiting the Paris exhibition'.

Page 164. *whether pigs have wings*: see note 2 to page 81.

Page 168. *you're only a sort of thing in his dream*: see Martin Gardner, *A.A.*, pp. 238-9, for discussion of the possible metaphysical background to the Red King's Dream.

Page 173. *the White Queen*: Dodgson denied that she owed anything to Mrs. Wragg in *No Name* (1862) by Wilkie Collins, but admitted that they 'might have been twin sisters' ('Alice on the Stage': *The Theatre*, April 1887; *Hamlyn*, p. 237).

Page 178. *in a shop*: as Williams and Madan pointed out (*Handbook*, 1931, p. 239), Tenniel in his illustration seems to be reproducing the shop at 81 St. Aldates, Oxford—remembering to put everything backwards as it is through the looking-glass.

Page 179. *teetotum*: a top spun with the fingers, particularly one shaped like a cube with letters on its four flat sides. This was a favourite Victorian toy.

Page 180. (1) *Feather*: term used in rowing for turning the blades of the oars horizontally when drawing them back for the next stroke.

  (2) *catching a crab*: failing to 'feather', and so catching the oar in the water—or missing it altogether.

Page 183. *I should like to buy an egg . . .*: Elma K. Paget in her life of *Henry Luke Paget*, 1939, p. 62, says: 'Luke would point out that there are references to Christ Church happenings in the two *Alices*. Alice, for instance, can buy two eggs cheaper than one at the Sheep's shop. "Only you must eat them both", said the Sheep, and a Christ Church under-graduate knew that if he ordered one boiled egg he was served with two, but one was invariably bad.' Paget (1852–1937) went up to Christ Church in 1872.

Page 186. (1) *Humpty Dumpty sat on a wall*: nursery rhyme or riddle, current by 1803 (*J.O.H.*, p. 51, no. ccxvi; Opie, *Oxford Book of Nursery Rhymes*, no. 233).

(2) *With a name like yours, you might be any shape, almost*: for the logical background to Humpty Dumpty's theory see Peter Alexander, 'Logic and the Humour of Lewis Carroll', *Proceedings of the Leeds Philosophical Society*, vi, Pt. viii, 551–66 (May 1951), esp. p. 558.

Page 190. *When I use a word*: cf. Dodgson's *Symbolic Logic*, 1896, p. 165 for the logical implications of this.

Page 191. (1) *Impenetrability*: meaning very suitably, 'unfathomableness'.

(2) *the meaning of the poem*: see *supra*, notes to page 134.

Page 194. *In winter, when the fields are white*: if this is a parody and not simply a straightforward nonsense poem, no 'original' has yet been found for it. John Mackay Shaw (*The Parodies of Lewis Carroll and Their Originals*, pp. 10–11) suggests Longfellow's 'Excelsior':

> The shades of night were falling fast
> As through an Alpine village passed

but the poems share only a very common verse-form.

Page 200. (1) *Anglo-Saxon attitudes*: Dodgson noted in his *Diary* for Saturday, 5 December 1863: 'Christ Church theatricals, given in Berners' rooms. The pieces were . . . *Alfred the Great* [historical extravaganza by Robert Brough]. . . . Mrs. Liddell and the children were there . . .'. A particular point was made of the Anglo-Saxon costumes, settings, etc. in this production. (See T. Vere Bayne's *Scrapbooks* in the Library at Christ Church.)

(2) *Haigha*: the Tenniel illustrations make clear that the two Mes-sengers are the March Hare and the Mad Hatter with their second names reproduced in would-be Anglo-Saxon forms. (See Harry Morgan Ayres, *Carroll's Alice*, Columbia, 1936, pp. 67–8 for possible origin of the 'Saxon' names.)

(3) *I love my love with an H*: popular Victorian game. *J.O.H.*, p. 32, no. cxxiv, gives the version for 'A':

> I love my love with an A, because he's Agreeable,
> I hate him because he's Avaricious.

He took me to the sign of the Acorn,
And treated me with Apples.
His name's Andrew,
And he lives at Arlington.

Page 201. (1) *sal-volatile*: aromatic solution of ammonium carbonate, much used in Victorian times to cure or prevent fainting; often known as 'smelling-salts'.

(2) *Nobody*: as so often Dodgson is using language literally; but this sequence was probably suggested by the well-known incident in *Odyssey* IX.

Page 202. *The Lion and the Unicorn* . . .: *J.O.H.*, p. 18, no. lviii; an old nursery rhyme current by 1708; found as a song with other verses in chapbook of 1806. Supposed to be a political rhyme referring to the Union of England and Scotland under James I and VI when the Lion and the Unicorn became the supporters in the combined Royal Arms: the Liddell children were collecting crests and sticking them in books (see *Diaries*, 1 August 1862) and would have given pride of place to it.

Page 204. *How fast those Queens can run!*: Queens can, of course, go from end to end of the chessboard in a single move.

Page 205. *It was just like a conjuring-trick*: Dodgson had noted in his *Diary* on 6 April 1863 while at Cheltenham: 'Went with the party in the evening to see Herr Dobler, a conjurer.' The party was the three Liddell girls with whom he had spent the day at Hetton Lawn, Charlton Kings, and Miss Prickett the governess. Unfortunately there is no mention of what tricks Herr Dobler performed.

Page 207. *the Lion twice as much*: i.e. 'the lion's share'—see Babrius, *Fable lxvii*, and Phaedrus, *Fable v*—particularly the former, in which the Lion divides the spoils into three equal portions and claims two for himself, leaving only one for the Onager (wild ass).

Page 211. *It was a glorious victory*: this suggests the line which ends most stanzas of Southey's 'The Battle of Blenheim' (written 1798): 'It was a famous victory.'

Page 212. *mice on the horse's back*: Cecil Headlam suggested in the issue of *Literature* for 19 February 1898 that the White Knight was suggested by *Hudibras*, and quoted (1. i. 315 *et seq.*):

For, as we said, He alwayes chose
To carry Vittle in his hose.
That often tempted Rats, and Mice. . . .

On 5 March 1898 R. Brimley Johnson wrote (also in *Literature*) quoting a letter from Dodgson dated 16 May 1893 in which he answered his own suggestion of the same source: 'I have certainly no consciousness of having borrowed the idea of the inventions of the White Knight from anything in *Hudibras*, of which poem all that I ever read, to the best of my recollection, is contained in the little book of selections herewith enclosed . . .'. (Johnson adds that none of the relevant passages are contained in the selection.)

The other passage, I. i. 409-12, which· Headlam and Johnson had both thought suggested the White Knight's lack of skill as a rider, describes how Hudibras mounted his horse so vigorously

> That he had almost tumbled over
> With his own weight, but did recover,
> By laying hold on tail and mane,
> Which oft he us'd instead of Reyn.

Page 214. *The great art of riding* . . .: Dodgson noted in his *Diary* during the visit to Cheltenham (7 April 1863): 'Went over for the last time to Charlton Kings, and walked into Cheltenham with Alice, Edith and Miss Prickett, and left them at the Riding School, where the children are going to have a lesson.'

Page 218. '*The name of the song* . . .': this is a logical difficulty known as 'metalanguage'. See Martin Gardner's excellent notes in *A.A.*, pp. 306-7, and Robert D. Sutherland, *Language and Lewis Carroll*, 1970, pp. 118-20.

Page 219. (1) *it's 'I give thee all* . . .': the metre of the poem is that of Thomas Moore's *My Heart and Lute* (*Collected Works*, 1841, v. 195):

> I give thee all—I can no more—
> Though poor the off'ring be;
> My heart and lute are all the store
> That I can bring to thee. . . .

(2) *I'll tell thee everything I can*: in his letter about *Hudibras* to R. Brimley Johnson quoted above, Dodgson concluded: 'It may interest you to know that the verses on the Aged, Aged man were written long before Alice was thought of, and appeared in a magazine called *The Train* in the year 1856, as a parody of Wordsworth's poem "Resolution and Independence". The character of the White Knight was meant to suit the speaker in the poem.'

The original poem (*The Train*, ii. 255-6, October 1856) was called 'Upon the Lonely Moor', and is a parody of the subject matter but not the metrical form of Wordsworth's 'Resolution and Independence, or The Leach gatherer' (1807). Dodgson seems also to have been recollecting another poem by Wordsworth, 'The Thorn', as it originally appeared in *Lyrical Ballads* (1798); cf. stanza x (l. 105), 'I'll tell you every thing I know', and stanza xi (ll. 111-14) begins:

> I'll give you the best help I can:
> Before you up the mountain go,
> Up to the dreary mountain-top,
> I'll tell you all I know.

(Dodgson's original parody 'Upon the Lonely Moor' is reprinted in all collected editions, e.g. *Hamlyn*, pp. 241-3.)

Page 220. Rowland's Macassar-Oil: the most famous brand of hair-oil of the nineteenth century—the name is perpetuated in 'antimacassar', the decorated material hung over the back of an armchair to keep the hair oil from marking it.

Page 221. (1) *limed twigs*: twigs smeared with adhesive bird-lime, an old method of catching small birds.

(2) *the Menai bridge*: Telford's famous suspension bridge carrying the London to Holyhead road over the Menai Straits between North Wales and Anglesey, opened in 1826. Dodgson crossed it by coach (the railway bridge, the 'Britannia Tubular', was not opened until 1850) when going on a family holiday to Beaumaris when he was about ten years old.

Page 222. when I get to that turn in the road: the Knight's move in chess is L-shaped. He is presumably returning to KB5, the square he occupied before capturing the Red Knight.

Page 223. The Eighth Square at last!: Alice, as White Pawn, has reached Q8 and so has become a Queen.

Page 228. fiddle-de-dee: title of a song published 1719, and first line of nursery rhyme 1740. See *J.O.H.*, p. 86, no. ccccxxiii, and Opie, *Oxford Dictionary of Nursery Rhymes*, pp. 112-13. Since 1784, also an exclamation synonymous with 'Nonsense!'

Page 230. (1) *putting her hair in papers*: curl-papers round which the hair was wrapped overnight to produce 'corkscrew-curls'.

(2) *Hush-a-by lady*: parody of the well-known nursery lullaby 'Hush-a-bye baby on the tree top'. See *J.O.H.*, p. 83, no. cccxiv.

Page 233. 'To the Looking-Glass world . . .': parody of Sir Walter Scott's song, 'Bonnie Dundee', from his play *The Doom of Devorgoil* (1830), II. ii. The first stanza and chorus run:

> To the Lords of Convention 'twas Claver'se who spoke,
> 'Ere the King's crown shall fall there are crowns to be broke;
> So let each Cavalier who loves honour and me,
> Come follow the bonnet of Bonny Dundee.
>> Come fill up my cup, come fill up my can,
>> Come saddle your horses and call up your men;
>> Come open the West Port, and let me gang free,
>> And it's room for the bonnets of Bonny Dundee!'

Page 235. 'What impertinence!' said the Pudding: probably suggested by Cuthbert Bede's drawing in *Punch*, 19 January 1861 of the Plum Pudding getting up on the dish and saying to the diner who is about to help himself: 'Allow me to disagree with you'.

Page 236. (1) *First the fish must be caught*: these verses do not seem to be a parody. The answer to the Riddle is 'An Oyster'. Although this is apparently obvious, other solutions have been proposed; but Dodgson's definite intentions are shown in a letter to Macmillan the publisher in November 1878 about a metrical solution which appeared anonymously in *Fun*, xxviii. 175 (30 October 1878) which he (Dodgson) had amended and corrected. The last stanza runs:

> Get an oyster-knife strong,
> Insert it 'twixt cover and dish in the middle;
> Then you shall before long
> Un-dish-cover the OYSTERS—dishcover the riddle!

(2) *extinguishers*: the conical silver extinguishers used to put out bedroom candles.

Page 237. *a voice from the soup-tureen*: perhaps suggested by the lines from another 'Ballad from Bedlam' in *Punch's Almanack* (1862):

> And hidden in a soup-tureen
> No mortal eye should find us!

Page 239. *I'll shake you into a kitten*: Martin Gardner (*A.A.*, p. 336) points out that 'this is Alice's capture of the Red Queen. It results in a legitimate checkmate of the Red King, who has slept throughout the entire chess problem without moving.'

Page 245. *A BOAT, beneath a sunny sky . . .*: an acrostic poem, the first letters of each line making ALICE PLEASANCE LIDDELL.

Page 246. *Christmas-Greetings*: First published in *Phantasmagoria* (1869), p. 194; reprinted separately 1884; included in *A.U.U.*, 1886, p. 96. Not included in *Alice's Adventures in Wonderland* until 1887. Also printed at the end of *Through the Looking-Glass* from 1897.

Page 247. *To all Child-Readers of 'Alice's Adventures in Wonderland'*: printed separately as miniature pamphlet of 4 pp. ($4\frac{3}{16} \times 2\frac{3}{4}$ in.) in December 1871 and inserted in first edition of *Through the Looking-Glass* (December 1871) and the 1872 edition of *Alice*. Reprinted only in *Letters to Child-friends* (1933), p. 246, and *Hamlyn* (p. 223).

Page 248. *'An Easter Greeting to Every Child who Loves Alice'*: printed separately as a miniature pamphlet (as the above) for Easter 1876 and inserted in copies of *The Hunting of the Snark*. Reprinted in *Through the Looking-Glass* (People's Edition) in 1887 and in *The Nursery Alice* (1889). Also in *Hamlyn*, pp. 226-7.

PRINTED IN GREAT BRITAIN
AT THE UNIVERSITY PRESS, OXFORD
BY VIVIAN RIDLER
PRINTER TO THE UNIVERSITY